A Puzzling Occurrence

Mysteries of Sparrow Island®

A
PUZZLING
OCCURRENCE

Sunni Jeffers

Guideposts Books

CARMEL, NEW YORK

9546

www.guideposts.org
(800) 431-2344
Guideposts Books & Inspirational Media Division

Cover and interior design by Cindy LaBreacht
Cover art by Gail W. Guth
Map by Jim Haynes, represented by Creative Freelancers, Inc.
Typeset by Nancy Tardi
Printed in the United States of America

For my dear friend Karen Larson, who always has a true-life adventure to share and a word to encourage me. May God bless your journey.

A special thank-you to Daniel, my nephew and expert on Global Positioning Systems.

My prayers go out to all who care for the orphaned and lost children of this world. God has a special crown for you.

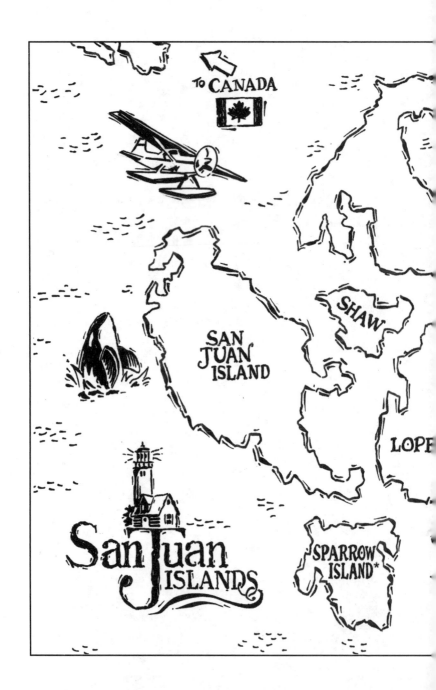

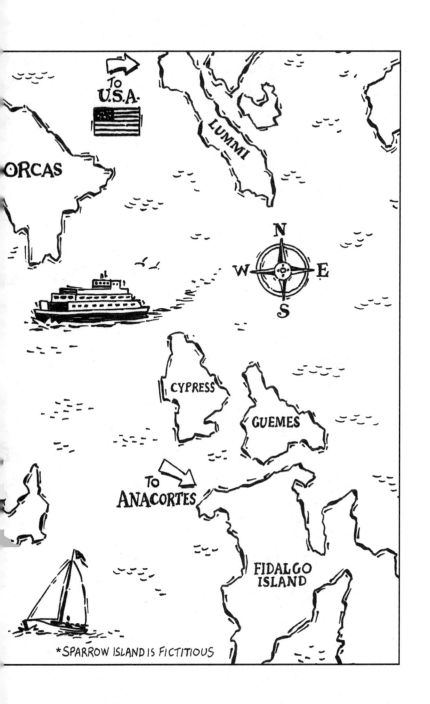

CHAPTER ❦ ONE

D R. ABIGAIL STANTON leaned back against her boss's desk, pen and pad in hand, jotting reminders for him and notes for herself as he sorted papers and arranged them in his briefcase. Abby's affection for Hugo Baron went deeper than that of an Associate Curator for her boss. They shared a passion for conservation and a deep love for God's creation.

Pushing her glasses up, Abby glanced around the room. Spotless, as usual. Everything about Hugo announced order and control, from his conservative, gray business suit, to the way he perfectly aligned the spines of the books on his shelves, to his desk, devoid of papers, pen set lined up precisely with his empty inbox. Only his tie hinted at his enthusiasm for nature.

Abby liked order, but she also liked having her work readily at hand. She kept her papers and reference materials in neat piles and knew exactly where to find anything she needed.

"Do you have the case studies on our flight cage?" Hugo asked, looking over his shoulder at her. "I'd love to interest a benefactor or two in building a permanent facility."

"Yes. I have it here," she said, handing him a folder. "There's a CD in the packet with pictures of our magnificent rough-legged hawk from the time he came to us with a broken wing and mangled feathers to yesterday, when I caught pictures of him flying the length of the cage. Put these on a large screen, and it's guaranteed to touch the heartstrings of your audience."

"And their pocketbooks," Hugo said. His snow white mustache, which matched his thick, neatly combed hair, curved up at the corners. The little crow's-feet at his eyes crinkled as he smiled. He placed the folder in his briefcase. "Do you think he'll be ready to release before I return?"

"Possibly. He gets stronger every day." As an ornithologist, Abby kept meticulous records of her studies and observations. She preferred field studies and would much rather be tromping around outdoors than working in her office. Her sensible apparel and short, straight haircut testified to her preference for a casual, yet tidy, appearance. Her years of experience as a researcher at Cornell University and her no-nonsense approach to her current administrative duties contributed to the efficiency that gave her time to pursue her scientific investigations.

Part of Abby's job involved finding grants and patrons, but Hugo did most of the public appearances, which suited Abby fine. Operations and expansion required Hugo's continuous fund-raising efforts, which meant travel.

Hugo had founded the Sparrow Island Nature Conservatory in 1981. With the help of grants and generous donors, he'd added the Nature Museum a few years later. The past summer, a team of wildlife biology students from Washington State University had built a one-hundred-and-twenty-foot-long temporary flight enclosure during an internship program. In six months, the cage had proven its value, enabling large injured birds, such as eagles, hawks and owls to exercise their wings during recovery at the conservatory. Constructed of tall wooden beams and mesh netting, the enclosure would suffice for several years, but a more permanent structure would be needed eventually.

Hugo straightened up and turned to Abby, giving her a resigned half smile. "I almost regret agreeing to speak in Florida next week, but I've given my word."

Hugo's reticence surprised Abby. "That's a very prestigious international symposium. An invitation to speak there's a great honor. I wish I could hear you. Besides, you'll bring back new ideas and meet lots of prospective patrons. You usually look forward to sunshine and warmer climes this time of year. Are you feeling all right?"

"I'm fine, and I'm aware of the honor. I wouldn't have the opportunity if it weren't for the interest and respect you've brought to the conservatory." Hugo's smile lacked its usual spark. "I guess I'm getting old. Two weeks in hotels, hopping from city to city and eating rubber chicken every night at these fund-raisers doesn't hold much appeal. Besides, I hate to go off and leave you with all the work. I'd like to be here to see our patient's release."

"Not much to do here. We don't have any big projects underway, and things are so quiet. By February I'll be twid-dling my thumbs, staring at my bird feathers." Abby counted on the slow winter months to research and catalog findings from more active times of the year. "Nothing happens on Sparrow Island in mid-winter. The only thing you'll miss is Mary's social at the church."

"I suppose that's true. I'm sorry to miss that, though. I promised your sister I'd procure the use of several tropical bird statuaries from a friend in Seattle for her Hawaiian theme. I'd hoped to drive down and pick them up myself. It sounds like her committee's planned quite a shindig."

"Really? She didn't tell me. Her committee has been mum on their plans. Where you're going, it'll be like Hawaii, not just a room full of tropical decorations and desserts."

"Yes, but it's a business trip and I won't spend much time outdoors in the sunshine."

"True. Don't worry about the statuary, though. I'll be happy to pick up the birds from your friend in Seattle."

"I'd appreciate that. The birds are handmade papier-mâchè, and quite durable, but I wouldn't want anything to happen to them. My friend has an import business in Seattle. He's willing to ship the birds, but I'd rather they were hand-carried."

"No problem. Maybe Mary will want to go along. She hasn't been to the mainland for a while."

"Good. Here's his card. I'll call and let him know you're coming." Hugo took a business card out of his briefcase and handed it to Abby.

Abby glanced at the brightly colored, glossy card, then put it into the pocket of her brown corduroy pants.

Hugo shut his briefcase with a decisive click. He reached up and adjusted the intricately tied knot at his throat.

"Love your tie. Is it new?" Abby asked. An osprey in flight spread its wings lengthwise on the tie, gray and white and regal against forest green and brown pine boughs and a deep, turquoise sky.

Hugo smiled. "Yes. Beautiful, isn't it? My sister-in-law gave it to me for Christmas. She has impeccable taste."

"It's perfect for your presentation tonight in San Francisco. Too bad it's not an endangered species though," she said, grinning.

"True. A bald eagle would be more sympathetic, but the similarities should still draw a response. Although I would hope environmentalists would know the difference between a bald eagle and an osprey from a distance." He shrugged.

"I'm sure it will help our cause," she said. Hugo's history of conservation efforts around the world in the years before his wife died and his mission to preserve the natural habitat of Washington's San Juan Islands endeared him to conservationists wherever he spoke.

Hugo slipped on his overcoat and picked up his briefcase. "I guess I'm off then," he said.

"Have a good trip, and let me know how things are going," Abby said, pushing away from the desk. "I'll keep you in my prayers."

"I appreciate that," he said. Their mutual belief in the power of prayer gave them another strong bond.

He turned and went out and down the hall. Abby followed him as far as her office, then went inside and checked her schedule.

With nothing urgent pending, she put away her work and picked up the telephone, dialing her sister's flower shop, Island Blooms. Perhaps Mary would like to take a break and meet her for lunch. Abby wanted to learn more about the plans for a

Hawaiian-themed event at the church. Mary was spearheading the committee to plan the winter diversion. So far, she'd kept the details quiet, letting little hints leak out to the residents to spark interest. Everyone knew something was happening at Little Flock Church for the community, and the islanders loved a social event.

MARY REYNOLDS SAT in her wheelchair behind a worktable in the back room of Island Blooms. Her manager, Candace Grover, had stepped out to deliver a bouquet to the Dorset, Sparrow Island's premier hotel. The front door opened. Next to her, Finnegan lifted his head and pricked up his ears. It still amazed Mary that the wonderful yellow Labrador, golden retriever mix service dog reacted so instinctively to her every need. When Candace was present, Finnegan ignored the shop's front door unless prompted by Mary. Now he looked up at Mary, waiting for her command. She reached over and patted the silky hair on his head.

"Shall we see who's here?" This time of year, Sparrow Island saw few tourists, so Mary expected a familiar face. Finnegan rose and walked beside her as she wheeled to the front of the shop.

"Terza. How nice to see you," Mary said to her diminutive, dark-haired friend. Terza and Martin Choi owned the Bird Nest bed-and-breakfast inn next door to Mary's shop. "Are you here for flowers?"

"Yes. I saw Candace leave, but I called early this morning, so my arrangement should be in the case." Terza opened the refrigerated case, then stood still for a moment, inhaling deeply. She let out her breath. "*Mmm*, I love coming in here. It reminds me of the beautiful Chinese gardens in springtime.

Sweet and spicy and woody all at the same time. No wonder you possess such tranquility, Mary. You fill your spirit with these sweet scents every day."

Mary laughed. "Tranquil? Me? I've been accused of being a butterfly, flitting about, but that's not exactly tranquil. You're confusing me with Abby. She's the quiet sister."

Terza cocked her head to one side, making her straight black hair swing gracefully. Her dark brown eyes warmed Mary with their kindness. "Quiet is not what I mean. You have a stillness in your spirit that shines, Mary. That is a desirable virtue in my culture."

"Thank you, Terza. That's a great compliment. You have that tranquility too."

She nodded slightly. "God has blessed us with much."

"Yes. I'm proof of that," Mary said, smiling at her friend.

Terza picked up an arrangement of carnations, lacy chrysanthemums, deep purple roses and ferns and shut the glass door to the case. "Sometimes little things can steal our peace though," she said, her brow knitting in little wrinkles.

"Has something happened to disturb your peace?" Mary asked.

"Not mine, exactly, but our guests have complained of losing sleep because of strange noises and lights flickering in the night. I don't know what to think. I sleep light. I didn't hear any noise. Martin sleeps like a rock. Nothing wakes him." Terza's Chinese accent became more pronounced, making Mary realize the depth of her friend's concern.

"Something might have blown onto the roof. The flickering light could be a coincidence. Have you called Rick DeBow to take a look?" Rick worked at handyman jobs for the Chois and Little Flock, and repaired engines at the marina.

"Martin checked the lights and said it's fine. He went around the house, looking at the roof, but he didn't see anything. He wants to climb on a ladder to get on the roof. I told him no. I said to call Rick." Terza shook her head. "Men," she said with such vehemence, Mary almost smiled, although she agreed with Terza. The thought of Martin climbing onto the third story roof gave her chills. Accidents happened so easily.

"I hope he waits until Rick can help him."

"Yes. I better get home and make sure that crazy man doesn't get on the ladder. Please put this on our account, and say a prayer for my Martin."

"I will. Call me when you find out what's causing the problem and let me know Martin is all right."

"Yes. Thank you, Mary." Still frowning, Terza took her arrangement and hurried out the front door. Mary whispered a prayer after her.

WHEN ABBY WALKED through the gift shop into the restaurant area at the Springhouse Café, Mary waved at her from a table across the room. As Abby made her way through the tables, she saw Finnegan lying close to Mary's wheelchair. The service dog's eyes rolled upwards, watching her approach as a retriever traces the movements of a bird, still, but alert. He greeted her with a slight twitch of his ears, but didn't so much as raise his head.

Mindful that the dog was on duty, Abby didn't greet him, although she loved that dog almost as much as her sister did. She pulled out the chair across from Mary and sat.

"I'm glad you decided to come in to town for lunch," Mary said. "I needed a break."

"Busy today?" Abby opened the menu.

"Yes. I guess everyone has the winter blahs. Flowers are in demand. Terza came in just before I left. Candace was making deliveries, so Terza and I visited for a while. Seems there's something odd going on at the inn—strange noises and lights flickering in the middle of the night."

Abby couldn't resist anything mysterious, though this no doubt had a logical explanation. "What kind of noises?"

"Terza isn't sure. Some of their guests complained about being kept awake for the past two nights. Seems to be a scraping noise. Neither Terza nor Martin heard it."

"Probably the wind. We've had a bit the last few nights. Has Martin checked that big maple tree in their yard? Could be a branch rubbing against the house."

"She said it isn't touching the roof. He's planning to climb up on the roof to investigate, which worried Terza."

"I should think so! That roof is three stories up. I hope he doesn't try it alone."

"I suggested she call Rick."

"Good. Maybe I'll stop by after lunch and see if they followed your advice."

"Hi, Mary, Abby," Ida Tolliver said, setting a glass of ice water in front of each of them. "Have you decided what you want? We have a really good turkey and cranberry croissant sandwich today." Ida smiled, but Abby thought the young waitress looked a bit blue.

"That sounds delicious," Mary said. "I'll have that."

"I'm in the mood for a roast beef on rye," Abby said, handing Ida her menu. "How are you doing?" she asked, searching Ida's features. Ida's face was an open book when it came to her emotions.

"I'm good. Wouldn't mind a bit of sunshine though. Wish

we could put that on the menu. Grilled sunshine with a side of Cole slaw and a glass of fresh lemonade. Or maybe something Hawaiian," she said, laughing. Her light, high-pitched laugh always reminded Abby of a gurgling brook. When she gave Mary a conspiratorial glance, her eyes brightened, bringing out the startling violet—the color of the asters that grew wild on the island.

"That will do the trick, guaranteed," Mary said, returning Ida's glance with a wink.

"I can't wait." She slipped her pencil over the top of her ear. "I'd better turn in your order."

After she left, Abby turned to her sister. "Tell me about your Hawaiian party. You've piqued my curiosity with your secrecy."

Mary smiled smugly. "Our publicity campaign is working. That was Ida's idea. Everyone wants to know what we've planned. We've said it's Hawaiian, and people can come in Polynesian costume, but that's all we've revealed."

"I'm amazed. Patricia's good at keeping secrets, but Janet? She can't resist telling a good story." Patricia Hale and Janet Heinz were the other members of the committee for the winter social. The tall, gorgeous red-haired daughter of a famous Hollywood actor, Patricia was married to the pastor of Little Flock. She loved the church and the people of Sparrow Island and helped organize many of the church events. Janet's friendly, bubbly personality made her an asset as the church secretary. Her compassion for those in need was only exceeded by her wild imagination and talkative personality.

"Janet loves a mystery more than a good gossip," Mary said. "She's in charge of publicity. When we're ready to spill the beans, she'll make sure the word gets out."

"Well, I promised Hugo I'd pick up your tropical birds for you, so I'm part of the secret now. You might as well tell me the rest," Abby said.

"All right." Mary looked around, to make sure no one was listening, then leaned forward. "We've planned an ice cream social," she said in a lowered voice. "But it won't be like an ordinary church social. We're going all out on the decorations to make it look like a luau on the beach. We'll have Hawaiian music and real flower leis for everyone, and Janet convinced Margaret Blackstock to take photographs of everyone in front of a special backdrop of palm trees. She has a fancy digital camera and she's taken some beautiful photographs. Margaret volunteered Joe to set up a printer and reproduce the pictures right there. I've ordered little picture folders to put them in, so everyone gets to take home a picture."

Abby stared in wonder at the sparkle in Mary's eyes. The townsfolk would get a boost out of the event, but Mary already glowed. Her excitement reminded Abby of what Jesus said in Acts 20:35: "It is more blessed to give than to receive." Mary and Ida had received pleasure just from planning the event and anticipating the fun. Abby was glad she'd volunteered to help out. She could already feel the joy.

CHAPTER ❦ TWO

"THERE'S NOTHING UP HERE," Rick DeBow shouted from the roof of the Bird Nest. He had a rope tied around his waist that was secured across the roof from the other side of the house.

Abby shielded her eyes from the midday sun, which had finally made an appearance. A chilled breeze ruffled her short hair despite the sunshine, so she zipped up her windbreaker. Beside her, Martin and Terza watched the repairman descend the tall extension ladder. Abby breathed a sigh of relief when his feet hit the ground. Out of the corner of her eye, she saw Terza mouth a silent "Thank You, Lord." She agreed.

"Nothing's accumulated up there since I cleaned out the gutters last fall, Martin," Rick reported. He ran his hand through his grayish-brown, curly hair, then pulled a Dallas Cowboys hat out of his back pocket, shook it open and plopped it on his head. Despite turning his back on his former high-stress career as a stock broker and moving from Dallas to the laid-back life on Sparrow Island, he remained a fan of the Dallas football team.

"Thank you, Rick. I don't know what to think." Martin's creased brow on his normally calm features added years to his age, which surprised Abby. Martin was about her age—mid fifties—but she thought of him and Terza as younger because of their smooth, youthful appearance.

"I'd say maybe your guests are hearing things in their sleep," Rick said. "Your electrical wiring is fine too. Nothing to explain flickering lights, unless the island power fluctuates in the middle of the night. I never noticed a power surge, but then I hit the sack pretty early."

"Hit the sack?" Terza repeated, looking perplexed.

"Sorry. I go to bed early," Rick explained. The Chois spoke excellent English, but the slang people used could be confusing.

"Ah. I understand," Terza said, nodding. She held her hand above her mouth and giggled. "Hit the sack," she repeated, her eyes crinkling with laugh lines. Terza was the epitome of politeness and would not have shown such a reaction around strangers.

"Maybe I caused the noise and lights blinking," Martin said. "I made a goof-up on New Year," he said, shaking his head. "The fish I cooked for dinner was not good."

"Your fish was delicious, Martin. I'm sure that's not it." Abby and Mary had been guests for the Chois' Chinese New Year celebration dinner.

"No," he said, waving his hand. "It was not enough."

"It is traditional to have leftover fish for luck," Terza said. "It means there will be blessings and profit that year. That's superstition, Martin," she said, shaking her head at her husband.

"It is tradition," Martin said. "Then I swept the floor on New Year's Day. Very bad omen."

"One of our guests broke a glass. You had to clean up the pieces, so no one would get hurt," Terza reasoned.

"Traditions are part of all holiday celebrations," Abby said. "We have them too. They're fun and symbolic, but they aren't necessarily real."

"I believe in Jesus, not the old ways," Martin said. "But look at what has happened. Sometimes traditions come from wisdom and experience."

"That's true. I'm sure there's a logical explanation for this disturbance," Abby insisted.

"I agree with Abby," Terza said, which surprised Abby—not that Terza thought she was right, but that she said so. She'd never heard Martin and Terza disagree in public. "Please, will you come stay tonight?" Terza asked. "You can hear the sounds and find the answer."

Abby's reputation for solving mysteries had become well-known on the island. "I . . . I'll have to ask Mary. I'm usually at home to help her." Abby found the idea intriguing though, and it might give her friends peace of mind. Besides, she'd always wanted to stay at the inn and enjoy the Chois' fabulous breakfast. "Do you have an empty room?"

"Yes. I will make sure it is ready," Terza said.

Martin looked resigned to his wife's machination. He turned to Abby with a gracious nod. "We would be honored to have you as our guest."

"Thank you. I'd love to help you solve your mysterious events. I'll let you know this afternoon."

Satisfied that her friends were safe, Abby returned to the conservatory.

ABBY WORKED IN HER OFFICE for an hour. Wilma Washburn looked up from behind the reception desk when Abby came out to the front of the museum.

"Looks pretty deserted out here," Abby said.

"We haven't had a visitor or phone call all afternoon." Wilma closed a ledger, put it in a drawer and stood. The light caught the strands of silver in her long black braids. "I was just thinking about closing up. I listened to the weather forecast a little while ago. They're expecting high winds and rain tonight and tomorrow. I need to take in my patio chairs."

"It's nearly three thirty. I'll feed our hawk and check to make sure the mesh is secure."

Wilma reached behind her and pulled a colorful striped wool jacket off the back of her chair and slipped it on. "I'll help you, then we can both get out of here."

"Thanks." Abby admired Wilma's jacket, which had been made by one of the local Indian artisans. Wilma cherished her roots. Not only was she an exceptionally efficient and cheerful receptionist, secretary and bookkeeper, but Wilma made beautiful baskets in the manner of her Native American tradition.

The two women walked past lighted exhibits of birds, animals and sea creatures indigenous to the San Juan Islands, dioramas of extinct and endangered species, and the Native American and Early Settlers exhibits. Abby extinguished the museum lights, leaving only the dim night lights glowing before they went down the hall past the offices and workroom, then out the back of the museum.

The wind had picked up, tossing large, dry maple leaves and brittle spruce needles skittering across the parking lot and winter-browned grass. Abby's windbreaker provided little protection against the chill in the air. She wished she'd worn a heavier coat. The gravel crunched underfoot as they made their way to the back of the conservatory building.

A long mesh-enclosed runway extended out from the building, twelve feet high and over one hundred feet long, where a full-grown rough-legged hawk perched on a pole. He looked good, considering his condition when they'd rescued him from a twisted pile of chicken wire. Feathers covered his legs down to his toes. This light morphed color variation of the species had a grayish brown back, wings with darker brown markings and a definite white U-shaped area across its breast. When he heard them coming, he swiveled his head and stared at them with his sharp, piercing eyes. Deciding they weren't a threat, the bird languorously rose and spread his wings, extending them out to an impressive four and a half feet. Lifting off, he swooped down the length of the flight cage.

Captivated, Abby held her breath. She'd observed thousands of raptors over her lifetime, but the beauty and power in their flight never ceased to amaze her. Although this was a smaller species than the eagle, she pictured the Lord's hands gently lifting this bird, whose wing had been broken and his feathers ripped and mangled. "He gives strength to the weary and increases the power of the weak. . . . those who hope in the Lord will renew their strength. They will soar on wings like eagles," Abby quoted out loud from Isaiah 40:29, 31.

"He's magnificent," Wilma whispered. "He's healed now, isn't he?"

"Yes, although I'd like him to gain a bit more strength before we release him."

After Abby set out food for the bird, she and Wilma walked both sides of the cage, making sure the mesh ties were secure. They met at the end.

"Everything on my side should hold," Wilma said.

"My side looks good too. I'm sure our raptor will seek the shelter near the building if it gets too blustery. I'll check him again in the morning."

Abby retrieved her bag, then the two women walked to the parking lot.

"See you Monday," Wilma said. "Have a good weekend."

"You too." Abby got in her car as Wilma started hers and drove out of the parking lot.

As she drove through town and out onto Oceania Boulevard toward home, Abby could feel the gusty wind buffeting her car. She turned on the radio to a local station, but she'd just missed the news. She pulled up and parked next to Janet's car, which was blocking the garage door.

The wind whipped her pant legs, propelling her toward the front door. When she opened the door, a gust nearly ripped it out of her grasp. She held on, then pushed it closed behind her.

"Phew!" She laughed as four pairs of eyes stared at her when she entered the living room. She could just imagine what she must look like with her short gray-streaked brown hair spiked by the wind and her clothes disheveled.

"GOODNESS! Look what the wind blew in," Janet said, grinning. "You'd better come in here where it's safe and snug."

Finnegan raised his head to check out the newcomer. Seeing it was Abby, he wagged his tail a couple of times, then laid his head back on the rug in front of the fireplace and closed his eyes.

Mary chuckled at her sister's tousled appearance. "You do look as if a bird got caught in your hair. Come join us. We're just finalizing plans for the ice cream social."

"I'll join you in a minute. Let me comb my hair," Abby said, pushing her tangled hair back with her fingers. She hurried upstairs.

Patricia Hale set her empty coffee cup on the table. "That cake was delicious, Janet. I hope it doesn't spoil my dinner. Are we finished?" she asked. "I need to get back to town. James was working on his sermon while Toby napped, but I'm sure he's awake by now."

Janet stood and picked up their empty dessert plates. "I've seen your son when he first wakes up. He can go from angel to rocket-man faster than a speeding bullet. Rev. James won't get much done with Toby awake."

"I remember when my Zach was a two-year-old. He did keep me hopping," Mary said. "I think we're finished with our business."

A small branch blew across the deck, clattering against the wood slats, drawing their attention.

"I heard it's supposed to rain tonight," Janet said.

"Well, I'd rather it rain now than next weekend," Mary said. "I'm praying for sunshine."

Abby came down the stairs just then, her hair neatly restored to order. "The way the wind's blowing, this should move through quickly," she said as she entered the living room. "Are you leaving?"

"I need to fix an early dinner," Patricia said. "James has a meeting tonight."

"I need to go too," said Janet. "I'll leave the rest of the coffeecake here, Mary. Abby can have some, and you can have it for breakfast. I have another one at home."

"Thanks, Janet," Mary said. She didn't need the extra calories, but Janet was a great cook. Bobby McDonald usually visited on Saturday, so she could give him a piece. Their ten-year-old neighbor had a sweet tooth, but he kept very active, so he worked it off.

After Janet carried their cups and plates to the kitchen sink, Abby saw the ladies out. Mary's Persian cat, Blossom, jumped up in the armchair Janet had vacated and began grooming herself. Abby returned and poured a cup of coffee, then sat on the couch. Finnegan got up, stretched, then ambled over to greet Abby.

"Hello Finnegan," she said, scratching his ears. He laid down on the floor between her and Mary.

"Terza called to find out if you're going to stay at the inn tonight. She invited us to dinner. Poor Terza. She apologized that they don't have a way for me to stay too. Martin had looked into making the inn handicapped accessible, and the cost is more than they can afford right now. Goodness. I certainly understand, and I told her so. I prefer my own bed, anyway. It's all set up for me. But you know how the Chois want to accommodate everyone." Mary shook her head. "Are you going to investigate their noises?"

"I'd like to give them some peace of mind. Martin seems to think he brought on the disturbances by failing to keep certain traditions. I'm sure there's a logical explanation for the sounds and flickering light. I don't want to leave you alone, though, with a storm coming in. Maybe I should call Terza and tell her I'll just come by tomorrow and look around."

"You should go tonight. The sounds occur in the middle of the night. We might get a few sprinkles, but the storm isn't due until midnight, and they're talking a little rain and wind. I'd be in bed before the storm hits."

"Are you sure you wouldn't mind if I stay at the inn?"

"Other than the fact that I'd love to stay there and enjoy their breakfast, which I've heard is wonderful, I don't mind at all. Finnegan and I will be fine, and I can always call Neil and Sandy if I need anything," Mary said. "So go get your things together."

"All right, if you insist." Abby grinned. "As soon as I finish my coffee. I'll forego Janet's coffee cake though. I don't want to spoil my appetite."

Mary could see the sparkle in her sister's eyes. Abby had the probing mind of a scientist and the curiosity of a cat. She couldn't resist a puzzle, and she was amazingly good at sniffing out answers.

"We'll go in your van, then I'll come home with you and get my overnight case."

"We can take two cars. That way you don't have to come back here."

"I insist. It might be raining by then. Honestly, Mary. I know you and Finnegan can handle it by yourselves, but I'll worry if I don't see you safely tucked in."

Mary placed her balled hands on her hips, pretending offense. "Safely home is all right, but that's all. You haven't had to tuck me in for months, little sister."

Abby finished her coffee and stood. "I know. You're amazing. I'm so proud of you."

Mary smiled and Finnegan sat up and looked at Abby expectantly. "And you, too, Finnegan," she said, petting his head. "I'll be ready to go in a few minutes." She headed for the stairs.

Finnegan moved closer to Mary and looked at her for instructions.

"You heard Abby say go, didn't you?" Mary asked, petting her dear companion. "I suppose I'd better get my jacket and purse and put on your harness, so we'll be ready." Mary backed and turned her wheelchair. Finnegan stayed beside her as she went into her bedroom. As she did daily, Mary gave thanks for her sister, for Finnegan and for her friends. Her life was rich and full, thanks to them.

TERZA LEANED FORWARD at the formal mahogany dining room table at the Bird Nest. They were dining in the room usually reserved for guests of the inn. The Chois served breakfast and sometimes other meals by special arrangement. Terza glanced toward the kitchen, then spoke in a low voice. "You're so good to come here, Abby." She threw up her hands and shook her head, causing her straight black hair to swing against her neck. "I don't know what to think, we haven't even heard the noises. Maybe these people made them up to get a refund."

"Would they do that?" Mary asked just as Martin came through the doorway from the kitchen. He set a platter of grilled salmon and a bowl of steaming rice on the table.

"I don't think so," Terza said, "but you never know."

Martin glanced at his wife, but didn't comment. He was too polite to question her in front of guests. He sat at the foot of the table, his back to the doorway and bowed his head. "Thank You, Lord, for these gifts and for our honored guests. Amen." He stood again and carried the platter around the table to serve Abby and Mary. Stir-fried carrots, snow peas and broccoli surrounded the delicate pink fish. He spooned a portion on their plates, then went on to serve Terza. Abby was aware that she'd been seated in the position of the honored guest, facing the doorway. Mary sat next to her. Abby helped herself to the rice and passed the bowl to Mary.

"This looks wonderful, Martin."

Martin made a slight bow with his head. "Thank you." He sat and made sure his friends were eating before he began, although that went against Chinese tradition. Terza had explained that the host in China ate first, but that they had become westernized—especially since they'd become innkeepers. Abby still removed her shoes at the doorway and slipped on one of the pairs of slippers Terza kept in a basket at the front door. There was a separate basket for used slippers, so they could be laundered. Abby loved the thoughtful tradition, but few people noticed the slippers or removed their shoes.

"I'm sorry to impose on you, Abby. Terza insisted on calling for your help. You have a talent for uncovering the truth." He gave Abby and Mary a perplexed look and turned his head side to side. "I can't find a logical reason for the noises, but we had another complaint today. I've seen investigations of spirits in haunted houses on television. This is a very old house, you know. Perhaps I did something to upset them."

"I don't investigate spirits, Martin. I don't believe that spirits or unexplainable phenomenon haunt houses. There is a reason for the noises, and we'll find it."

"I hope so," Terza said. "I see on the travel channel that some people like to visit haunted inns and old houses, but we want our home to be a place of peace and rest. We don't want anything bothering our guests." She wiggled her shoulders as if shivering at the thought of the noises.

Mary smiled at Terza's dramatics. "If anyone can find the cause, it's Abby. I'm sorry your peace has been disturbed, but I have your puzzling occurrence to thank for this wonderful dinner. This is delicious."

Martin and Terza gave Mary dismayed looks. "We invited

you as friends," he said. "It is true that our problem made the invitation sooner."

"Mary is teasing you, Martin."

"Oh yes, I am," Mary said, giving the Chois a hearty smile to prove it. "Tell us more about the strange sounds."

From the twinkle in her eyes, Abby knew Mary was as curious about the noises as she was. "Have they said what direction the sounds come from?" Abby asked.

"Mrs. Horner heard noises last night. She tried to wake her husband. When he wouldn't wake up, she turned on the light. That's when the flickering light started. Mr. Clark also has complained. They both have rooms on the north side of the house. We offered to move them to different rooms. Mr. Clark didn't want to move, but the Horners accepted our offer."

"So that room's empty?" Abby asked.

"Yes. We thought you could stay there, if you're still willing. You might not get much sleep."

"Oh yes. More than ever," Abby said. "I can sleep any time."

CHAPTER ❦ THREE

THE WIND HAD SUBSIDED when Abby went home with Mary, then returned to the Bird Nest. Abby had seen some of the inn's rooms, but she'd never been a guest. She admired the blend of Chinese and American antiques, giving the old home the chinoiserie decor popular during the Victorian period. Deep rose-red silk wallpaper covered the walls in the entry and stairway. A tall Ming-style vase next to the stairway held decorative grasses, peacock plumes and cattails.

A gold and red floral Oriental carpet and stair runner accented the polished hardwood floor and muffled their footsteps as she followed Terza up the wide, steep staircase. The plush carpeting would allow a person to move about in the bed-and-breakfast during the night and not be heard, Abby thought. However, the strange sounds reportedly came from overhead, likely the attic, where the floor was bare. The attic was probably an open room, too, so sounds would be amplified.

Abby remembered the first old house she'd lived in as a doctoral candidate in upstate New York. The large, three-story house had been converted to apartments. She'd been the only one living on the third floor, with a big, empty attic above her. A door went from her bedroom to the attic, and it hadn't had a lock, which had given her the willies, especially with all the creaky noises of an old house. When she began hearing boards squeak, footsteps and scraping sounds overhead, she'd reported it. The maintenance man had checked it and told her she was hearing old house sounds and the wind whistling through a vent.

Not long after that, she'd heard it again. She'd waited until the next day. Armed with a heavy flashlight, she'd gone up to investigate for herself. The dusty room showed no signs of habitation. There were foot prints, and some furniture had been moved around, but the maintenance man had been up there.

Somewhat reassured, she'd gone back to her apartment. She still heard sounds. Sometimes she'd lay there and listen, wondering if she'd imagined it. Just to be safe, she'd wedged the back of a chair under the doorknob, so no one could enter her bedroom from above, and she kept the heavy flashlight next to her bed.

She remembered lying in bed night after night, studying, listening for sounds with one ear, glancing toward the door at every sound, watching the doorknob, waiting to see it turn. For two months, she'd been exhausted every day and her work had suffered, until the day a neighbor called the police to report a burglar climbing down the fire escape at the other end of the house. The police caught the man—a transient—who'd been living in the attic. Abby had insisted the owner of the house install a deadbolt on the attic door in her apartment. There'd never been a repeat of the noises, but she never slept well the year she'd spent in that old house.

The Chois' noise was probably the wind blowing in through a vent or boards expanding and contracting. Old house sounds were spooky, especially when you weren't used to them. She strongly doubted anyone was sneaking into the Chois' attic. Not on Sparrow Island.

Remembering the intruder so many years ago gave Abby chills, but she'd never let a little fear keep her from investigating an unexplained phenomena. She had no idea what to expect, but she wasn't alone in this house. Besides, the reward of a scrumptious breakfast awaited in the morning. Abby was ready.

Soft wall sconces lit the upstairs hallway. Abby heard muffled voices coming from a guestroom down the hall from the one Terza unlocked and opened for her.

In the soft light of the bedside lamp, a muted green wallpaper patterned with lilies and pheasants covered the walls. The raised ceiling kept the tall, ornate Eastlake headboard and the mirrored dresser from seeming too large in the small room. A pair of upholstered chairs flanked a round skirted table covered with a lovely silk scarf in one corner. Green velvet drapes were tied back, showing delicate lace panels over the tall windows.

Abby turned and smiled at her hostess. "What a lovely room, Terza. Thank you for letting me stay here. You and Martin did a wonderful job of decorating your home."

"I thought you might like the birds," Terza said. "Would you like to come have a cup of tea with us before you retire? I will serve in the gentlemen's study, if you want to join us."

"I'd like that. I want to hear more about the sounds, so I'll be prepared."

"Come down when you're settled." Terza left, closing the door behind her.

Abby inspected the room. A chandelier hung from the middle of the ceiling. She flipped on the light switch, and soft electric candlelight illuminated the room. She had thought perhaps the candles would flicker, but the light was steady.

Pulling back the lace panels, she gazed out the window. There was a small balcony with an overhanging roof outside the window, but no door to access it. She'd have to climb out through the window. She decided against that, as Rick had checked the roof all the way around the house.

The old-fashioned streetlamp illuminated Holloway's Hardware across the street and the bare branches of an alder tree bending and twisting in the wind. Looking out the other corner window, she saw the outline of a tall spruce tree, swaying and bending between the house and Bayside Souvenirs next door. The Bird Nest bed-and-breakfast was located on Shoreline Drive, the main street in town. Through the inn's backyard, guests could access the beach at Randolph Bay.

Setting her overnight case on a chair, Abby retraced her steps downstairs. Terza and Martin were already in the gentlemen's study, a handsome room at the back of the house that served as a den, with vintage wallpaper, wainscoting, bookshelves and a wonderful view of the bay. Chairs were arranged around a low coffee table.

Martin rose from his easy chair and offered Abby the best chair in the room. As always, his manners were impeccable, but Abby thought he seemed distracted and a bit morose, as if their problem weighed heavily upon his shoulders. As she sat, Terza poured tea into a delicate china cup and handed it to Abby. She took a sip and tasted a hint of peach.

"*Umm.* Delicious."

"It's oolong tea. Very low caffeine," Terza said. Terza's

reverence for tradition added to Abby's enjoyment of the tea, transporting her mind to a place of peace and beauty.

Abby loved the way Terza served tea, taking the time and care to prepare it as if it were a special event.

"Did you know tea is supposed to awaken us to the truth of our existence?" Martin said.

Abby smiled. "What an interesting thought. It certainly is delightful." She lifted her cup toward Terza and Martin. "I thank God for the tea leaves that made this soothing drink and for the pleasure of dear friends with whom to share it."

Martin raised his cup in response and smiled. "You are right, Abby. That is one truth of our existence."

"So tell me how you get into the attic, Martin. I assume you've been up there to check for the source of the noises."

"There's a service stairway at the back of the house. It goes from the kitchen to the basement and upstairs all the way to the attic. I went up to the attic yesterday, but I couldn't hear or see anything. Nothing looks disturbed. I don't see anything loose that could be causing a noise."

"Do you have flashlights so we can investigate when we hear the noises tonight?"

"Yes." Martin rose. "I'll give you one now, but you must *not* go up to the attic alone. You will have to wake us if you hear a noise. There is a bell cord in your room that rings in the kitchen. I don't usually tell the guests about it. Our bedroom is off the kitchen, so I will hear it if you ring."

He left and returned a moment later, handing Abby a small, powerful flashlight.

"Thank you, for this and for the tea. I believe I'll turn in now. Perhaps we can get a little sleep before the show starts."

"Show?" Terza repeated, giving Abby a perplexed look.

"The noisemaker—whatever is causing your disturbance," Abby explained. "I'm guessing we won't hear it until everything in the house quiets down. It could be a normal sound that people don't hear above the daily noise."

"Ah." Terza rose. "We will say good night then. I hope you get some rest, but I do hope we discover the cause of the noises tonight."

"Me too," Abby said. "Good night." She made her way up the stairs. All was quiet. She went down the hall to the back doorway. Martin had locked the door to the stairway. She approved, but still had an urge to wedge a chair against the knob. She smiled at her fanciful thoughts. She wasn't a college student anymore, and there was nothing spooky about the Chois' lovely home.

Her watch said ten thirty when she unlocked the door to her room and went inside. She stood still for a moment, listening. All she heard was the ticking of the grandmother clock in the hall and the rustle of evergreen boughs dancing in the wind outside.

ABBY STARED at the papered ceiling that matched the walls. She'd left the overhead light on, so she could tell if it flickered. So far, nothing.

Three stripes of different patterns and shades of green and peach bordered the paper around the edge of the ceiling. At each corner, a square framed a tuft of bamboo leaves and a colorful bird in flight with outstretched wings. She tried to decide what kind of pheasant it depicted. From the blue patches on either side of its beak and the dotted stripes down its rust colored wings and breast, Abby guessed it was a Temminck's *Tragopan*, one of China's rare birds. She admired the art as she reclined against the bank of pillows, snuggled beneath crisp linen sheets and a light down blanket, reading a mystery she'd brought with her and listening. She hadn't expected the bulky antique bed to be so comfortable.

She heard a swoosh of water from a faucet or shower somewhere in the house. She knew from experience that every house had its unique sounds, which became evident at night, when all else grew quiet. Especially old houses. When she'd returned to the island, she'd discovered that all over again, staying in Mary's house alone while her sister recuperated and received physical therapy and training at a rehabilitation facility.

Abby tried to identify the unique sounds of the Bird Nest. She traced a knocking sound, like the tapping of a hammer, to pipes expanding and contracting as hot water circulated through old radiators, heating the rooms. She recognized the sound from old buildings where she'd worked at Cornell University. In the darkness, to someone used to electric heat, that could sound very strange.

A mournful cry wailed outside, setting her nerves on edge with its unearthly groaning, like a troubled spirit crying out its lament. It was the wind, keening around the roof and balcony. At least the Chois had modernized the windows, so the wind stayed outside. Could that be the noise?

The whistling subsided. She tried to read, but she couldn't concentrate. She was listening. The rapid ticking of her watch kept counter-time to the pendulum clock in the hall. A car drove by. A deep, resonant bong came from the hall, then another and another. Abby counted them. Twelve in all. The midnight hour. She'd heard a lot of strange sounds, but still no scratching sounds above her head.

The bong of the clock penetrated Abby's senses. She felt like she was hearing from a long way off. She opened her eyes. The overhead light still shone. She'd dozed off. She thought she'd only heard one bong, so she hadn't been asleep long.

A board creaked, then another and another. It sounded close, as if someone was walking on the floor in her room. Feeling a bit spooked, she looked around, thankful that she'd left the lights on. Listening intently, she tried to discern the direction of the sound. She could feel her own heart beating. She found it interesting, how the power of suggestion could put irrational thoughts in her mind.

Abby got up and peered out the window. Bare tree branches dipped and clawed in the wind, bony specters backlit by a streetlamp. *Just a tree*, she told herself, but she checked the windows to make sure they were locked, then double-checked the door to make sure she'd bolted it. Everything was secure. Nothing could enter her room.

Marking her page, Abby put her book down and tried to sleep. She had no doubt any loud or eerie sound would wake her. She closed her eyes and lay still. Every sound registered in her overactive imagination. Finally, she tucked her hand under her head and concentrated on the ticking of her watch. As she lay there, she prayed for Martin and Terza, for Mary, for her parents, her niece's family and her nephew, for Hugo, and for every one of her friends, and for world peace.

The bonging of the hall clock penetrated Abby's senses. She opened her eyes. The light still shone overhead, but natural light seeped in through the lace curtains. Pushing to a sitting position, Abby looked at her watch. Seven o'clock. *Goodness*, she thought to herself. Guilt swept over her. Some detective she was! Evidently she'd fallen into a sleep even the dead couldn't rise from. She'd slept later than usual.

She'd heard plenty of unfamiliar sounds before she'd fallen asleep, but no scratching noises other than the trees outside. Somehow, she didn't think she'd heard the sound that was causing all the concern.

Pulling back the covers and swinging her legs over the side of the bed, she got up. She dressed quickly, then descended the stairs. Terza was in the dining room, serving omelets to a middle-aged couple. She looked up and gave Abby a smile.

"Good morning." Terza's eyebrows lowered slightly. "Did you hear it?"

"No," she said sheepishly. "I'm afraid I fell asleep." Abby glanced at the couple. They must be the ones who had changed rooms. "Did you hear any unusual sounds last night?" she asked.

"All night," the woman said. "I didn't sleep a wink."

"Oh dear, I'm sorry," Terza said. "I hoped changing rooms would help you sleep better."

"I slept like a rock," the man said.

"You always sleep through anything," his wife grumbled.

"Not the night before," he said. "That scratching and knocking kept me awake. But last night was just wind."

"Please, let me introduce you," Terza said. "Abby Stanton, this is Mr. and Mrs. Horner."

Mr. Horner stood and reached out his hand. "Dale Horner," he said. "This is my wife, Evie."

"Nice to meet you," Abby said, shaking his hand.

"Sit down and I'll bring you coffee," Terza said. Abby glanced up at Terza, giving her a grateful look. She felt bad accepting the Chois' hospitality when she hadn't done anything to help them. Terza gave her a nod. When Abby sat, Dale resumed his seat.

After Terza went into the kitchen, Evie leaned toward Abby. Her eyes widened. "I think this house is haunted. Maybe someone was murdered here or died from some awful disease. Do you know if there are any stories about this place?"

"No, nothing. I grew up around here and I never heard of anything. Mrs. Choi warned me there'd been noises reported at night, so I expected to be wakened. Did you hear the scratching noises last night? I must have slept through it," Abby said.

"I didn't hear *those* noises," Evie admitted, "but I laid awake listening, and I heard creaking and knocking sounds and . . . like . . . footsteps all night long. I don't know if it was just wind, but I didn't get a minute's sleep, I tell you."

"Old houses make noises," Dale told his wife, patting her hand. "That's part of their charm."

"Then I don't like old houses," Evie said, frowning.

Dale turned to Abby. "I can assure you, the nightly disturbance is real. We heard it the night before last, didn't we, sweetheart," Dale said, looking at his wife for confirmation.

"Oh yes. It was awful. It gave me the creeps," she said. "I wanted to leave, but the Chois were so nice and offered us a different room. Well, it wasn't much better. Maybe it wasn't the same scratching, but all the sounds kept me awake. If we weren't leaving today, I'd check out and go stay at that Dorset hotel down the street, even if it costs more."

Terza came out just then. Evie looked down and took a bite. The noises didn't seem to have upset her appetite.

Terza poured a cup of coffee for Abby. "I'll bring you an omelet and Martin's special apricot tart. Would you like crab or ham?"

"Please, don't go to any trouble," Abby said.

"I insist," Terza said. "I know you like crab. I'll bring one of them." She turned and disappeared into the kitchen.

"The crab is delicious," Evie said. She glanced around, as if expecting to see something. "Too bad the place is haunted. Are you staying here long?"

"No, I'm a friend of the Chois," Abby said, reluctant to disclose her reason for staying at the inn. "Can you describe the strange sounds?"

Evie leaned down and forward, as if sharing a secret. "It was like fingernails scratching," she said, her voice low and mysterious. Then her eyes widened. "Like something digging to get in . . . or out, and lights blinked on and off." She turned to her husband. "You heard it too," she said.

Dale nodded. "I did. At first I thought it was in our room. I turned on the light and looked around. That's when the light began flickering. I looked out in the hall. The fellow in the next room was standing in the hall. I asked him if he'd heard the sounds. He turned and stared at me with those dark, piercing eyes, but he didn't say a word. Just went into his room and shut the door. I heard him lock the door. I'm sure he heard it too."

Evie looked around, as if the man might appear at any moment. "Maybe it was him. I don't trust that man. He's hiding something. Maybe he's a robber and he's hidden something in the attic," she said.

"The man's just antisocial," Dale said. "Being unfriendly isn't against the law. I agree though. He's kind of strange. I suppose he's got things on his mind."

"Well, he's rude," Evie said. "He looks at you like he's looking right through you, you know?" She picked up her coffee and took a drink.

Terza came in and placed a warm plate in front of Abby. The omelet was steaming hot and smelled delicious.

"Thank you," Abby said, smiling up at her hostess.

Terza patted her shoulder. "Eat now. We'll talk later." Terza took the Horners' empty plates and went back into the kitchen.

"Excuse me," Abby said. She bowed her head and silently thanked the Lord for His blessings and prayed for the Chois. When she opened her eyes, the Horners rose and excused themselves and left Abby alone to enjoy her breakfast.

Abby took two bites of the crab and avocado omelet, then couldn't resist tasting the tart. It melted in her mouth. She was savoring the sweet, buttery pastry when a man came into the room and sat at the far end of the table. He ignored Abby and stared down at a magazine he'd brought with him.

Not one to stand on ceremony, Abby said, "Good morning. It looks like the wind has died down. Should be a nice day."

The man looked up and stared at her as if analyzing her. The lack of emotion in his piercing black eyes disconcerted her. They were just as Dale Horner had described. He glanced out the window, gave a "humph," then returned his attention to his paper.

Refusing to be ignored, Abby said, "Did you hear any strange sounds last night?"

He looked up again, glaring at her, daring her to persist in her attempts at conversation. "You mean the ghost?" He smirked and laughed, a short, biting sound. "I don't believe in ghosts." He picked up his magazine and held it in front of him, pointedly snubbing her.

She'd learned what she wanted to know. At least she hadn't slept through an occurrence. Whatever it was, it hadn't happened during the night. Abby picked up her empty coffee cup and plate and went through to the kitchen. Martin was making a fresh omelet. Terza was washing a pan. They both looked up. Terza set the pan in the water and grabbed a towel. Wiping her hands, she reached for Abby's dishes.

"You didn't have to clear your own dishes. You are our guest," she said.

"I know. Thank you for the delicious breakfast. Your apricot tart is even better than I'd heard, Martin, and my friend raved about it. I'm sorry I wasn't able to track down your nocturnal noise last night. Neither the Horners nor the man in the room next to mine heard anything. I heard normal house and wind noises, but that's all."

Martin nodded. "I should have known it wouldn't come out. It knew we were trying to catch it," he said, as if they were dealing with an intelligent being.

"Trying to catch what? What do you think it is, Martin?" Abby asked.

"A bad spirit," he said. "I have upset the elements. I must correct the cycle."

"What if it's something simple, like the wind getting into the attic? Could we look around the attic, Martin?"

"We can look," he said. "After Mr. Clark has breakfast, I will take you up there. I looked before, but found nothing."

Abby knew Martin was too polite to tell her she was wrong. She didn't want to contradict him, either, but it had to be something logical. "I need to call Mary. I'll meet you in the living room in, say, a half hour?" Abby said, glancing at her watch.

"Yes. That will be good." Martin slid the omelet onto a warmed plate, folding it in half in the process. Holding the plate with a linen towel, he went through to the dining room.

Terza watched him go, then shot Abby a grateful look. "I hope you find something, so Martin can stop worrying about bad luck."

"I hope so too," Abby said. She went back upstairs where she found her cell phone and called Mary.

"How was your night?" she asked when Mary answered the phone.

"Good," Mary said. "No noises here. Bobby's here. I shared the leftover coffeecake with him, and now he's out sweeping the patio. The wind made a mess out there, but no damage."

Bobby often came over to play with Finnegan and help the sisters with a variety of chores. He and Abby had become buddies when he began coming to the conservatory after school to help out. Abby had suggested Bobby become a junior docent.

Abby had expected a challenge keeping Bobby entertained. She'd worked with thousands of college students over the years, but had little experience with young children. Bobby had surprised her with his enthusiasm and unquenchable curiosity. He'd become her faithful assistant, always eager to learn and willing to do anything she needed.

"I'm glad you had something special this morning. Now I won't feel too bad for savoring Martin's wonderful breakfast. I can't say it was quiet here last night, but I didn't hear the scratching noises. I talked to a couple who've heard it though. It certainly spooked them. I'm going to inspect the attic with Martin in a few minutes. He's been up there, but perhaps he missed something. After I leave here, I'll swing by the conservatory to check on my feathered patient, then I'll be home."

"Don't hurry. I'm going to the shop for a while. We have bouquets to prepare for a wedding."

"Anyone I know?"

"No. It's a party staying at the Dorset. I'll see you later."

After she hung up, Abby took her jacket and the flashlight Martin had given to her the night before and went downstairs. She was early. She put on her shoes and went outside, walking around the building, looking up at the roofline, shining the light on dark corners and crevices. Nothing appeared out of place.

Even discovering a natural cause might not reassure Martin, who seemed certain they were experiencing bad luck because of his own failure to observe proper customs. Although the Chois had become Christians, old Chinese traditions and culture were deeply ingrained in the couple who'd immigrated to the United States as adults. For Terza and Martin's peace of mind, Abby prayed they would discover the cause this morning, so they could put a stop to the disturbance.

As she came back around the building, the front door banged shut and the taciturn guest bounded down the steps and strode down the walk. Abby had no wish to be rebuffed by him, so she backed up and waited until he reached his car. He was dressed in faded jeans, a sweatshirt and sturdy, scuffed boots and carried a backpack and jacket. He looked around to his left and right, as if someone might be watching him. He never glanced backward, or he might have seen Abby standing just around the corner of the house. He opened the rear door of a newer model economy car with Washington license plates and tossed his pack and jacket in the back, then got in, started the engine and drove off, never once looking in Abby's direction.

Very odd man. Strange behavior. He seemed like a man with a mission, she thought. She ruled out sightseeing. He didn't look like a typical tourist. Besides, late January wasn't exactly tourist season. She eliminated birding or wildlife viewing. Too early for bird migration or spring births. She wondered what would draw a man like that to Sparrow Island. Since any answers would be pure speculation, Abby gave up her musing and returned to the living room to meet Martin.

CHAPTER ✤ FOUR

T HE ATTIC DOOR CREAKED loudly as Martin opened the door for Abby and Terza. He stepped inside first and surveyed the room, listening for sounds. When he heard nothing, he allowed Abby and Terza to enter.

Abby stepped through the doorway and stopped, flicking on the flashlight and shining the powerful beam into the dim interior's corners. Short, vertical knee walls raised the attic ceiling by several feet on the steeply pitched sides, so they were able to stand easily.

The room had the musty, closed-up smell of dust, old furniture, papers and clothing. The gable windows were dingy from the accumulation of dust, stale air and dead flies. A couple of flies buzzed noisily at the window. It reminded her of the attic in New York. *Seen one old attic, seen them all*, she thought. *Obviously, the Chois use this one very little.*

Nothing moved. Abby wasn't surprised. She shined the light around the large dusty room as Martin and Terza watched. Several sets of footprints were visible in the dusty floor, leading from the doorway into the attic, then back. Martin's and perhaps Rick's, no doubt, from their previous investigations. She looked for other kinds of prints, but saw none. Abby took a few steps into the room, looking around and listening for any scurrying or scratching noises. A thump-thump-thud resounded loudly behind her, making her jump. She whipped around, shining the light.

"Sorry. I knocked over a chair," Martin said. He picked it up and set it upright.

Giving up any pretense of silence, Abby went through the attic, looking in corners and around old pieces of furniture stored in the dusty room.

"Most of this came with the house," Terza said. "Someday we will sort through it. Maybe we'll use it or sell it or maybe send it to the junkyard when we have time." She laughed softly. "I'm so far behind, I haven't even opened all the mail from Christmas."

A small, intricately carved trunk sat against the far wall. It had a round brass escutcheon plate on the front with a long, tubular padlock.

"What a lovely trunk," Abby said. "Surely it wasn't here before. It looks Chinese."

"It is," Terza said. "It came from my father's mother." She looked at Martin, who was staring at the trunk. "We used to keep small mementoes in it, but I think it's empty. Martin, where is the key?"

"I don't know." He tugged on the lock. It didn't open. "I'm sure I left the key in the lock." He shrugged. "It must be here somewhere. I'll find it later." He turned and paced off several steps away from the outer wall. "Your room is under here," he said.

"So the light fixture is under your feet," Abby said, making a quick calculation from the corner and far wall. The wiring is under here then?"

"Yes. Beneath the floorboards. Rick checked the wiring from the ceiling in the room and he said it was fine," Martin said. "It knows we're looking. We won't find anything here unless it wants to be seen."

"If what wants to be seen, Martin?" Abby asked.

His eyes widened. "The spirit that plays tricks on us."

"Martin!" Terza said in the strongest tone Abby had ever heard from the tiny, gentle woman. She gave Abby an imploring look. "You don't believe spirits are here making noises, do you?" Terza asked, her accent more pronounced than usual.

"No." Abby glanced at Martin, who didn't look convinced.

"I read it in the Bible," Martin said. He looked embarrassed. "I looked up *spirits* in the back. God sent a tormenting spirit to make King Saul depressed. I found it in the book of Samuel" (1 Samuel 16:14–16). He crossed his arms and looked at them, his jaw set, as if that settled it.

Abby didn't know how to respond. She didn't deny that spirits existed. Even Jesus talked about spirits, but Abby didn't believe anything unnatural was causing the problem in Martin's attic. Although she'd seen documentaries supposedly investigating spirits through the use of meters and such, she'd never seen or heard of any real proof. But she couldn't convince Martin unless she discovered the source of the noise. She glanced around for loose boards, papers or something that might move if the wind hit it. "Perhaps the noise will happen tonight," she said.

"Please stay here again," Terza said. "We won't get any peace until we find the cause and fix it."

Martin acquiesced. "I hope you're right. Whatever it is, it drives away our guests, and that is bad luck."

"I'll check with Mary to see if it's all right with her. Tomorrow's Sunday, and I usually help her get ready for church. Now I need to go to the conservatory and check on our injured hawk to make sure he's okay. The wind was strong last night." She'd heard the wind and so had the other guests, which seemed to rule it out as the cause of the disturbing noises. She didn't know what to think.

"I will begin to set the elements right," Martin said. "Then we shall see."

Abby didn't know what the elements were. Clearly she hadn't convinced Martin that there had to be a natural cause for the disturbance.

LATER SATURDAY MORNING, Martin marched through the door and up to the counter of Island Blooms. Mary could see him from the table in the back room, where she sat securing pieces of white voile netting around individual white roses and sprigs of baby's breath with white floral tape. She would add orchids and lily of the valley to complete the bride's bouquet.

Although Mary had turned the day-to-day management of her flower shop over to Candace, Mary loved arranging bouquets and often came to the shop to help. Candace sat across the table making bouquets of pink and lavender roses, freesia and tulips for the bridesmaids to carry.

"We're back here, Martin," Mary called out. "Come on back."

Martin appeared in the open doorway. "Good morning, Mary, Candace." He nodded as if making a slight bow.

"What can we do for you?" Candace asked, finishing a sprig of flowers and setting them down.

"You don't need to stop. I can look around. I need some plants. I . . . er . . . thought I would surprise Terza with some flowers to make her think of spring."

"What a lovely idea. She'll be thrilled," Candace said, walking out to the front of the store. "We have a nice selection of flowering plants. The chrysanthemums are very hardy and you can plant them outside this spring."

"I have a list," he said, taking a folded piece of paper out of his pocket and opening it. He looked at it. "Chrysanthemums are good. I like the yellow. Do you have bamboo and crassula?"

"We have bamboo. I'll have to look the other one up, unless . . ." Candace turned to Mary. "Do you know what crassula is?"

"That's a jade plant," Mary said. "We have one. How about red kalanchoes," she suggested, knowing Martin favored red.

He consulted his list. "Yes, I like red," he said. "I'll take two of these, also," he said, picking up a dark pink azalea that was covered with buds.

By the time he made his selections, he had eight flowering plants.

"That's a lot of plants," Candace said. "They all need window exposure to light."

He looked at the profusion of plants hesitantly. "Yes. We will find room," he said.

"I can deliver these in the van," Candace offered.

"No, no. It is a short way next door. I can take them. It isn't too cold this morning," he said. "Thank you, ladies."

Two at a time, he carried them out the front door and piled them onto a garden wagon he'd pulled with him.

After holding the front door open for him, Candace came to the back. "Terza may be overwhelmed by his gift," she said, shaking her head.

"Curious," Mary said, frowning thoughtfully. "Martin often buys flowers for the inn, but that's the first time he's bought so many plants all at one time."

The front door opened, and Abby came in.

"I just saw Martin pulling a wagon full of flowers."

"He just about cleaned us out," Candace said, grinning. "Good thing I have an order coming Monday."

"I think the unexplained noises in their attic are getting to him," Abby said. She pulled a chair up to the table and sat beside Mary's wheelchair. "Hey, Finnegan," she said, leaning down to scratch around the dog's ears. The dog looked up and gave a deep sigh of contentment.

"I'm going to load up the van with the wedding flowers," Candace said. Picking up an arrangement, she went out the back door.

"What are your plans tonight?" Abby asked Mary.

"Henry's coming over. He's bringing a pizza. I said I'd make Caesar salad to go with it. Will you be home?"

"I need to go out to the conservatory to check on things, then I thought I'd stop and see Mom and Dad. I might have a bite with them. The Chois asked me to stay another night."

"You said yes, of course."

"I told them I'd talk to you. I could come home early in the morning to help you get ready for church."

"Now, Abby, I'm perfectly capable of getting myself ready for church, just as I got myself ready this morning and many other mornings. Go solve this mystery so poor Martin can calm down." She grinned at Abby. "Otherwise, Terza will run out of places to put plants."

"It is odd. Martin's usually so calm and collected. I can't believe he's so disturbed by this noise. All right. I'll stay there tonight and meet you at church in the morning. Besides"—

Abby gave her a wink—"that will give you a nice, quiet evening with Henry."

"You know you're always welcome when Henry's there," Mary said. Sgt. Henry Cobb, San Juan County Deputy Sheriff, was Mary's beau, although they had no future plans. Abby knew that, but she liked to tease and play matchmaker. At fifty-five, Abby still played younger sister. And Mary loved it. She also loved having her sister home, living with her after over thirty years of separation.

So much had happened since Abby had come home to help her after her accident. The relationship that had been strained since their teenage years had healed and blossomed into a flower more beautiful than any rose or orchid in Island Blooms, and Mary thanked God for their second chance. When the Lord promised to work all things for the good of those who loved Him and were called according to His purpose, Mary had never in a million years considered being confined to a wheelchair for the rest of her life, but God had turned her accident into so many blessings she couldn't begin to count them.

Unconsciously, she reached down and stroked Finnegan's head. He lifted his large head and laid it in her lap. A bubble of joy gurgled up inside Mary, making her heart feel full. Yes, she had many, many things to rejoice about.

"You'd better get going. Give Mom and Dad a hug for me. Tell Mom I'll bring Henry to dinner after church tomorrow."

"Will do." Abby stood. "Call me if you need anything."

"I will if you'll call me when you solve the mystery."

"At midnight? That's when it usually starts scratching around, you know."

"Well, maybe you could wait and tell me in the morning."

Abby's laughter trailed back as she went through the shop and out the door.

DRY LEAVES HAD BLOWN UP against the side of the flight cage, the only evidence of the winds the night before. The rough-legged hawk sat on a perch inside the cage, one wing outstretched, preening his feathers. He raised his head to observe Abby's approach. Unconcerned, he returned to his ministrations.

"Hey fella," Abby said in a quiet, gentle voice. "Looks like you survived the wind with no ill effects." She wanted to see him fly, but he ignored her. She went inside the conservatory building and got some raw fish out of the refrigerator where they kept food for their patients. He watched her carry it to the far end of the cage, where she tossed it inside. It smelled very fishy. Wrinkling her nose, she stepped back against a tree and waited to see if he would be hungry enough or curious enough to investigate. He waited, watching her to see what she would do. When she didn't move, he rose up, stretched out his wings and swooped down the long corridor. When he landed beside the fish and began eating, Abby slowly moved away. She skirted the perimeter of the flight cage, then went inside to wash her hands. Satisfied that both her charge and the flight cage had escaped any damage from the windstorm, Abby left the conservatory and drove back toward town, turning off at Stanton Farm.

As she pulled into the farm yard, Sam Arbogast waved at her from the top of a ladder leaning against the barn behind the house. Sam worked for her father, doing the heavy chores around the farm. If Sam was on the ladder, her father was sure to be at the bottom, so Abby walked around the house.

Sure enough, George Stanton stood at the bottom, holding the ladder steady. When Sam called out "Howdy," George turned to see who was coming. A smile spread across his face when he saw his daughter.

"Hi, Dad, Sam." She looked up at the farmhand. "What's broken?"

"The loft door blew off its track in that wind last night," her father said. "This might be a wasted effort. We're supposed to get more wind tonight. Sam thinks he can secure it so it won't blow off again. At least it might keep it from blowing all the way down."

"There, that ought to do it," Sam said, descending the ladder. He released the catch on the extension ladder to pull it down, then picked the ladder up. "I'll put this away."

George removed his work gloves. "We're finished here. We'd best go see your mother." He started walking with her toward the house. "So what are you up to?"

"I went out to check our hawk at the conservatory. He's fine. No wind damage that I could see. So I thought I'd stop by and see how you're doing." She tucked her hand around the crook of his elbow. Abby adored her father. He shared her love of the outdoors and wildlife—birds in particular. He had encouraged her to follow her dreams and become an ornithologist, even though it took her thousands of miles away for many years.

"Good. Your mother talked to Mary this morning. She said you spent the night at the Bird Nest. You and Mary didn't have a falling out, did you?"

"No. No fear of that happening," she said, squeezing her father's arm. "You know Mary's my best friend, as well as my sister."

"I know. I thank the good Lord for that, and for bringing you home," he said, smiling down at her. "So what's happening at the Bird Nest that needs your attention? The Chois all right?"

"Yes. They're having problems with a strange disturbance

that seems to be in their attic. Guests have complained of scratching noises in the middle of the night. Martin thinks it's some kind of bad luck omen. He and Rick looked for signs of something getting in, but they didn't find anything. Oh, and lights have been flickering, which could be a coincidence or the wind, but it occurred simultaneously."

"Did you find it?"

"No." Abby shook her head. "Martin says the spirit knows we're looking."

"Could be mice or a squirrel."

"He doesn't think it's an animal. They checked around the house pretty thoroughly, and there's no sign of a way into the attic. I'm thinking more along the lines of loose boards. Maybe the wind has loosened a roof vent or the seal around an exhaust pipe or sheathing around the chimney, or perhaps it's the siding. The wind could get under boards and create an awful sound. Then there's a guest who acts odd, like he has something to hide."

"You think he went snooping in their attic?"

"I'm not ruling anything out. He was seen prowling around in the middle of the night. But Martin thinks it's an angry spirit because of some omission on his part. Whoever or whatever it is, it didn't make noise last night."

"A bad spirit? You don't buy that, do you?" George asked. He was a pretty down-to-earth man, not given to flights of imagination in the supernatural.

"No, but it doesn't matter. If I don't find the source, Martin will continue to think it's an unhappy spirit. Any ideas?" Abby valued her father's judgment. He was a practical man, but also very observant. She credited her own persistence and thirst for knowledge to him.

"Your ideas are all possible, but I'd be looking for an animal. Maybe something got in when a door was opened. Isn't there a stairway all the way up the back of the house?"

"Yes. I suppose something could get in that way."

"Critters are smart," he said, chuckling. "Do you remember the skunk that got into our basement?"

"I sure do. Mom had a fit. She put Mary and me in the car, drove us to town and said we wouldn't come back until it was gone. I wanted to stay and help you, but she refused to let me. I seem to recall you made a smoke bomb that stunk up the house for weeks."

"And your mother never let me forget it," he said, chuckling. They'd reached the kitchen door. George opened it for Abby. They stepped inside and began removing their coats, hats and boots. The smell of chicken and dumplings filled the room, making Abby's mouth water.

"Well, I hope you're wrong about what's causing the ruckus at the Chois'," she said. "I don't want to resort to such tactics at the Bird Nest. Poor Martin is already convinced this is some kind of bad luck. I don't want to drive his guests away."

"I have some old traps if you need to catch a critter," George offered.

"I'll remember that." Abby gave her mother a kiss on the cheek. "I came to invite myself to dinner. It smells delicious. Do you have enough?"

"I always have enough for you, dear. And it's ready to put on the table. Go ahead and wash up."

Abby wasted no time obeying. She was back in a flash, pulling up a chair at the old, round white oak table that her father had made when she was a child.

Ellen handed Abby a wooden bowl of salad greens and a

cruet of dressing, then set a steaming bowl of chicken on a trivet on the table.

When they were all seated at the table, after George said grace, Abby smoothed her hand over a worn spot in the finish that always reminded her of dinners and laughter around the table. How good it was to be part of a loving family.

"Have some chicken," Ellen said, passing her the hot dish.

"Thanks." She spooned a piece of chicken and gravy over the rice on her plate and topped it with a large, juicy dumpling.

"What brings you out this way?" her mother asked.

"I was checking on the conservatory and thought I'd stop to make sure you didn't have any wind damage last night." Abby leaned over her plate and inhaled slowly. She let out a satisfied sigh and gave her mother a happy smile. "Besides, I just knew you were making something special tonight. I couldn't wait until tomorrow."

"She came to get my expert advice," George told his wife.

"I gather you were telling Abby how you evicted the skunk from the basement." She looked at her daughter and frowned. "I hope you have better sense than that. Whatever you do, don't take your father's advice. At least not in this instance."

Abby laughed. "All right. I won't. Promise. Besides, I don't think we're dealing with anything so intrepid as a skunk."

"I hope not," her mother said. "The Bird Nest would never be the same again."

CHAPTER ❧ FIVE

I'M JUST LEAVING THE FARM. Do you need anything before I go to the Bird Nest?" Abby asked her sister over the telephone.

"No. Henry is here. He got a weather alert to expect high winds tonight. He checked to make sure everything's battened down here and got out the battery lantern for me, in case the power goes out."

Abby frowned. "Maybe I should come home instead of going to the Bird Nest."

"No, no. Henry doesn't expect any problems. He's more concerned for fishermen who might have boats in the water. Most pleasure boats are in storage for the winter. He thinks the storm will move through quickly, like last night."

Abby bit her lower lip. "Are you sure? Terza and Martin would understand."

"Stay at the inn and figure out what's going on. Finnegan and I are fine, and I can always call Neil. Henry wouldn't leave me alone if he thought there was any danger."

"True." Abby knew how much Henry adored Mary, and they could count on their neighbors, the McDonalds, to respond immediately if Mary needed help. "All right. Stay in and keep warm. I'll call you in the morning."

Abby said her good-byes, hung up and went out to her car. The wind had picked up a little, but nothing alarming. She hoped the disturbing phenomenon would occur tonight. Much as she enjoyed the beautiful bed-and-breakfast, she didn't want to spend many more nights at the inn.

THE NIGHT WAS STILL CALM when Abby climbed into the antique bed and pulled the down comforter up to her chin. Hoping to block outside sounds, she closed the heavy velvet drapes. She felt like a pampered princess in the plush bed, cocooned in the lovely room with the exotic bird decor.

Abby read from her Bible, keeping her ears attuned to the night sounds of the house, listening for sounds overhead. Within minutes, however, she was engrossed in the book of Joel, with its story of devastation to a rebellious people. She loved God's promise of restoration and the promise of His Spirit and blessings upon His repentant people.

A *scritch-scratch* registered on her mind. She opened her eyes and realized she'd fallen asleep. Her Bible lay open against her chest. Blinking, she looked up. She'd fallen asleep with her bifocals on. The light overhead flickered once. She blinked again. Had she imagined it? She listened. *Scritch, scritch, scratch*, reverberated around the bedroom. She couldn't tell what direction the sounds came from, but they seemed close. It did *not* sound like a loose board or siding flapping. It didn't sound like pipes expanding or wires shorting or the old house settling. *Could it be something in the walls or in the floor?* The light flickered again. Abby's heart began pounding with anticipation as she sat up in bed. *This is it.*

She looked at the floor around the bed, although she didn't expect to see anything. The scratching continued. She threw the covers back and climbed out of bed.

Scritch, scratch, screeeeek. Louder, nerve-prickling, like fingernails on tinfoil. Deep moaning, like someone in pain. *Plrr-plrr-plrr-plrr.* Almost like rhythmic drumming. The lights blinked again. *What in the world?*

The sounds were eerie, but not unnatural. She was used to discerning different sounds in nature. Someone who lived in a city, in a townhouse or apartment—someone with a fertile imagination—might mistake the sounds for something unearthly. Abby began to think her father was right. It sounded like an invasion of some kind of wild creature. Rats? Cats? It didn't sound like birds. Squirrels? Something must have gotten into the house and found a way to the attic.

Abby pulled the cord that would ring in the Chois' quarters and alert them. Then she slipped on her bathrobe and tied the sash around her waist. She stepped into her slippers as she ran her hands through her short hair and rubbed the sleep out of her eyes.

She tiptoed around the room, listening, trying to locate the sound. It seemed loudest in the corner closest to the room next door. She wondered if the taciturn man in that room was awake, listening to the sounds. If so, she hoped he didn't come out to complain. She didn't want to scare away the culprits until they solved the mystery.

Scritch, scratch, scritch, squitter, squeak, squeak, scratch. It sounded like an army of claws and critters. Abby pictured a pack of furry, frenzied creatures clawing through the ceiling, landing in her room. She grabbed the flashlight next to her bed, picked up her long-handled umbrella and tiptoed to the door. Slowly she unlocked the latch, turned the knob and pulled open the door.

Martin and Terza rounded the top of the stairs and moved stealthily toward her. In the dim light of the hall, they looked like a couple of thieves, sneaking around. Terza had on a midnight-blue and gold kimono. Her pale complexion and wide eyed look gave her a ghostly appearance. In a dark kimono, carrying a fireplace poker, Martin looked like an avenging warrior. As they reached her, Abby put her finger to her lips and nodded toward the attic steps. Martin and Terza nodded in sync. Martin moved ahead and unlocked the door, then led them up the steep, narrow wooden steps to the landing outside the attic door.

They crept slowly, making as little noise as possible. Abby cringed at every creak, hoping the sound wouldn't carry and scare away the intruders. At the top of the stairs, Martin slowly turned the doorknob. It didn't make a sound. Abby listened as he pushed the door open.

As they stepped into the darkness, sounds of scratching and low, rhythmic *purrup-purrup-purrup-purrup* reverberated around the large room, surrounding them. Something was purring. The sound echoed, amplified by the large open room.

Abby stopped. Martin and Terza bumped against her and stopped. Abby could feel the tension in her hosts. Clicking on her flashlight, pointing it at the floor, Abby turned to Martin and Terza. Their two pairs of eyes stared at her, eerily shiny in the dark, reflecting the narrow beam of light. Assuming they had heard the sounds and realized it was animals, she nodded toward the far wall.

Abby moved forward a step and stopped. The scratching continued, nerve shattering, like claws on metal. Keeping the light pointed down at their feet and the space just in front of them, she moved forward two steps and stopped. Extending her arm, she brought the light up and shined it near the corner of the wall. The light hit the small, ornate trunk and reflected off the shiny brass escutcheon plate, sending something white, a moth perhaps, flying away.

Martin gasped and grabbed Abby's sleeve. Startled, she dropped her flashlight.

Pandemonium broke loose. *Hiss. Hisssss. Ch-ch-chitter-ch-ch-chitter-ch-ch-chitter*, loud, high pitched, rapid and furious, it sounded as if they were surrounded by a jungle filled with frantic monkeys.

Terza stifled a scream, which came out like a strangled squeak. Martin stepped forward, raising the fireplace poker, ready to fight off the army in his attic. Abby raised her hand, gesturing for the Chois to be still and silent. She picked up the flashlight and aimed the light around the trunk in the direction of the deep growling. It seemed to come from the trunk. It sounded like a large wild-cat.

Or raccoons, she thought. They had a large vocabulary of sounds, could be ferocious and would attack if provoked or cornered.

"Let's turn on the attic light," Abby suggested. If the raccoons were hiding, the light should keep them from coming out.

The overhead light bulb clicked on, illuminating them and

sending dim light into the corners. It wasn't very helpful. Abby moved forward.

"Stop!" Martin insisted. "Don't go near the trunk. They're inside." He pushed Terza back toward the door. "We must wait. I will make amends."

"I think your intruders are behind the trunk, Martin. Probably in the wall."

"It sounds ferocious," Terza said, her eyes wide. "What is it?"

"I'm reasonably certain it's raccoons. We'll have to search tomorrow, when they go out to forage, and block their entrance."

"Raccoons in my attic? It sounds bigger than that. It sounds like—"

"Dragons or angry spirits," Martin said, herding the ladies to the door.

Abby almost laughed. Martin couldn't be serious. But one look at his face sobered her. Martin was very upset.

"There are no dragons or spirits," Terza said, shuddering. "It sounds like tigers or rats. *Some* people might consider them lucky," she said, glancing at Martin, "but not me. I'm calling an exterminator first thing in the morning. We'll get rid of them all right."

"I don't favor rats," Martin replied defensively. "They're not part of my lucky element. It can't be a tiger." He turned off the light, ushered them out onto the stairway and locked the attic door.

"Please don't call an exterminator," Abby said. "We'll get rid of them. I think we can board them out, and my father offered his traps if we need to catch and release them out in the woods. The raccoon is actually related to the red panda," Abby said.

"I love pandas," Terza said. "I don't want them in my house though."

"You talk like this is some harmless animal in our attic. This is not the case. We will lock it in and leave it alone until we reverse the cycle," Martin insisted, ushering them out of the attic. He glanced back toward the locked door. "I'll go to the Asian market tomorrow and get some pomelos and lychee nuts and fish."

"We don't need lucky food," Terza said. "We will let Abby help us get rid of them. There are no spirits in our attic. That is old superstition."

"Then we'll call Rev. Hale to come pray for our house. Maybe his blessing will help."

Abby thought prayer was a good idea. At the very least, it would help Martin and Terza find peace of mind.

They entered the second floor. Martin shut the door loudly. He locked it.

Terza put her finger to her lips. "Please keep quiet before we wake all the guests."

"Sorry," he said.

Abby started to laugh, then saw the seriousness on Terza's face and stopped. "I think we already woke everyone with our commotion. Maybe the pests will leave since we disturbed them. We can't do anything tonight, though, so get some sleep."

"You, too, Abby. Thank you for helping us discover what's disturbing our guests," Terza said, giving Abby's hand a squeeze, which, for the quiet, reserved woman was tantamount to a big hug. "I hope they don't disturb you more tonight. Martin will make apricot tarts for you for breakfast."

"Yes. I'll make tarts for you and our other guests." Martin bowed to Abby. "Thank you, our friend."

As Abby let herself back in her room, she could hear Martin and Terza discussing their course of action in loud whispers, as if no one could hear them. Abby knelt by the big bed and said a prayer for her friends and for the nocturnal visitors to leave so she could help them restore peace in their lovely home.

Before she climbed back into the bed, Abby opened the drapes. As she pulled them back, ice cold air, trapped between the window and fabric hit her. She looked outside and gasped.

Snow swirled around the posts supporting the overhanging roof of the balcony outside her window. The wind dashed big, fluffy, wet flakes against the window, leaving lacy white flocking, a sight both beautiful and alarming. Abby loved snow—in New York. Sparrow Island didn't get snow. Not often, and not so thick that she couldn't see across the street. She cupped her hands against the cold window and peered out between her hands, staring into the storm. She barely made out the faint glow of the street light as a yellow orb in the world of white.

Mary. Her sister was probably asleep, unaware of the storm outside her house. At least the electricity was still on. She doubted her small hybrid car would make it the several miles through the snow to Mary's house. In New York, the snowplows would already be out clearing the roads, but since it rarely snowed on Sparrow Island, they were not prepared for the elements. That meant no snowplows. No road clearing equipment. No sand trucks or salt to melt the snow. No snow shovels to clear the sidewalk.

Fretting, Abby turned off the overhead light, then picked up her Bible and climbed into bed. She clicked on the bedside lamp and opened her Bible to the Psalms. She had tucked a ribbon in one of her favorites. She began reading a verse she'd highlighted. "If you make the Most High your dwelling

—even the Lord, who is my refuge—then no harm will befall you, no disaster will come near your tent. For He will command His angels concerning you to guard you in all your ways" (Psalm 91:9–11).

Mary was safe in the Lord's care. Abby knew that didn't mean nothing would ever hurt Mary or her. God had allowed Mary's accident and paralysis. But God had spared her life and Mary had said she knew the Lord was with her during that frightening time trapped in her car and through her recovery and physical therapy. Besides, Henry would be monitoring the storm and any damage. He'd check on Mary.

Abby closed her Bible and removed her glasses, setting them on the bedside table. Mary was safe inside from the storm, and Abby thanked the Lord for His presence with Mary and with her. Snuggling down under the downy comforter, Abby closed her eyes. Tomorrow might be more challenging if the critters in the attic decided to stay instead of venturing out in the blizzard, but that was a problem for tomorrow.

CHAPTER ❧ SIX

T HE LOWING CRY OF THE wind woke Mary on Sunday morning. Beside the bed, Finnegan sat up, ears alert. Mary listened for a moment, unable to identify what sounded different.

"What is it, boy?" she said to the dog. He looked at her and whined, then came over and laid his head on the bed next to her pillow and looked at her with his big brown eyes. She reached over and petted him.

"It's just the wind," she said. Still, there was something different about it. A haunting heaviness, as if the trees were burdened, rather than dancing in the wind. She'd closed the blinds before going to bed, so she couldn't see out. Her bedside clock registered seven o'clock. Time to get up.

Shifting her upper body, pushing up against the pillows, Mary pulled back the covers, baring her legs, and reached for the overhead bar. Grabbing a secure hold, she heaved herself out of bed and into the wheelchair next to the bed. She'd become proficient moving around, so she gave her actions mere cursory attention, positioning her legs, checking the brakes on the wheelchair, making sure her grip was sure and balance aligned properly.

Tucking a lap blanket around her legs and slipping on a bed jacket, Mary wheeled out to the living room. As she passed the chair in her bedroom, her white Persian cat, Blossom, opened one blue eye, then tucked her head deeper into the cushion and went back to sleep.

The sight beyond the patio doors stunned Mary. She wheeled closer and stared outside.

A shower of fluffy white flakes swirled horizontally, flying up under the patio roof, pelting the glass doors like a swarm of little white moths attracted to the light.

Snow? She peered out, straining to see through the thick whiteness. Tree branches bent and hung low under the weight of snow. She guessed the snow piled on top of the patio railing was somewhere between six and eight inches deep, and it was still snowing. The chairs and storage chest were snow-covered. Mary couldn't see the cedar fence at the edge of the yard, much less the waters of the Strait of Juan de Fuca beyond.

"Oh dear. I don't think we'll be going anywhere today," she told Finnegan, who stood next to her, looking out. He whined.

"You need to go out, don't you?"

Finnegan answered with a soft woof. Mary wheeled to the front door and unlatched the door. The dog grabbed the leather strap with his teeth and pulled. The knob turned, unlatching the door. He backed up, pulling it open. He went through, then tugged the door shut from the outside.

"Thank You, Lord," Mary said out loud, looking heavenward. "What would I do without Finnegan? Thank You for sending him to me. He's so smart and so capable, I'm not the least bit afraid of this storm." She wheeled over to the patio doors to watch him.

Finnegan wasted no time. He ran around to the back, a large bouncing ball of gold plowing through deep snow. The wind and snow created a white-out condition, so she could barely see him. The snow covered his legs completely, showing the depth of the snow.

As she watched Finnegan disappear into the woods edging the yard, Mary considered her situation. She didn't dare try to drive anywhere. She had no idea if her van would navigate the snow, and she wouldn't chance getting stuck. Abby's car wasn't equipped for snow either, so she wouldn't be able to drive out from town. Mary wasn't concerned about being snowed in. She had power. She had supplies. She had Finnegan. Just then, her dog came bounding out of the woods, retracing his path through the snow. Mary wheeled into the bedroom and got a towel out of the bathroom cabinet, then she went back to the front door to meet Finnegan. She heard him outside the door, his collar jingling as he shook off the snow. Then he pulled the cord, which opened the door, and came inside.

"Hold still while I dry you off," Mary said. He came close and waited patiently while she reached over and toweled his back and head. "Good boy."

Mary wheeled into the bedroom and got dressed. She'd just finished her morning routine when the phone rang. She reached into the pocket of the embroidered denim bag fastened to the arm of her wheelchair for her cordless phone.

"Hello?"

"Mary. It's Abby. Are you up? Have you seen the snow? Do you have power?"

Mary laughed. "Yes, yes and yes. Isn't it amazing? I haven't seen this much snow in years. And I'm fine. Finnegan was just out. The snow came up to his belly. I don't think I'll make it in to church this morning. Are you all right in town?"

"We're fine. I was concerned about you, though. You'd better not try to get out in this mess. I don't think my car will make it out there. I'll try to get a ride."

"Don't bother. I'm warm and snug and enjoying the view. I have lots of food. How was your night? Did you discover the source of Martin and Terza's noise? Oh, I think someone's knocking on the door. Hang on." Mary wheeled to the window and peered out. "It's Neil and Bobby. Gotta go, but I do want to hear all about your night."

"I'll tell you about it later."

"All right." Mary hung up. "Finnegan, open the door."

Finnegan went to the door and tugged it open.

Bobby and his father took off their snow-crusted stocking hats and shook off the snow before stepping inside and shutting the door. Bobby had a plastic bag in his hands.

"Hey, Mary, did you see the snow?" Bobby asked, jumping up and down, his cheeks bright red and his eyes sparkling. "I can't wait to make a snowman. Dad says I have to wait until it stops snowing though."

Mary laughed. "Good morning. That's quite a sight out there. It's snowing so hard. You're brave to go out in it."

"Good morning, Mary," Neil said. "I'm glad to see you're up. Everything okay?"

"I'm fine. Thanks for checking."

"Bobby, give Mary the bread," Neil said.

"Oh yeah, I almost forgot." He held out the sack. "Mom sent this. She baked it this morning."

Mary took the sack and looked inside. The scent of fresh bread escaped. She closed her eyes and inhaled the sweet, yeasty aroma. She pulled out a loaf of raisin bread, still warm and held it between her hands, warming them. Her eyes teared up at the loving gesture. She blinked and gave Bobby a smile. "How wonderful. Tell your mother thanks for me."

"Okay. Can we shovel your driveway?"

"It's sweet of you to offer, but I'm not planning on going anywhere," she said. "Would you like some hot chocolate before you trudge back through the snow? I was just going to make some coffee, but this is definitely cocoa weather. I could toast some of this bread to go with it."

Bobby looked up at his dad expectantly. "Can we, Dad?"

Neil ruffled Bobby's tussled hair. "How about a rain check? We'll come back and clear your walk and patio after it quits snowing."

Mary started to refuse their help, but stopped herself. One of the things she'd had to learn was to accept help graciously. Even if she weren't wheelchair bound, shoveling all that snow would be difficult. "Thanks. I'd love to have the company. I don't intend to go anywhere in this, though, and it'll quit and warm up before long. In a day or two, this will all be gone."

"They've issued a blizzard warning for the entire Northwest coast. An unexpected arctic air mass moved down and mixed with this moisture coming up from the southwest," Neil said. "They canceled the ferry today. I've never seen that happen before. They said the storm could stall and dump as much as a foot of snow on us." Neil worked for the ferry service, which ran between the many islands and the mainland.

"We have almost that much snow now," Mary said. "You don't need to worry about me. I have my telephone and my cell phone, so I'll call you if I have a problem. I'm just grateful knowing you're next door if I need you."

"Be sure you call, okay? I can be here in a couple of minutes, and I'll be thankful for an excuse to get out of the house," Neil said. "Well, son, let's go, before your mother wonders if we got lost. We'll see you later, Mary."

"Thanks, Neil. Bobby, maybe you could come play in the snow with Finnegan. I'm sure he'd love it."

"Can I, Dad?"

"Sure."

"I'll see you later then," Mary said.

"You bet. Bye, Finnegan." Bobby gave the dog a hug, then pulled the damp hat back on his head and followed his father out the door.

The phone rang again.

"Hello."

"Mary, are you snowed in?"

"Hi Henry," she said when she heard his voice. "I just said good-bye to my company."

"Company? In this weather? I hope it wasn't someone stuck in a ditch."

"No. Neil and Bobby came over to check on me. Wasn't that sweet? And I suppose you're concerned too. I'm fine," she said. "More than fine," she added. "I'm having an adventure."

Henry chuckled. "I should have known you'd find this exciting. Do you have power?"

"So far. And I'll be fine, even if the power goes out. I have plenty of wood and kindling, and the cupboards are full. I can take care of myself, you know." Henry was a protector at heart. He had enough rescuing to do without worrying about her too.

"I know," he said, his voice turning serious. "Just promise me you'll stay in. It's a mess out here. We've got reports of accidents and cars off the road all over the islands. They've canceled the ferry service until it stops snowing. That could be all day. I'll get over there as soon as I can."

"Don't worry about me." She glanced down at the sack of bread in her lap. "I'm as warm and snug as the fresh loaf of bread Sandy sent over. I'll save you a piece."

"Sounds good. Did Abby make it home?"

"No. She's still in town. I'll be fine. Honest. You just take care of all the people in distress. I'm sure you have your hands full."

"That I do. I'll call you in a couple of hours. Don't hesitate to call the emergency number if you have any problems."

"I won't. Please be careful." Henry was a trained and experienced law officer, and very capable. He had found and rescued her after her accident. She hated to think of any harm coming to Henry as he battled the blizzard, going out to rescue others. He was careful, but he wouldn't hesitate to do whatever was required to save someone else.

Mary wheeled over to her favorite spot beside a table and lamp. Turning on the light, she took her Bible out of its denim pocket on her wheelchair and opened it to the concordance in the back. Storms. She turned to Psalm 107:28–29 and read: "Then they cried out to the Lord in their trouble, and he brought them out of their distress. He stilled the storm to a whisper; the waves of the sea were hushed."

Closing the Bible, Mary asked the Lord to protect Henry and his deputies and everyone who might be caught in the snowstorm.

AFTER TALKING TO MARY, Abby felt better. Not much rattled her older sister. Besides, the McDonalds would make sure Mary was all right. Other worries crowded in to occupy Abby's thoughts, like the creatures in the Bird Nest's attic. The attic might not be a bird's nest, but the raccoons considered it home.

She wondered how her parents were at the farm. Her father had a generator, but she hated the thought of his working out in the elements. She dialed their number and stood, looking out at the blizzard as their phone rang.

"Hello?"

"Mom! Am I glad to hear your voice. How are you?"

"We're fine. Are you home?"

"No. I'm at the Bird Nest. I just talked to Mary. You'd think she was on an adventure."

"That sounds like her. Your father went out to milk the cows. He told Sam to stay put until the storm passes. It's snowing so hard, I can't see the barn, so I made your father tie a fish line to the kitchen door and take it with him, in case he needs a guide to find his way back. I told him, if he isn't back in an hour, I'm coming after him."

"Call me when he gets back to the house."

"I will. Don't worry about us. We'll be fine."

"Okay. I'll check on you later. I love you, Mom." Abby's stomach grumbled. With the image of Martin's apricot tarts in her mind, she hurried downstairs to see how her hosts had fared.

"Good morning," Terza called to her from the dining room. She set plates of food in front of a couple who had checked in the night before. Across from them, a young man with longish red hair and a thin red mustache and goatee glanced up briefly, then took a bite of food.

"Good morning. How are you?" As always, Terza looked fresh and serene. Abby sat at the table, next to the couple.

"I'm fine." She turned to the other guests. "How are you this morning?" she asked.

"Awful," the man said. When he turned toward Abby, she saw dark circles beneath his eyes. "I don't know what was going on last night, but it sounded like we were being raided. Then this snow." He shook his head.

"We're stuck here." His wife looked ready to cry. "We just stopped here for one night, on our way back from Victoria. This inn looked good in the brochure, but all that noise! And we're supposed to fly out of the Seattle airport today, but the ferry won't run until this storm stops. Grant has an important meeting tomorrow." She glanced at her husband. "If we don't leave by noon, he'll miss it. I can't believe our luck."

The young man across the table looked up and scowled. "At least you're not stuck out in the storm or at the airport," he said.

Terza came back into the room, carrying a plate of fresh tarts. "I'm so sorry your plans are ruined," she said. She introduced the couple to Abby as Grant and Tanya Niven, then she told everyone, "We have plenty of room, and you can stay as long as you need to."

"No way. We're checking out," the woman said emphatically.

The young man took a tart and popped it in his mouth. He swallowed it down quickly. "When does Dr. Clark usually come down for breakfast?" he asked Terza.

"Dr. Clark?" Terza asked. "Oh, Mr. Clark didn't say he was a doctor. Do you know him? He comes down early and goes out every morning, but I haven't seen him yet."

"I came here to speak to him," the man said. He looked at

his watch. "I suppose he's seen the snow. Otherwise, he'd be down here by now." He looked at Abby and the Nivens. "Everyone else is here," he muttered, almost to himself. He stood and put his napkin down. Without even a thanks to Terza, he stomped out of the dining room and ran up the stairs. A moment later, they heard him banging on a door.

Terza looked alarmed, but schooled her features to hide her feelings and offered the couple coffee. She refilled Abby's cup. "Excuse me," she said, and went into the kitchen.

Abby could hear Martin's voice, raised above his normal calm. With the events in the night and a guest upstairs banging on doors, Abby could understand Martin and Terza being disturbed. Terza came out, carrying a plate of steaming hot salmon cakes and fluffy scrambled eggs. She set it in front of Abby as the young man bounded down the stairs.

"He didn't answer his door. I knocked loud enough to wake the dead," he said.

"How do you know which room he's in?" Abby asked.

"Simple deduction," he said, giving her a condescending look. "I know what rooms you're in. That only leaves one. He's not there." He went to the window and looked out. "Is his car out there?"

Abby got up and looked out the front window. The car she'd seen him driving was not parked out front. "It's gone," she said.

"He didn't come back last night?" Terza asked.

"Not unless he got up early and went out in this mess," the man said.

"There're no footprints in the snow," Abby said.

"I've been up since early and he didn't go out," Terza said, her accent thicker than usual. She turned and hurried into the kitchen. "Martin, there's something bad," she said as soon as she entered the kitchen. Her words drifted back into the dining room.

Martin came into the room, wiping his hands on his white apron. Terza was right behind him.

"You're certain Mr. Clark isn't here?" he asked.

"Yeah. He didn't answer his door. His car is gone."

"He could have parked down the block. Maybe he's sick. I'll go see." Martin went up the stairs. Uninvited, the young man ran after him, taking two steps at a time. The woman stood, as if to follow, but her husband grabbed her arm. He gave her a withering look, and she sat down.

Abby was curious, too, but she refrained. Martin could handle his disagreeable guest. No sense letting the delicious breakfast get cold. She bowed her head and said a silent prayer, then took a bite of eggs, enjoying the delicate seasoning and light texture while she listened, trying to hear what was happening upstairs. The eggs had soft cream cheese, mushrooms and snipped dill mixed in, complementing the salmon patty with creamy lemon sauce. If she was snowed in there for very long, she'd lose her girlish figure for sure, she thought.

She'd finished her eggs when Martin came down the stairs, the young man trailing behind him. Abby could see Martin was upset.

"Mr. Clark didn't come back last night," he said. "We need to call Sergeant Cobb."

"Maybe he decided to stay somewhere else," she suggested.

"His clothes and luggage are in his room," the young man said.

Martin frowned at the man, then looked at Abby. "Excuse me. I must make a call." He went into the kitchen.

"You know Dr. Clark well, Mr. . . ?" Abby asked, raising her eyebrows.

"No. He's just an acquaintance," the man answered shortly. He didn't give his name.

"Odd. You seem familiar with his sleeping habits. Would you have any idea why he might not come back here? What's his business on the island?" Abby asked.

The man gave her a sharp glance, then shrugged. "Beats me. That's what I came to find out."

"What does he do?"

The man glared at Abby.

"It might help us find him, if we know why he's here."

He smirked. "I suppose you're going out in the snow to find him."

Abby refused to be baited by the man's ill manners. "I might. I've done search and rescue here and back in New York."

Nonplused, the man stammered, "I don't know. He's . . ." He clamped his lips together and frowned. "I just heard he was here. That's all."

CHAPTER ❦ SEVEN

"THE STORM'S LETTING UP. I'm going to walk down to the church and see what's going on," Abby said. She doubted many would show up for Sunday service, but a few brave souls would be out. "It's not far, and it's the one place in town people are likely to congregate. Anyone want to go with me?"

The young man who had finally identified himself as Terry, was pacing in front of the living room windows, stopping once in a while to peer outside, then utter a grunt and continue his pattern. The unhappy couple was sitting in the living room. The wife was flipping the pages of a magazine. From her scowl and abrupt motions, Abby doubted she was seeing what she was looking at. Her husband was playing solitaire at a small round table. They all looked up at her invitation. Grant scooped up his cards and stood.

"Sounds good to me. Tanya?"

"No thanks. Don't be gone long. I want to leave as soon as possible."

"We'll go as soon as the ferry starts running again," he said.

Terry stared at Abby for a moment, then said, "I'll come. Beats staying here."

"I hope you have warm clothes," she said. "Tennis shoes will get soaked in two minutes out there."

"I've got hiking boots," Terry said.

"I'm going to change my clothes. I have to grab some warmer things from my car. I'll meet you here in twenty minutes," Abby said.

She went through the kitchen and borrowed a broom from Terza. Martin insisted on shoveling a path for her, so she put on her coat and waited on the front porch for him. He came around the house, slogging through the knee-high snow, carrying a short-handled square-nose shovel, which reminded Abby of the snow shovels she'd used in New York.

Although Martin worked fast, the snow stuck to the steel blade, making his job difficult. The wind had lessened, but still blew icy darts into the air, pelting them as large clumps of snow fell from the trees. Martin finally cleared a narrow path to her car. Following him, Abby's ears burned from the cold and her cheeks stung. She tucked the broom handle under her arm and stuck her hands in her pockets to keep warm.

"Thanks, Martin. This snow is unbelievable. I've got waterproof boots and warm gear in the car, so I can make my own path down to the church. Do you and Terza want to come to the church with us?"

"I think not. We will try to clear the snow around the house and the sidewalk. Since our guests are stuck here, I'll cook dinner for everyone. If there's anyone at the church needing a meal, please invite them to join us. And I'd be grateful if you would say a prayer for us at the church. All this snow is another bad omen."

Abby put her hand on Martin's shoulder, hoping to give him some reassurance. "This storm is unusual for our area, but we do get snow once in a while. I remember a storm like this when I was a teenager. It's a natural occurrence. It will melt in a few days. The raccoons will leave the attic at some point to get food too. Then we'll get rid of them and things will return to normal."

"I don't know," he said, shaking his head. "Mr. Clark is missing. And that other man, Terry Jones, he's not nice. He pushed his way into Mr. Clark's room as if he owned it. I couldn't stop him. It's not good."

"Perhaps he's just concerned," Abby said, although she agreed with Martin. Terry Jones was rude and secretive. "If Mr. Clark didn't leave the island, Henry and his search team will find him. There are places he could get shelter, so I'm sure he's fine. But I'll be happy to say a prayer for you and Terza and Mr. Clark."

"Thank you." Martin turned and began shoveling his way back up the walkway, widening the path.

Abby swept snow off the roof and driver side of her car, then opened the rear door and retrieved a duffel bag of clothing and gear. She swept off the hood and trunk, then shook the snow off the broom and trudged back into the house, carting her duffle bag.

Removing her shoes at the front door, she hurried upstairs to change.

When she returned moments later, Grant and Terry were waiting. Both were wearing hiking boots. Grant had an expensive-looking leather flight jacket over a turtleneck sweater. Terry was better prepared in an olive green snow-boarding jacket. Abby knew what it was because so many of her college students at Cornell had worn them. She'd thought about getting one herself, for her winter forays into the woods when she was checking on the bird population, but then she'd moved back to Sparrow Island where the winters were milder and it never snowed. *Ha. Oh well. My insulated windbreaker and wool turtleneck should keep me warm and dry*, she thought.

"Shall we go?" She put on a stocking hat and gloves. Grant pulled leather gloves out of his pocket and put them on. Terry put on ski gloves. She headed out, the men following right behind her.

"This is very unusual," she told them as they tromped through the deep, unplowed snow. The wind had blown some of the snow off the road into drifts on the curb and sidewalk, so they broke a trail down the center of the street. Vehicles were buried in white along the street. No tire tracks or human tracks marred the pristine white powder.

Colorful light spilled out the beautiful stained glass window in the front of Little Flock, beckoning them inside. As no foot-prints approached the front door, Abby figured Rev. Hale had gone from the parsonage behind the church, through the back door. The tall, narrow wooden structure, with its side steeple and drifts of untouched snow against the white walls looked like a Christmas card.

Abby was relieved when one of the double doors opened easily.

"Welcome," Rev. Hale said as they entered the lobby. "You're the first brave souls I've seen." The sandy blond, boyish-looking pastor had always reminded Abby of a California surfer, but today, in jeans and a pullover sweater, she could picture him snowboarding with Terry. She hoped the sullen young man would warm to her pastor.

Rev. Hale reached out his hand toward the men. "I'm James Hale, the pastor here."

"This is Grant Niven and Terry Jones," Abby said. "They're guests at the Bird Nest," she added. "I stayed there last night too."

Rev. Hale gave her a curious look, but didn't ask for an explanation. He smiled at the guests. "Looks like you may be stuck for a while. Life certainly is an adventure, isn't it? We may not have a regular service, but we're here to help in any way we can. Would you like some coffee or tea? I put on the pots in the recreation room." He turned to Abby. "Is Mary at home? Have you spoken with her?"

"Yes. She insists she's fine. I should be with her, but I'm pretty well stuck too. Neil and Bobby went over early to check on her, so I know she's in good hands."

The front door opened, letting in a cold rush of air. Mike Bennett, one of the sheriff's deputies stationed on Sparrow Island, came inside. He stomped his feet on the mat just inside the door.

"Morning," he said, removing his dark green baseball style hat with a hat badge announcing San Juan Co. Sheriff Dept. on it. "How are you all doing?"

"We're fine," Abby said. "How does the island look?"

"Roads are bad. Don't try driving unless you have four-wheel drive or chains. Most of the island has power, but we have a few trees down on lines. Road crews are out now, trying to get roads open and check on people. We've got one missing person." He looked at the men. "We'll be organizing a search as soon as Sergeant Cobb gets here. Should be soon."

"The man was staying at the Bird Nest," Abby told Mike. "When he didn't come down for breakfast, Martin checked his room. His suitcase is still there."

"Maybe I'd better have a look. Were you there when they discovered he was missing?"

"Yes. I stayed at the inn last night, so I'm stuck in town. If you have a chance, I'd appreciate your checking on my sister. Mary's at home alone."

He gave Abby a searching look, but didn't ask why she'd stayed at the inn. "We'll do that."

"Since the church is already open and warm, you're welcome to use it for a command post," Rev. Hale said. We can set up cots if anyone needs a place to stay or just to get warm. My wife's making a big pot of chili and rolls, so we'll have something warm and nourishing available."

"Thanks. I'll spread the word. Don't know how much outside help we'll get. All the islands got hit pretty bad," he said. "Call my cell phone if you hear of anyone needing assistance." He wrote the number down and handed it to the pastor.

Rev. Hale took the paper and put it in his pocket. "I will. We'll get a prayer chain going too. Either of you interested in helping out?" he asked the two men with Abby.

"I'll help find Dr. Clark. He's the missing guy," Terry said.

Grant looked around. "Might be able to help around town, but I'm not prepared to go tromping around the island in the snow. I took a vacation to rest up. Recuperate. We have a flight out of SeaTac Airport this afternoon. I didn't expect to get stuck here. Soon as the ferry starts running, we'll be leaving."

"If you've got a room at the Bird Nest, you might as well stay. All the airports in the area are closed. Flights are all canceled until at least tomorrow morning. I heard hotels are all full around the airport. Better to be stuck here than sitting on the floor at the airport," Mike said. He turned to Abby. "Do you know the missing man?"

"Not personally. I had breakfast with him yesterday morning, but he wasn't talkative. If you want to go check out his room, I'll go with you."

"Sure. Four eyes are better than two."

"I'll go too," Terry said.

Mike looked at the young man. "You stay here. Sergeant Cobb should be here soon," he said.

Abby could see the young man's inner struggle. He was determined to find Dr. Clark, and not happy about being left out, but not quite ready to go against a law officer either.

The door whooshed open again and Janet and Doug Heinz came in with Sam Arbogast.

"Brrr," Janet said, stomping her feet. "Don't know if I've ever seen that much snow in such a short time around here, and I've been here most of my life." She looked around. "Looks like everyone is stuck at home. Shall I start calling and checking on people?" As church secretary, Janet kept track of the Little Flock members.

"Good idea. Did you drive in?" Rev. Hale asked.

"Sam gave us a ride in his truck," Doug said. "I talked to Frank Holloway. He's offered to go get people or take supplies to them in his truck, whatever's needed."

"Great. I spoke to Rick earlier. He's out cutting up a tree that's blocking Dorothy McCullough's driveway off Cross Island Road. She can't get out. He'll bring her to town."

"I'm going out to the farm. Do you want to go with me?" Sam asked Abby.

"If you don't mind waiting a bit, while I go back to the Bird

Nest with Mike. We need to check on a missing man. I'll hurry."

"Missing man? Hope he found shelter. Go ahead," he said, waving her off. "I'll have a cup of coffee here." He removed his work gloves and heavy jacket, but left on his bright red stocking hat that was rolled up on the edges and fitted tight on his head. Sam only stood a couple of inches taller than Abby, but his stocky, muscular build always made Abby feel petite.

"Thanks," Abby said. "I talked to my mom this morning, but she wouldn't admit they needed help unless it was an emergency. Would you mind taking me out to the conservatory? I need to check on the hawk we're rehabilitating and make sure he has food. It won't take long."

"Sure. We'll swing by there first. How about I pick you up at the Bird Nest in twenty minutes?"

"Perfect."

Abby caught Janet as she headed for the church office. "I'm going out to the farm with Sam. We can check on people out that way. Call me if there's anything we can do."

"Okay. Be careful. It's nasty out there," Janet said. "You'll be fine with Sam. He knows how to drive in this stuff."

Abby and Mike trekked through the snow where she'd made tracks before. Grant Niven went with them, but Terry stayed behind. He'd given them a sullen look as they left. Abby was glad Mike had refused his company. There was something about the young man that didn't sit well with Abby. He seemed anxious to find Dr. Clark, but claimed not to know the man personally.

They left Grant downstairs with his wife, and went up to the missing man's room with Martin, who unlocked the door.

The room was cold. Martin explained he'd turned down the thermostat to conserve electricity.

Abby took a quick glance at the decor. Cerulean green silk wallpaper formed wainscot on the walls with a border of fancy goldfish swimming around the room. Several paintings of goldfish with various exotic flowers and fancy Chinese calligraphy lined the walls. A pair of small, intricate bronze lamps hung on the wall on either side of a mirrored dresser. Cutouts of fish circled the lamps. She had stayed in the pheasant room, and this was the fish room. She wondered what motifs were in the other two rooms.

A suitcase sat on the floor next to the antique oak dresser. A spiral notebook sat open on the bedside table.

"Don't disturb or take anything," Mike said. "We don't have a search warrant."

"You don't, but Martin and I are just concerned citizens, looking for possible clues as to where the man went," Abby said. "Don't worry," she added, at Mike's dismayed looked. "We won't bother anything." She glanced down at the notebook. It had doodles and wavy lines and letters and numbers scrawled across the sheet. At first she thought about map coordinates, but the numbers weren't latitude and longitude or hours and compass points. She saw no clues in the unintelligible notations.

Abby noticed a stubby, rounded piece of something striated and whitish-gray with jagged ends sitting on top of the dresser. "Look at this," she said.

"It looks like ivory," Martin said. "Like a piece of a horn of some kind."

Abby picked it up and turned it over. A smudge of brown

came off on her fingers. "It still has dirt on it," Abby said. "He must have found it here on the island."

"You think he's some kind of rock hound or archaeologist?" Mike asked.

"Possibly, although this could be just a chance find. If I saw something like this, I would pick it up to examine further," Abby said.

"Yes, but you're a scientist," Mike said.

"True, but we scientists don't have a corner on the curiosity market. You might start looking for him in some of the more rocky areas on the island. Try the old quarry and rocky areas around the beaches or cliffs."

"I'll tell Sergeant Cobb."

She heard a horn toot and looked out the window. "There's my ride," she said. "I've got to go. I hope you find him."

ABBY PUT ON HER HAT and gloves and hurried out to Sam's truck. When she had her seat belt secured, he put the truck in drive. His tires spun, then grabbed purchase and he steered out into the road. A few vehicles had been out, leaving tire tracks down the street.

"This reminds me of New York, except we'd have several feet of snow on the ground most of the winter," Abby said. "I didn't realize it, but I've missed it. I hope no one's hurt. The coast just isn't prepared for all this white stuff."

Sam slowly turned onto Primrose Lane and headed out of town. "Yeah. We'd get snow like this in Spokane. I don't miss it at all. We're lucky the power's on," Sam said.

"I'll say." She spotted a tan sedan in the ditch. "Look, Sam. There's a car off the road," she said, pointing.

Sam slowed. Abby looked closer. The car was deserted. As they drove along, they saw several other vehicles off the road.

"Look, there's someone walking," Abby said. A woman was waving her arms at them. She carried a black case and the hood of her jacket was pulled up over her head. "It looks like Dr. Randolph."

Sam stopped in the road. No one was coming. He unrolled his window and leaned out. "Hey Doc, climb in. We'll give you a lift," he yelled.

She hurried around the front of the truck. Abby opened the door and scooted over.

"Dana! What are you doing out here?" Abby reached out and took the doctor's hand, helping her climb up into the cab.

"I was going to check on Opal Collins." Dr. Dana Randolph removed her gloves and blew on her hands. "It must be well below freezing out there. Opal has bronchitis. When I talked to her on the phone last night, she sounded worse. I called in a prescription, but she couldn't get to town to get it. Now I'm worried that she might have pneumonia. I don't want her getting out in this weather, so I thought I'd deliver the medication and check on her."

"Did you make it out there?" Sam asked.

"No. I was on my way. I can't believe I got stuck. I have an SUV, you know."

"Four-wheel drive is no guarantee on snowy roads," Sam said.

"Opal lives near the conservatory. Sam, could you drop Dr. Randolph at her house, while you take me to the conservatory? Then we can pick the doctor up on our way back." She turned to Dana. "We're stopping at my folks' farm. Is that all right?"

"Fine. Beats walking to town. Maybe I could call and see if there's a tow truck available, although I'm sure they're all busy."

"Didn't you have your cell phone with you?" Abby asked.

Dana sighed. "Yes, but the battery's dead. I forgot to recharge it."

Abby took out her cell phone and called the church. She relayed the message that the doctor's car needed a tow. Janet told her everyone she'd called was safe, trees were down all over the island, cars lined the ditches, no one could get out, and Henry had arrived. The ferry was running again and a search party had formed to look for the missing man. Unfortunately, they had no idea where to start looking.

"Well, there's good news and bad," Abby announced as she hung up. "According to Janet, the island is devastated, but thank goodness no one's hurt." She looked at Dr. Randolph, then Sam, giving them a cheerful smile. "I do love a good adventure. Gives God a chance to really show His power."

CHAPTER ❧ EIGHT

ABBY SAW THE DAMAGE before Sam parked his truck in the conservatory parking lot. She was out of the truck and plodding through the snow before he turned off the engine. He hurried after her.

The flight cage was destroyed. The tarped top had caved in under the heavy snow. The sides had buckled under the weight. Poles tilted precariously. Some had snapped.

Abby opened the building and found a couple of shovels. "Help me get this snow off," she said, handing a shovel to Sam.

Fearing the worst, Abby listened for the sounds of a distressed bird as they worked at the end closest to the building, clearing the roof above where the hawk roosted. The wind keened through the pine trees. Snow plopped in thuds off laden boughs. She heard the grunts of their labored breathing as she and Sam strained at their work.

"The mesh is torn here," Sam said, stabbing the shovel into the snow. He grabbed the tarp with both hands, lifted and shook it. A shower of snow rained down on them.

Abby shook off the snow, set her shovel down and went over to help Sam. Another shake dislodged most of the rest of the snow. Sam poked the shovel under the tarp and lifted. Abby grabbed her shovel and added her strength. More snow slid off the tarp, freeing it. Abby scrambled beneath it, searching for the injured hawk.

"It's not here." She looked at Sam in disbelief. "I think it escaped. There's no bird and no blood."

"Look." Sam held up a feather. "It was stuck to the mesh where it ripped."

Abby took the white feather. It had the distinctive light brown markings of the light morph rough-legged hawk. He'd escaped. Relief filled her. He'd been flying well.

"He may not have eagle's wings, but he should be strong enough to make it, as long as he wasn't hurt before he escaped." She picked up her shovel. "That's it, Sam. He was our only boarder right now. We'll need major repairs on this flight cage, but that can wait until spring. Just in case he comes back looking for food, I'll set out some raw meat for him. Then let me make a quick check of the museum before we go."

Abby upended a wooden box and set a chunk of raw hamburger on it near the end of the flight cage. If it snowed again, the meat would be high enough that it might not get buried.

They entered the main building through the back door. Soft lighting dimly illuminated the interior. Everything looked fine. They exited the same way and Abby locked up.

"Thanks, Sam. I couldn't have cleared that snow by myself."

"At least not as fast," he said, shrugging off his helpfulness.

The wind increased, whipping up ground blizzards of swirling snow, making navigation difficult and slow as they drove to pick up Dr. Randolph, then on to Stanton Farm.

Ellen met them at the door and ushered them in to the warm kitchen.

The aroma of fresh bread and cinnamon reached her before she entered the room. "Yum. I didn't know I was hungry until I smelled that," Abby said, giving her mother a kiss on the cheek.

"Come in and sit down," Ellen urged. "Give me your wet hats and gloves. I'll dry them by the fireplace."

"Where's George?" Sam asked.

"Out at the barn. He'll be here in a minute."

"I'll go see if I can help him," Sam said, already on his way out the back door.

"I'll put our things by the fire, Mom, if you could make something hot to drink." Abby took their wet things to the living room and hung them over a rack her mother had set up. Cheery flames crackled in the fireplace. Abby held her hands up to the fire and felt the welcoming warmth soothe away her chill. She rubbed them together, then went back to the kitchen.

"Dana was just telling me about Opal," Ellen said. "I'll have to take her some cinnamon rolls and chicken soup."

"That would be wonderful," Dana said. "I don't think she's eating very well."

"Mom's chicken soup will cure anything," Abby said. "These rolls must be medicinal too," she said, grinning. "*Umm*. They're still hot." She served a piece to Dana and got one for herself, then pulled out a chair and sat down.

"I'll get a chicken out of the freezer," Ellen said, going out to the utility room.

Abby took a bite just as her cell phone rang. She swallowed quickly and licked her fingers, then answered the phone. The lit screen read Janet.

"Hi. What's up?"

"Rick DeBow is on his way to pull Dr. Dana's car out of the ditch. Where are you?"

"We're at the farm. Can he come here first and get Dr. Dana? Then she can drive back to town and he can follow her to make sure she doesn't get stuck again. There are cars all over the place."

"So we've heard. I'll tell him to pick her up."

"Thanks. Anything else?"

"Just that we've got another storm warning. More snow and frigid temperatures. Looks like this is going to hang around for a while. They're trying to get crews over here to clear the main roads, but they're stretched pretty thin, with all the islands and the mainland in a mess. When are you coming back?"

"Soon. My folks are fine, but I think Sam's going to stay and help my dad. Maybe I'll get a ride with Rick and Dana. I'm not needed here." Much as she'd love to stay and have a bowl of fresh chicken noodle soup, she needed to help the Chois with their raccoon problem. She hung up and quickly finished her sweet roll.

A *beep-beep* alerted them to Rick DeBow's arrival. He came up to the door, but declined Ellen's invitation to come inside and have a cup of coffee and a cinnamon roll. He'd been out helping people and his boots and clothes were wet and dirty, he said.

"Hard to believe it's barely noon," Abby commented as they rode back to town in Rick's truck. "I feel like I've been through a full day already. I nearly forgot about the Chois and their uninvited guests."

"I imagine they've filled up with extra people needing a place to stay," Dana said.

"These are four-legged guests," Abby said. "I'm pretty sure, from the sounds, that they have raccoons in the attic. They've been scratching around, waking the guests. We pinpointed their location. I'm supposed to help evict them this afternoon if we can find their entry, so we can board it up. I might need your help, Rick."

"Give me a call. If I'm available, I'll be happy to help," he said.

A county road-grader came at them out of the blowing snow. Rick steered as far to the edge as possible. The back wheels of his truck started to skid. He slowed to a crawl, gently pumping his brakes. The large grader crept past them, blade down, pushing snow. Not exactly a snowplow, but at least it was moving some of the snow off the road.

MARY STARED OUT the back window at the winter wonderland. Trees bowed under thick white frosting. Bare trees had turned into fanciful white sculptures. The storage shed and the bird feeders were snow covered. Gusty wind tossed sparkly white powder into the air like fairy dust.

"You think we need to cancel the ice cream social?" she asked Janet on the telephone.

"I think we need to postpone it. Who wants ice cream when it's freezing outside? The news said this arctic front's staying awhile. It won't be gone by next Saturday." Mary heard a long sigh. "I'm so disappointed," Janet said.

"What do Ida and Patricia think?"

"Patricia agrees. She's busy feeding workers and she said we should get through this crisis, then think about doing the social in a few weeks, after all this melts off."

"I suppose she's right. I wish I could help."

"Don't even think about going out in this snow, Mary Reynolds. We've got enough to contend with without your getting stuck driving in this. It's a mess."

"Don't worry. I won't."

Janet began relaying the plight of other islanders. After several accounts, Mary knew if she stayed on the phone much longer, Janet would tell her every detail about every person on the island. Janet loved to share what she knew. She didn't mean any harm. She just loved to talk. "I'll go along with whatever you and Patricia and Ida decide," Mary said, turning the conversation back to the Hawaiian social. "I doubt we'll get our flower orders this week anyway, unless the wind blows this snow out of here."

"Okay. Gotta go. Some of the rescue crew just came in. Bye."

Mary had to smile at Janet's abrupt good-bye. She was efficient and caring and loved to be in the middle of everything. From the sound of things, Janet had plenty to keep her busy. Mary hung up her phone and stared at it, half expecting it to ring again. She'd talked to more people today than on a normal day when she went in to the flower shop. When the phone didn't ring, she slipped it into the pocket attached to her wheelchair arm.

Finnegan lay sleeping on the rug in front of the fireplace. Henry had laid kindling and logs in the fireplace, and the day begged for a cozy fire, but Mary hadn't lit it. If the power went out, she would need that warmth. A *whoosh* drew her attention outside. A pine bough bounced in relief after dumping a load of snow.

Although she was warm and cozy, a sense of chill and isolation descended on her. She caught a glimpse of what cabin fever meant. She couldn't get out, and others couldn't get in easily.

Not that she was truly alone. She had her beloved Finnegan, who lived to serve her, and Blossom, who lived to serve herself, as cats were prone to do. In the hierarchy of residents, Blossom was the queen of Mary's castle. And Mary didn't mind a bit. She thought about her situation for a moment. Without Abby, her home seemed empty. Though it hadn't been that long ago that their lives were separated by almost three thousand miles and a rift as deep, Mary couldn't imagine life without her sister.

She'd become so comfortable and close to Abby, she hoped she didn't take her sister for granted. She reached for her telephone to call Abby, but her hand landed on her Bible instead. Lifting it out of its pocket, she smoothed her hand over its quilted cover. She unzipped it and opened it to the bookmarked page in John where she'd been reading.

Picking up where she left off, she read, "I will ask the Father, and he will give you another Counselor to be with you forever—the Spirit of truth. . . . you know him, for he lives with you and will be in you" (John 14:16–17).

For He lives with you. She'd read that many times before. She'd highlighted a verse farther down. "Peace I leave with you; my peace I give you. I do not give to you as the world gives. Do not let your hearts be troubled and do not be afraid" (John 14:27). *It might look like I'm isolated and alone,* she thought, *but God is right here with me.* He'd proven that to her over and over—especially during those days right after her accident. "Thank You, Lord, for reminding me."

Finnegan looked up when he heard her voice. Realizing she wasn't speaking to him, he laid his head back down on his front paws and closed his eyes. "Let me see the snow as a blanket of Your peace and comfort, not a prison," Mary said. "It really is beautiful outside, Finnegan."

At the sound of his name and "outside," Finnegan jumped to his feet and shook. Ready for duty.

"I do wish I could go outside and play with you," she said.

He came over to her and put his head in her lap. As he did, the phone rang.

"Hi. This is Bobby. Can I come over and play with Finnegan?"

"You certainly may. He needs to get out and get some exercise."

"Great! I'll be right there. Thanks."

Bobby hung up. Mary hung up the phone and put it away. Reaching out, she smoothed her hand over Finnegan's soft head.

"Looks like my wish is granted. It may not be me outside with you, but I'll have the joy of watching you and Bobby romp around. And I won't be the one getting wet and cold," she said, chuckling.

CHAPTER ❦ NINE

ABBY, MARTIN AND TERZA crept up the stairs to the attic, wearing soft-soled slippers and armed with a remnant of plywood, scraps of board, a hammer and nails that Martin had found in his shed. Martin had gone along with their plan reluctantly, still not convinced there were real animals in his attic. Abby didn't expect to find the raccoons there in the middle of the day, but she didn't want to take a chance. At the door, she stepped aside and let Martin unlock the door.

He hesitated before carefully turning the doorknob, opening the door silently. He entered and stopped, holding his arm out to the side, preventing the ladies from entering until he was satisfied it was safe.

He stepped in and listened for a moment, then motioned them forward. The three advanced carefully toward the small trunk against the north wall. Terza stepped on a squeaky board.

Hisssss.

The sound stopped them in their tracks. A deep growl followed the hiss. Hissing and growling echoed in the open room, surrounding them with nerve-jarring menace.

Martin grabbed Terza's arm and pulled her back toward the door. Abby stood still, listening, trying to determine the location. It sounded like it came from behind the trunk. She'd assumed the animals would leave during the daytime, but evidently she'd been wrong.

"Abby, come away from there," Martin whispered loudly. "They might be dangerous."

Abby joined her hosts. The raccoons remained hidden. Wild animals could be dangerous and could carry diseases, so she didn't want to take a chance without proper equipment.

"Leave the light on, Martin. If they're nocturnal, they won't like light. That might encourage them to leave," Abby said.

"I don't know. We shouldn't disturb them," Martin said.

"Actually, we should disturb them, so they'll leave. They don't like light or loud noise. We could put a radio up here."

"Leave it on," Terza said. "We want them to leave."

Martin shut and locked the door. "No radio," he said. "We want to placate them, not disturb them. I will prepare a special meal. You will join us, Abby?"

"Thank you, Martin. I've imposed on your hospitality enough, and I should go home. Mary has been alone since yesterday."

"I don't think your car will make it. Too much snow," he said.

"I hope Mary is all right," Terza said. "You're stuck here because of us. If you can't get home, we'd like you to stay."

"Let me call Mary and see how she's doing. I'd like to keep an eye on the attic and see if the raccoons decide to leave at some point. My father mentioned putting flour on the ground, so their tracks are visible. The snow will serve the same purpose."

"I'm going to start dinner," Martin said, leaving them on the second floor landing. He was frowning as he descended the stairs.

Terza shook her head. She glanced around. They were alone. The Nivens had left and Terry was still gone with the search crew. "Martin thinks there's a bad spirit in the attic," she said. "He knows that's not real. I told him he was acting like a super-stitious old woman. He said it can't hurt to align the elements."

"He mentioned elements before. What are they?" Abby asked.

"Chinese years revolve in ten-year cycles. Different years are controlled by different elements. They are wood, which is Martin's element, earth, which is mine, fire, metal and water. Each element has a color and certain qualities. Martin values ethics and generosity and he's a good businessman, but he can be stubborn," she said, sighing and shaking her head. "I'm more practical. He's going to do things to make us lucky now, but it won't work. Your way's better. We need to get rid of the animals in the attic."

"Cooking a lucky meal can't hurt anything," Abby said gently. "It will help him keep his mind off the trouble. Maybe Rick or Sam can help us evict the unwanted guests."

"Our other guest is still missing too. I worry about him. He was a strange man. Very secret. He could be hurt somewhere. I know it's a coincidence that he's staying here, but I pray for him, that he is safe and the sheriff's men will find him."

"Henry and his men will find Mr. Clark. But I'm sure prayers will help. Now don't let me keep you from what you need to do. I'll go call Mary."

"I'll be in the den. I need to go through the mail. I'm so far behind, I haven't looked at all the Christmas cards yet, and I like to answer them."

Terza went downstairs.

Abby went into her room and got her cell phone. She went over by the window and looked out as she punched in Mary's number. Leaning closer to the window, she stared at the snow.

How odd, she thought, looking closer as she waited for Mary to pick up the phone.

"ABBY! I'M GLAD YOU CALLED. Did you get rid of the Chois' intruders?"

"Unfortunately, no. They seem to be living there full time. I suppose they haven't been heard during the day, because inn guests don't spend the daytime in their rooms. When we went up this afternoon, the animals hissed and growled at us. Poor Martin is certain they are some other-worldly visitation. I'm going to call Rick to come help evict them, but how are you?"

"Having a fairly quiet, but enjoyable day." She glanced out the patio door and grinned. Bobby waved at her. She waved back just as Finnegan jumped up on the boy and knocked him off his feet into the snow. They wrestled for Finnegan's ball in the white powder. Mary laughed. "Bobby's here, playing with Finnegan. They've made a mess of my beautiful, pristine snow, but they're having a blast. I was wishing I could join them, but they've both got to be soaking wet and freezing cold. I'll have to make Bobby some hot chocolate."

"Bless his heart. What a sweetie to come over."

"Yes. It's been that kind of a day. He and Neil scraped snow off the walk. And I think I've talked to everyone I know today. Zach called. Nancy called. They both heard about our snowstorm on national news."

"Hugo called me from Florida. He heard on the news too."

"So we've become famous," Mary said. "That's okay. Any excuse to hear from my son and daughter are welcome. Nancy put the children on the phone. I can't believe how grown-up Emily sounds. Much older than seven. She told me she's praying for us. And Nicholas. I nearly cried when his little voice said 'Hi, Gamma.' And Henry's called three times from various parts of the island. He's out on a manhunt, but you know about that."

"Sounds like you had a perfect day," Abby said, smiling, knowing how much her sister adored her children and grandchildren. "Have they found Dr. Clark?"

"No. They don't know where to look, so they're trying to cover the entire island. They've rescued a couple of residents, though, so all's not in vain. Henry says there are lots of trees down and cars stuck in ditches. He gave me a strong warning not to leave the house, dear man. I promised."

"The snow's too deep for my car," Abby said. "They're plowing with the road department's only grader, so it could take days. I thought I'd ask Rick or Sam to take me home. When this clears up, we can come back in the van to get my car."

"Don't come, Abby. No sense both of us being stuck here. I'm fine. Sandy and Neil keep checking on me. I invited them to come over for stew, which is simmering in the crock pot. Sandy's bringing fresh baked bread. She's enjoying a forced day at home."

"Are you sure? I don't like leaving you alone."

"I'm sure. I'm enjoying being a pioneer." She laughed. "Of course, I have electricity and heat and indoor plumbing. Pretty cozy. Even if the power goes out, I'm fine. I expect Henry will stop by sometime this evening. He said he'd come for stew if he can take a break. All the sheriff's vehicles have chains, so they're getting around in the snow."

"All right. The Chois invited me to stay another night. Martin's cooking up a storm. He's determined to bring good luck back to his home. Getting rid of the intruders will help restore his peace of mind, I'm sure."

"I'm sure it will. Don't worry about me."

"I'll try not to. Love you," Abby said.

"And me, you. Bye, sis." Mary hung up the phone. Just talking to her sister left a warm glow in her heart. She put the phone in its pocket and wheeled into the kitchen. Bobby and Finnegan would be in soon. She filled the kettle with water and put it on the stove to heat.

LIGHT SNOW BEGAN FALLING outside the bedroom window. Abby studied the snow on the railing and posts around the small balcony. She hadn't been mistaken. Little prints like stubby human hands with five fingers and feet with five long toes left indentations in the snow. The upstairs denizens were getting in somewhere above her window. And they were mobile. If she calculated correctly, they'd gone in, not out. Now they had to wait until the raccoons left and hope they all left together.

Abby thought about walking down to Little Flock to pray for her sister, the situation with the raccoons and the missing Dr. Clark. The church always seemed the most peaceful, Spirit-filled place to pray, but Rev. Hale had invited the sheriff's office and the community to use the church as a refuge and meeting place, so the sanctuary might be full of people. Instead, she knelt by the chair next to the bed and picked up her Bible. She opened to one of her favorite Psalms and bowed her head. "Please, Lord, You hold the universe in Your hands. Calm this new storm. Let us have just enough snow to cover these tracks, so I can see when they leave. Protect Mary and Henry and my mom and dad. Help Henry find Mr. Clark and let him be safe. Restore Martin's peace of mind. Show him that their blessings are not luck, but Your favor. Show him You are more powerful than all the superstitions in the world. Amen."

Peace seeped into Abby's heart. She picked up her Bible and took it with her downstairs to join Terza.

Terza was sitting at a table in the gentlemen's study. Yellow chrysanthemums, red kalanchoes and dark pink azaleas lined the window, turning the room into a springtime garden.

Terza was sorting through a basket of mail and had made neat stacks around her. She looked up and gave Abby one of her gracious smiles. "Please join me," she said. "Would you like a cup of tea?"

"Yes, thanks. What a lovely teapot," Abby said, taking a seat across from her, facing the flowers.

"It's a blue lotus teapot, designed to look like two lotus leaves together."

Abby thought it looked a bit like a blue version of a genie lamp, with its squat body and long spout. As Terza poured tea into a matching cup with no handle, Abby said, "It looks so cheery in here with all the flowers. I could almost forget there's snow outside."

"Martin bought them from Mary's shop yesterday. There are more in the entry hallway." She sighed, giving Abby a resigned look. "They are for luck, you know." She added in a low voice, "Martin got out a book on Chinese holidays and traditions and spent hours reading it and making notes." Terza looked around and pointed to the chrysanthemum. "That one is ju hua, which means prosperity flower. All these plants are supposed to bring good fortune."

Abby smiled. "Well, they certainly bring cheer. Goodness, how do you keep up with so much mail?"

"I don't. That's the problem. I can't believe how fast it piles up."

"Sometimes I feel that way at the conservatory. It multiplies like rabbits, doesn't it?"

"Yes. It will take a month to answer all the Christmas and New Year's greetings." Terza placed another card with a holiday stamp on the growing pile. "Most of the cards are from former guests. At least our bill pile is small. I gave them to Martin as they came in. I hope none of them ended up in this basket."

She picked up a thick envelope and turned it over to see who it was from. She sighed. "I wish people would put their return address on cards. How am I supposed to write back?" Picking up her carved ivory letter opener, she slit the top of the envelope. As she pulled out a plain card with gold edges, something fell out and landed on the tablecloth with a clunk.

Terza picked it up and turned it over. "This is strange." She looked at the envelope again, then opened the card. "It says, 'What is unsought will go undetected.' It isn't signed. The tile has Chinese characters."

"May I see it?" Abby asked. Terza handed it to her. The flat, square piece of ivory had Chinese characters carved all over both sides. "It looks old. Do you know what these figures mean?" Abby asked.

"This single character in the corner is *qi*, which stands for the number seven. I don't know what the others are. The other side looks like part of a character. I can't tell what it means."

"Seven? Does that mean anything special? Is it a lucky number?"

Terza shook her head. "No. It's not lucky. *Qi*, or seven, sounds like the word *together*. A word or character is considered lucky or unlucky by what it sounds like. I don't know what *qi* or together has to do with anything."

"Perhaps Martin will have some idea," Abby said.

"I'll ask him later. I don't want to go in the kitchen. It's freezing in there."

"Freezing? What happened?"

"Martin has the window open. He'll get sick and then he'll blame it on the creatures in the attic. He'll say it's bad luck." She shook her head. "I can't convince him to close it."

Martin's superstitions made no sense to Abby. She was too logical by nature and training to consider anything lucky or unlucky. "Why would he want the window open when it's below freezing outside?"

"It's his element, which is wood. His lucky direction is east. He laments that the house faces north, but the kitchen window faces east, and it's supposed to be good for him to keep an east window open."

"Ah. Well, fresh air is good for him, and he's a healthy man. He won't get sick."

"He might if I bonk him on the head," Terza said very quietly.

With some effort, Abby kept a straight face. Terza never said anything disparaging about anyone—especially her husband. She'd be horrified if she offended anyone. Though Martin and Terza rarely touched in public, even after decades of marriage, the Chois' love for each other was obvious by their gentleness and respect for one another and the affectionate glances they exchanged when they thought no one was watching. Abby gave Terza a knowing smile. "You wouldn't do that."

Terza covered her mouth and giggled. "Only in my mind," she said, "and only enough to make him see sense."

Abby laughed. "I can think of a few times I've been tempted that way. Especially when I taught college."

Terza nodded. She picked up another fat envelope. "Look. It's like the other one." She slit it open and shook out another tile. Also ivory, with carving, this one was shaped like a triangle. "The card says, 'Search and you will find it.' Find what?"

"Maybe the tile tells you. Can you read the characters?"

She studied both sides, then tried putting the two tiles together. She flipped one tile and tried again. "Nothing makes sense. There must be more."

"Maybe there's another card. May I see the envelopes?"

Terza handed Abby the empty envelopes, then dug through the pile of mail.

The envelopes were hand-printed in precise letters, very even and straight. They were addressed to Choi Ching-kuo Xiansheng and Furen at the Bird Nest. One envelope had a Los Angeles postmark and the other came from Seattle, but there were no other markings, no return address.

"The addresses seem to be printed by the same person. What do the names mean?"

"They are addresses giving us high respect," Terza said. "It's like saying Honorable Mr. Choi and Madame Choi, which is very strange."

"Why?"

"It means a lady of high rank, which is ridiculous. I have no rank, no royal ancestors. This person is mistaken." She fingered one of the tiles, rubbing her thumb over its satiny smoothness and artistic etching. "Whoever sent these must be Chinese and have a classical education, or she is very old-fashioned. I don't know anyone who uses such formal language these days."

"You think it's a woman? Why?"

Terza laughed. "A woman takes more time. Martin learned good handwriting, but he hurries too much."

"I think Martin has beautiful handwriting," Abby said. "I remember the place cards he made for the Chinese New Year. They were lovely."

"Yes, when he wants to honor our guests, he does excellent calligraphy," she said. "When he makes a grocery list, I cannot read it."

Abby smiled. "Perhaps he has his own shorthand. Any idea who might have sent the tiles?"

Terza shook her head slowly. "I can't think of anyone who would send such a gift."

"It must be someone you know."

"Our friends and family would not call me madame."

"Perhaps a former guest," Abby suggested. "That would be the place to start solving this riddle." Abby glanced out the window. "Oh good. The snow's letting up. I prayed we wouldn't get another foot of snow. I saw footprints outside my window upstairs. I believe your visitors come in and out of the attic up there. With the new snow, we can watch for footprints, then go up and board up their entrance."

Terza's serene face broke into a smile. "That's wonderful news. I can't take much more of Martin's attempts to change our luck. Spring's supposed to be his lucky season. I can't wait that long."

CHAPTER ❦ TEN

Bobby AND MARY SAT IN the living room with mugs of hot chocolate. A cheery fire danced in the fireplace. Finnegan plodded over to the fireplace rug and laid down. He let out a big sigh, then shut his eyes. Poor dog. He was exhausted. Mary chuckled.

"You wore him out," she told Bobby.

"He wore me out," he said. "That was fun! I wish it snowed every winter."

"I bet they'll cancel school tomorrow."

"Yeah! Can I play with Finnegan again?"

"Sure. I know he'd like that. Maybe you could make a snowman for me."

"Neat. I want to go sledding. We have a sled in the garage from when we went to the mountains last year. Dad said he'd get it down for me tomorrow."

"What fun! I'd love to watch you. Maybe if the roads get cleared, you could go over to the hill behind the school. I could watch you from my van."

Bobby's hazel eyes lit up and even his freckles seemed to smile. "Sweet! Maybe I could find someone to race me."

Mary remembered sledding with Abby on a hill in the mountains near Snoqualmie when they were about Bobby's age. She could still feel the chilled wind against her cheeks, her pigtails whipping against her face, and her eyes watering. They'd end up rolling in the snow, giggling with delight until their sides hurt.

"That's a great idea, Bobby. You could organize a sled race."

"Really? Do you think I could?"

"Sure. Maybe your dad would help you."

"I'll ask him tonight!"

Mary's phone rang just then. Bobby picked up their empty cups while she answered it.

"Hey, Mary, it's Ida. How are you doing? Are you okay out there?"

"Hi Ida. I'm fine. Bobby's here. I was watching him play with Finnegan in the snow."

"Isn't it fabulous? I love it! I just made a snowman in front of the restaurant. I put a chef's hat and apron on him and tied a knife and fork to his hands." Ida giggled. "I haven't done that in years."

"That sounds like fun. I've been sitting here looking out and thinking how beautiful it is. Not a sight we get to see very often."

"Exactly. Janet came to the restaurant for lunch. She said everything's crazy at the church, and she needed a break. They served soup and chili and hot drinks to people all day long. I guess you heard about the missing man?"

"Yes. Henry's out looking for him."

"Henry and a bunch of people. I told Janet I think it's the guy who's been coming in here for dinner every day, except yesterday he didn't come in. I thought maybe he'd left. Odd guy. Wouldn't look you in the eye. I think he's hiding something. I told Sergeant Cobb that too. Maybe he's a criminal running from the law or maybe he got stuck while he was burying stolen loot." Her voice rose with every imagined scenario. "Maybe he's out there, buried in the snow, injured. They've got to find him. Even if he's a criminal, we can't let him die out there."

"I'm sure he's just a tourist who values his privacy. They'll find him, and he'll be just fine. He can't have gone far. The island isn't that big."

"They don't know why he's here, so they don't know where to look," Ida said. "I'm going to ask around. Who knows? Maybe I'll solve a mystery, like Abby."

Mary envisioned Ida, traipsing around alone, looking for the missing man. And what if he *was* hiding something illegal? "Promise me you won't go out on your own. Let the search and rescue team do the looking," Mary said.

"Oh, don't worry. I wouldn't do that. I'll just ask questions. And speaking of Janet, that's why I called. She thinks we should cancel the Hawaiian ice cream social this Saturday. She says this weather spoils the mood."

Mary adjusted to Ida's shift in topics. "She mentioned that to me too. It might be better to postpone it until the snow's gone."

"Let's have a snowman competition instead," Ida suggested. "Everyone could make a snowman in front of their house or store or in the park."

"The park's centrally located," Mary said. "Bobby wants to

have a sled race. The school isn't far from the park, and there's a good hill there."

"Hey, we could have a winter carnival!" Ida said, her excitement rising. "I read about one in Quebec that sounded fabulous. Course, we couldn't do anything that fancy, but we could have a festival in the park. It'd be fun."

Mary agreed. They should make the most of their unusual snow. Nothing elaborate. A few snow games and a snowman competition, perhaps. "I heard on the news that the artic temperatures will only be with us for a week. We'd have to hurry, but we could put something simple together for next weekend. Did you mention this to Janet and Patricia?"

"Not yet. I just thought of it. If you think we could do it, I'll talk to them." Ida's voice sounded hesitant but hopeful.

"By all means, talk to them. I can't get to town for a couple of days, but I could make phone calls."

"Super! Oh, this is going to be so much fun! I'll call them and let you know what they think. Thanks, Mary."

Mary laughed. "I didn't do anything."

"Yes you did. You listened, and you didn't think my idea was silly. Call you later. Bye."

Mary hung up and shook her head, smiling. Ah, the energy of youth. Ida and Bobby shared the same excitement about the snow. Mary hoped others would catch their enthusiasm and see the unexpected snow as a blessing instead of a catastrophe.

LEAVING TERZA TO FINISH going through her mail, Abby went upstairs to her room. Darkness came early at the island's northern latitude, and the cloud-cover made the dusk settle in even earlier. With the streetlights on, there was barely enough light reflecting off the snow to illuminate the balcony outside her window. She stared, squinting through her glasses, trying to focus on anything marring the white, powdery snow.

The fresh snow appeared undisturbed. Sighing, she started to turn away, when a slight movement caught her attention. Years of observing birds and nature had trained her to notice even the slightest motion. Standing still, barely daring to breathe, she waited for something to appear. The house was so quiet, she could hear the clock in the hall. She prayed no one would come upstairs or make a loud noise and warn away the creature. A minute ticked away slowly. She began to wonder if her mind had tricked her.

She sensed, rather than saw movement. Something was up in the corner of the balcony, at the roofline. As her eyes adjusted to the dim light, a sharp black nose surrounded by lighter, grayish hair appeared. A paw reached out and grabbed the post, then another. Slowly, a figure appeared. A raccoon. Just as she'd suspected. A pair of shiny, beady eyes, ringed in black, stared at her. She dared not look directly at it. She stood rigid, holding her breath. After a moment, a noise in the street distracted it, and it looked away. Abby took a deep breath. The raccoon descended the pole and another appeared.

It seemed she stood still for an eternity, as four raccoons descended from the roof and climbed down the pole, across the balcony railing, then down across the roof of the porch. She knew raccoons had an extensive repertoire of sounds with which they communicated, and she marveled that they'd discovered a way into the house. Martin and Rick had examined the roof and she had also studied the outside of the house. God's creation never ceased to amaze her.

The raccoons finally disappeared, and Abby jumped into

"Cool!" Bobby said, jumping up and shooting his fist into the air.

"Right now, let's eat while this is hot," Sandy said, taking a seat at the table.

After Mary gave thanks and as they began eating, Neil asked, "Have you heard any more from Henry?"

"He called two hours ago," Mary said, passing the bread to Sandy. "No sign of the missing man. The snow slows things down, but they're still searching. Henry said if they haven't found him by nighttime, he'll call off the search until daylight."

"I wonder where he could be." Sandy said.

"I saw him the other day when I was in Holloway's Hardware," Neil said. "Frank asked what he was doing on the island, just friendly-like, you know. The guy said he was checking out fishing spots. Seemed kind of funny. He didn't buy any fishing gear. He bought a pick ax and a shovel. Seemed more like he'd be digging for something." Neil was buttering a piece of bread. He held his knife in the air. "Strange guy, if you ask me."

"Maybe he's a pirate," Bobby said.

"Now, son, don't go getting any ideas," Neil warned. "I'm sure he's just a tourist who doesn't want anyone bothering him."

Bobby loved a mystery almost as much as Abby and aspired to solve every puzzle that came into his radar screen. He also had a vivid imagination. Turning the subject, Mary said, "I talked to Ida Tolliver today, and she wants to organize a winter carnival."

"Way cool," Bobby said. "What's a winter carnival? Is it like a circus, with rides?"

"Not exactly. Your idea of a sled race would fit in perfectly, though, if you could organize it."

Bobby's face lit up as he jumped in his seat. "Can we, Dad?"

"When is this, Mary?"

"She's talking about next Saturday. It's supposed to stay cold all week, so it should work."

"All right, son. We'll do it. But I have to work all week, so you'll have to make the arrangements."

"I'll be glad to help," Sandy said. "I can clear using the school hill."

"Sweet!" Bobby hollered, high-fiving the air. "I can't wait."

"Better eat your stew so you'll have some energy," his mother said, smiling at her son's enthusiasm.

ABBY, MARTIN, TERZA AND RICK crowded around the front window in the room Abby was occupying. Abby shined a flashlight on the snow outside the window. "See there on the railing?" she said.

The tracks were clear, and looked as if a large family of raccoons had exited. There were no tracks headed back.

Rick peered out at the paw prints.

"We need to act quickly, before they return," Abby said.

Martin let out a sigh. "Yes. We must keep them out."

Terza's tender look showed her concern for his feelings. She understood her husband's hesitations and deeply ingrained traditions, even when old fears and superstitions contradicted the freedom he knew he had in his faith. But Abby had to admit, there were times when she caught herself leaning back on old habits and traditions. Although she wasn't superstitious, sometimes old fears crept in. It was easy to trust when things went right. Not so easy when problems arose and everything seemed to go wrong.

"Let's go. I still have the plywood here," Abby said, picking up an unfinished scrap of wood.

"Lead the way, Martin. Let's get 'er done," Rick said.

Squaring his shoulders, Martin led them up the stairs to the attic. He glanced back at them with a warning look, then carefully unlocked the door and inched it open.

Light from the overhead bulb spilled out of the attic. The group advanced slowly and stealthily into the room, listening as they crept forward. Abby only heard their footsteps and breathing. Terza bumped into something and gasped. Martin stopped and turned to her.

"Are you okay?" he whispered.

Terza put her hands over her mouth and nodded. She giggled. Squeezing her eyes shut, she tried to stop, but the giggles kept spilling out. Terza had a good sense of humor, but Abby suspected her laughter was a release of tension and nerves rather than merriment.

Seeing she was all right, Abby and Rick moved forward. There'd been no hissing or growling, even with Terza's noise.

"I think their hiding place is behind that trunk," Abby said in a low, but normal voice. The trunk sat against the front wall in a gable that extended over the balcony off Abby's room and part of the room next door to hers. The gable ceiling was steeply slanted.

"Let's see what we've got," Rick said, bending down to avoid hitting his head on the pitched ceiling where it met the knee wall. He reached for the trunk.

"Wait," Martin said.

Rick stopped, his hands extended in midair.

"It's safe, Martin. I'm sure the sound came from the wall behind the trunk, and they're gone," Abby said.

Martin sighed. "All right." He watched as Rick set the small trunk aside and knelt down in front of the wall.

"I don't see anything," Rick said. "You're sure the sound came from here?"

"Yes. Somewhere along this wall. I'm pretty certain it would be near the area between the two bedrooms. The noise could be heard from both rooms. Isn't that right?" Abby asked, turning to Martin and Terza. Martin was eyeing the trunk.

"Yes. Both guests complained," Terza said.

Rick felt along the wall. "This paneling isn't original. Someone has added it to the walls."

Martin crouched down. He gave the trunk a wary look, then said, "Remove the wall."

"Will do." Rick put on his work gloves, then pulled a long screwdriver from his tool belt and used it to pry away the molding. As he worked to loosen a panel, the veneered particle board chipped and broke. A false wall had been erected several inches away from the outside wall, leaving a space that had been filled in with insulation.

"I'm sorry, Martin. I can't save the paneling."

"It is fake. Take it down. We will replace it with something real."

"We can secure it for now, and I'll help you tackle the walls later." Rick popped off a piece of paneling. The loose, blown-in insulation fell out, raising a dust cloud. It looked like shredded cardboard boxes that had gotten wet, then dried out.

"I'll get trash bags," Terza said. She hurried away.

Rick backed away from the wall and stood. He examined

the attic walls. "I'd guess the original attic was unfinished, and this paneling was added thirty or forty years ago."

"I should have removed it sooner," Martin said.

Terza reappeared with a large, heavy plastic trash bag, a broom, dust pan and cleaning materials.

Rick ripped back the paneling in both directions from where the trunk sat. Martin put on gloves and cleaned up the insulation that fell out of the wall. Suddenly Rick broke through a spot, and cold air poured into the room, bringing with it a sour odor.

"I found it," he shouted triumphantly. He opened it wider and cleared away the rubble with his gloved hands.

Abby, Martin and Terza squatted down, then crept forward on their knees. They peered into the opening. A screened vent, which had been hidden by the paneling, was ripped, allowing the raccoons to get inside the space between the outer wall and the false wall. Soggy insulation had packed down between the outer wall studs.

"Don't touch that with your hands," Abby warned. "It may contain dangerous parasites. There may be more nest area, but this looks like their entrance to the attic. When we get it cleaned up, we should wash it down with lye or ammonia," Abby said. "Animals are persistent. When they find this entrance boarded up, they may try to get through another way. The smell will deter them."

"If I can get out on your balcony, I can put up some temporary reinforcement," Rick said. "It seems to be up under the eaves, so it won't show. That's why we missed it. We can do more extensive prevention later."

Terza refused to let anyone else do the cleanup. She put on gloves, tied a cloth around her face, covering her nose and mouth, then got down on her hands and knees and soon had the area spotless. Standing, she stripped off the disposable gloves and threw them into the trash with the debris. She removed the cloth from her face. "Phew, they made a mess," she said. She scrunched her nose in a show of distaste. "I'm glad to get that cleaned up."

Rick nailed up the plywood, blocking the torn vent. "That should keep them out," he said. He removed more of the paneling and insulation to allow the area to air out. "Here's your electrical problem," he said. Wire came up through the wall and ran out to the rooms. "They don't look frayed, but I suspect the raccoons disturbed them." He wrapped the wires with black electrical tape. "That should keep them safe until we redo the walls."

Rick and Martin cleaned up the debris. Martin glanced at the small trunk. "At least they weren't inside the trunk."

Terza examined the trunk. "They didn't damage it. I wonder what happened to the key."

"It must be downstairs," Martin said. "We'll find it."

"No hurry," she said. "The trunk's empty."

Rick straightened up and put his tools in his tool belt. "We caught your pests in the nick of time, before they broke through into the attic room," he said. "From the scratches on the back of the paneling, I'd say they were working on it."

"Setting the elements straight worked very fast," Martin said, smiling with satisfaction.

"The raccoons' noise was a blessing in disguise," Abby said. "If your guests hadn't been disturbed, you'd never have known they were here until it was too late."

"If they'd exposed those wires, you could have had a fire," Rick added.

"Not bad luck after all," Terza said. "Very good fortune. God has blessed us, Martin."

Martin's eyes widened as he digested their comments. He stared at the boarded up wall, as if the realization left him speechless. "Thank you," he said in a solemn voice. He turned and carried the trash bag out and plodded down the back stairway to the kitchen.

Watching him go, Abby gave thanks that the raccoon incident ended so successfully for her friends. She hoped the puzzle of the anonymous cards would turn into a blessing too.

CHAPTER ❦ ELEVEN

THIS IS A FEAST, MARTIN. It feels like Chinese New Year all over again. I must remember to thank our raccoons if I ever see them again," Abby said as she picked up a bite of chicken and Chinese noodles with chop sticks.

"Thanks for including me in your feast." Rick used the fork Martin had provided to take a bite.

Martin's face turned a shade of red. Abby knew he was a modest man, and assumed the praise embarrassed him. He gave a small bow with his head. "I'm glad you like my humble offering. I wish I could say I prepared it to honor you, who have helped us so much. I made these to bring fortune back into our home. They are the same foods I prepare on Chinese New Year to insure prosperity and health."

Abby smiled at her host. "They've brought us good fortune tonight, because we get to enjoy them at your gracious table. Everything's delicious."

"Our good fortune is our friends," he said, raising his water glass to them. "Thank you for saving our home. I do not like to share our home with wild animals that destroy our attic and disturb our guests."

"Perhaps Abby will help us again," Terza said, glancing at her. "We have another riddle to solve."

Martin's eyebrows rose and his eyes widened with dismay. "The raccoons did not come back, did they?"

"Oh no. This riddle came in the mail. I haven't had time to show you. I will get it now." Terza excused herself and left the room.

"I'm sorry," Martin said. "We have taken enough advantage of you. You do not need to be bothered with our mail too."

"But this is very intriguing," Abby said. "I was with Terza when she opened the envelopes. However, I don't want to pry into your personal correspondence, so please don't hesitate to keep it private if you wish. You won't offend me."

"Now you have me curious too," Rick said.

"Then please stay and see Terza's riddle," Martin said as Terza came back into the room carrying three envelopes.

She handed one of the envelopes to Martin. "I found these in the basket of unopened Christmas cards and Chinese New Year greetings. I don't know who it came from. It isn't signed."

Martin's eyebrows raised as he looked at the first envelope, then he took out the card. The triangular ivory piece fell into his hand.

He turned the piece over and over. His eyes widened as he examined the markings. "It looks just like a piece of a puzzle I used to have. Remember my father's tangram, Terza?" To Abby and Rick, he said, "Puzzles are very common in China. Many pieces like this were made."

"Yes. It had pieces like that. Is that what it is?"

Martin fingered it, rubbing the smooth, cool ivory between his fingers. "Maybe. It could be a piece of a tangram or some other game, like a dissection puzzle. I can't make sense of the markings. Are there more?"

"I found two more. Abby was here when I found them," Terza said, handing Martin a second envelope.

Opening it, Martin took out the small square, similar in size to the triangle. He compared the two pieces. "They look like part of a set, but it can't be a dissection puzzle. It wouldn't have a square piece. These must be tans from a tangram puzzle. You said there is another?"

"Yes. The postmark is three days before Christmas from New York."

Terza handed Martin the third envelope. Abby leaned forward to see. Martin turned the envelope over and shook the piece into his hand. It was a larger triangle. He examined it, put the three pieces on the table and picked up the envelopes. Each was addressed in the same, precise handwriting.

"Which one has the earliest postmark?" Abby asked.

"The last one. It was at the bottom of the mail," Terza said.

Martin passed her the envelopes. She'd seen two of them, but reexamined them, then passed them to Rick.

Finally, Martin picked up the cards. He glanced inside them. "I don't know what order these cards were in."

"I'll arrange them," Terza said, reaching over. She put the cards in order. They looked identical on the outside. The thick white single-fold paper with gold deckle edges looked expensive. The envelopes were lined with gold foil.

Martin opened the first one and read. "'A small token of esteem.' That's all it says." He frowned as he looked at the second and third cards. Then he laid them open, in order.

"These together make a Chinese proverb. 'Search and you will find it.' Then, 'What is unsought will go undetected.' You were right, Terza. It's a riddle."

"These are handwritten. Either the sender doesn't use a computer much or wanted to be more personal. So what do you do with the three pieces?" Abby asked.

"An expert can make hundreds—in fact, I've heard claims of more than two thousand different shapes—by rearranging the pieces of a tangram, but this is not complete," Martin said. "There would be three more triangles and a parallelogram. This is useless without the other four pieces."

"Wait. I think I saw a piece like that," Terza said, jumping up. She hurried into the kitchen and came back with a plastic bin. She set the bin on a chair and began pulling items out of it. A pocketknife. A silk scarf. A folding umbrella. A single earring with dangly beads. A Seahawks T-shirt. She pulled out several more odds and ends. Finally she fished out a small piece and raised it triumphantly for everyone to see.

Grinning broadly, Terza said, "I found this in one of the rooms when I cleaned. I put it in my lost and found box. No one has asked for it."

"It looks like one of our pieces. Let me see it," Martin said, holding out his hand. Terza gave the triangle to him.

Next to the other pieces, it had the same hand worn look and creamy color of the other tans. Martin compared it to the small triangle. He looked up and smiled. "It matches. So these came from a guest. Did our guest lose other pieces and decide to send us the remaining pieces? Or did he leave us a puzzle to solve?"

"If you could figure out which guest left it, you might have the answer," Abby said. "Did you have any Chinese guests who stick out in your mind? Someone related to you perhaps? Or a friend of a friend?"

Martin laughed. "All of them. Most of the Chinese who come here are related or know someone in our families."

"There have been a few whose families we don't know," Terza said.

"We can look," Martin said.

"I hope you solve your puzzle," Rick said as he stood. "I'm afraid I need to get going. Thanks for the delicious meal. I don't often eat this well." He patted his stomach. Rick was lean and fit from physical labor.

Martin stood. "Please make a bill for me."

"Not this time. This one's on me. Besides, the meal more than repaid me."

"Thank you. We are indebted to you."

"Would you like a ride home, Abby?" Rick asked.

"That would be great." She turned to Martin and Terza. "I enjoyed your hospitality."

"I don't know why I thought we were unlucky," Martin said. "We are blessed many times over."

"If you need someone to help you look for tans, I'll be happy to give you a hand," Abby said, smiling. "You know I love a good puzzle. I'll call you tomorrow and make sure our raccoon blocker worked." She turned to Rick. "Give me five minutes and I'll be ready."

RICK PULLED HIS PICKUP TRUCK into Mary's driveway next to the sheriff's department silvery-tan cruiser.

"Thanks for the ride," Abby said.

"Streets should be cleared enough to drive your car tomorrow. Do you want me to come get you?"

"That would be great. However, Mary may want to drive the van if the road's clear enough. I'll call you."

Abby gathered her overnight bag and duffel bag and opened the door. She thanked Rick and got out. The McDonalds had removed the snow from the driveway to the front door. She silently thanked the Lord for good friends and neighbors. How blessed she felt for all those who had pitched in to help Mary and her throughout the storm and its aftermath.

Setting her bag down just inside the front door, Abby took off her shoes and padded to the living room. "There's just nothing as nice as home," she said, smiling at her sister and Henry.

Henry stood from his bent position. He'd been loading kindling into the fireplace. "This home, in particular," he said, smiling. "I've been in a lot of houses that lacked the warmth and welcome of this house."

Abby suspected Henry had seen the worst of society in his line of work, but his faith and good nature had kept him from getting cynical.

"Oh how nice. I love a cozy fire. We haven't used the fireplace since Christmas." She joined them by the fireplace and gave Mary a hug.

"Welcome home," Mary said, and her delighted smile made Abby feel very welcome indeed. She'd missed Mary, even though it had only been two days, and they'd talked on the phone several times.

"I had a fire yesterday, thanks to Henry," Mary said. "He had it all ready, and Bobby came over to play with Finnegan. They came in soaked, so I lit the fire and we had cocoa in front of it."

"Sounds like a perfect winter activity to me," Abby said, removing her jacket.

"Did you get rid of the Chois' ghosts?" Henry asked.

"Sure did. I watched them leave just before we uncovered and boarded up their entrance. Cute little creatures. I've always had a soft spot for raccoons, but they don't belong in a house." Abby sat on the couch. "Now the Chois have a new puzzle. Literally. Someone has sent them several ivory puzzle pieces."

"Not a whole puzzle?" Henry asked.

"No. They're missing three pieces."

"So you have a new mystery to solve," Henry said. "Will you have to spend more time at the Chois'?"

"No, although I may go over to help them search for pieces."

"Henry loves puzzles and brainteasers. Maybe he could help," Mary said.

"Sounds interesting. At the moment, however, I have enough to handle, trying to find the missing tourist," he said.

"Oh dear. You haven't found him yet?" Abby asked.

Henry planted his hands at his waist, his stance at ease. He'd probably had to answer questions about the search many times. Abby had the utmost respect for Henry's abilities, and had gone on a search with him, so she knew how exasperating a fruitless search was, especially when the weather played an adverse role in the outcome.

"No, and I called off the search for the night. Between the frigid temperatures and the ice and snow, it's just too risky. We don't need any injured searchers. We found a rental car along Wayfarer Point Road about a mile north of the road to Summit Stables. We're checking to see if it was leased by our missing man. I talked to Lindsay Buckminster at the stables, and she hasn't seen anyone. We had a helicopter searching this afternoon, concentrating on rocky areas around Arrowhead Hill and Mount Ortiz, but no luck. We even searched the rocky shoreline out by the lighthouse. I can't imagine where we've missed. Either he's hurt and can't respond to our searchers, or he doesn't want to be found."

"You think he's hiding something?"

"Doesn't seem likely, but everyone I've interviewed says he acted suspiciously. Trouble is, no one can describe what they mean," Henry said. "You talked to Terry Jones, didn't you? What do you make of him?" he asked Abby.

She frowned, thinking about the surly young man. "He reminded me of my brief encounter with Dr. Clark before he went missing. Disagreeable. Distant. Rather rude. I'm sure some of his behavior stems from his friend's disappearance, although I'm not sure they're friends. I think his concern had more to do with his personal reason for coming than worry for Dr. Clark's safety."

Henry rubbed his chin. "I got the same impression. I questioned him, but he insists he doesn't know Clark personally and he won't talk about the reason for his visit. Just says it's a private matter. He did say Clark is from Chicago, which matches Clark's registration at the Bird Nest."

"Did you trace the post office box he gave for his address?" Abby asked.

"It's a dead end. The street address on record led to an apartment. He doesn't live there anymore."

"He paid the Chois in cash, so you can't trace a credit card or check," Abby said. She'd asked Terza, thinking she might be able to help identify the man and find out where he might be.

"If he wants to disappear, he's done a good job of covering his tracks. I ran routine checks on Clark and Jones. There are too many Clarks to determine anything. We found one brain surgeon listed as J. Clark in Chicago. He was in surgery when we called the hospital."

"So you don't know what kind of doctor he is?" Mary asked, looking from Henry to Abby. "People use the term rather loosely. He could be a medical doctor, a professor, a veterinarian or a minister or it could be an honorarium. For that matter, you can buy an honorary degree off the Internet these days."

"That's true. He might not be a doctor at all," Henry conceded. "As for Jones, he delivers pizza and newspapers in Rapid City, South Dakota. He had four speeding tickets in the past three years. Otherwise, he's clean. But I've noticed he has no patience. I put him on James Hale's search team. If anyone can talk to him, the pastor can."

"Good idea. I'm sure Terry knows more than he admits." Abby frowned. "I can't imagine anyone would travel to an island looking for someone he doesn't know. That doesn't add up in my mind."

"My thoughts too. Terza said Clark's room was reserved for a week. He was to check out today."

"Maybe you'll hear from someone when he doesn't show up at home or at work tomorrow," Mary ventured.

"I hope so. Then we might learn why he's here and where to look," Henry said.

"We found a piece of ivory in Dr. Clark's room that still had dirt on it. Did Mike follow up on that?" Abby asked.

"He gave me your suggestions, which made sense to me. We searched the old limestone quarry, but we didn't find any signs of occupation. Of course, the snow could have covered his tracks. I sent a team to Paradise Cove, where he claimed to be fishing. No sign of him there, if he ever went there. Do you know of any other fossil sightings on the island?"

Abby thought for a moment. She'd found arrowheads and fossils of small sea snails and crustaceans, but nothing a collector would get excited about. She shook her head. "Nothing comes to mind. I'll think about it."

"Any ideas would help," he said. He finished arranging wood in the fireplace, then stood, arching his back and stretching. "I'd better get going if I'm going to make the ferry. I'm glad you're home, Abby."

"Me too, but I'm perfectly capable of taking care of myself," Mary objected.

Henry reddened. "You know I'm not questioning your abilities," he said. "You're amazing. But I don't want any woman being alone with the roads impassable and a missing man loose on the island."

"I have Finnegan," she replied. "But I'm glad to have Abby home too," she said, smiling affectionately.

"I'm the one who's glad," Abby said. "And I'm going to go upstairs and get comfortable. I've been wearing these clothes for two days. See you tomorrow, Henry."

Besides, Abby thought, *Mary and Henry don't need me around while they say good-bye.* Abby took her bag and went upstairs.

After she showered and changed into a fleecy sweatsuit, Abby logged onto the Internet and tried searching for rock clubs and geology groups in the Chicago area. She found pages and pages of bars and nightclubs, rock bands, rock concerts and a meetup site that wanted her to subscribe. Definitely not what she was looking for. A search for gem and mineral groups yielded several gem and mineral museums, stores and dozens of shows, a lapidary society, creative metal works and other businesses. She began clicking through the sites and searching for J. Clark, Dr. Clark, Clark.

Giving up the fruitless search, she typed in *ivory in Chicago*, which took her to the Web site of a national magazine article about a global ban on the elephant ivory trade. However, it said, ivory fossils were not considered endangered, so they could be bought and sold. It gave instructions on how to determine if ivory was elephant ivory or a fossil. Perhaps Mr. Clark, or Dr. Clark was an ivory merchant. Searching various sites for Clark brought up many references to the Lewis and Clark expedition.

Yawning, Abby realized it was getting late and she was tired from the search for live intruders at the Bird Nest. At least she had eliminated several possibilities in finding Mr. Clark. She shut down and headed for her own very comfortable bed.

CHAPTER ❧ TWELVE

MARY AND ABBY WERE JUST finishing breakfast Monday morning when the phone rang. Abby took the call. It was Rick.

"Hang on a minute," Abby told him. She covered the mouthpiece and turned to Mary.

"Rick says the roads are cleared. Shall I have him come get me or do you want to go to town?"

"I'll take you," Mary said. "I could use an outing. I'm not used to being cooped up so long. Let me call Bobby. I promised I'd take him into town to go sledding when the roads were cleared."

"Wonderful," Abby said. "Maybe I'll talk him into going to the conservatory with me too."

In less than an hour, they were headed into town in Mary's van.

"I'm glad you convinced me to come along," Sandy said from the backseat. "So much for my baking and sewing plans.

I'd much rather go play in the snow." She put her arm around her son's shoulders.

Mary carefully and slowly negotiated the roughly cleared road. The island had come back to life. Though not as busy as normal for a Monday morning, Green Harbor bustled with people, and cars lined the streets as they drove through town.

Holloway's Hardware and the Springhouse Café were particularly busy. Piles of snow were everywhere, shoved off sidewalks in front of doorways. Nothing had the groomed look of the mountain tourist towns. Sparrow Island was not prepared for a major snowstorm, and that's what they'd had. Looking around, Mary wasn't sure she could maneuver from her van into any of the buildings.

"What a mess! Thank goodness Janet and Patricia said they'll make contacts this morning. I don't think I could get around in this," Mary said. "My part in planning a winter festival may be restricted to the telephone."

"Maybe by the weekend, they'll have it cleared," Abby said. "It won't melt off. It's eighteen degrees outside right now, and the high predicted is twenty-two. It's supposed to drop into the teens tonight and all week."

"When I got up in the morning about three o'clock, the outdoor thermometer registered six degrees," Sandy said.

"Wow," Bobby said. "I've never been in weather that cold before, have I, Mom?"

Sandy laughed. "No, and you still haven't. You were snuggled down under your covers, nice and cozy."

"Aw, Mom. You know what I mean."

"Yes, and be glad it's not that cold right now. It might be too cold for sledding."

Mary slowed cautiously in front of the school, pumping her

brakes to keep from skidding. She pulled up as close as possible to the curb. Bobby and Sandy got out and retrieved Bobby's sled from the back of the van.

"I'll come by in about an hour and see how you're doing before I go to the conservatory," Abby said. "You can come with me if you'd like."

"Thanks. We'll probably be ready to get out of the cold by then," Sandy said.

Mary and Abby watched Bobby and Sandy trudge through the calf-deep snow to the driveway and parking lot of the school.

As Mary pulled away from the curb, she glanced at Abby. "I may have to drop you off at your car and go back home. I hadn't considered the difficulty of getting out in the snow."

"It looked like the sidewalk was cleared in front of Island Blooms. Maybe Candace cleared it."

Mary circled back to the flower shop. She usually parked behind the shop, but that would be full of snow. Two spots were cleared in front of the shop. Mary pulled into the handicapped spot. Sure enough, the snow had been scraped off clear up to the front door. With Finnegan and Abby's help, she made it into the shop.

Candace was cleaning out the refrigerated display case. "Good morning," she said when they closed the door.

Mary let go of Finnegan's harness. He moved ahead of her and stood waiting for instructions.

"Off duty," Mary said. Finnegan padded over to a corner and sat down.

"Smells good in here," Abby said.

"That's the wilted flowers I've crushed going through this case. I figured this would be a good day to do some cleaning."

"I'll help," Mary said, already looking forward to getting her hands in the flowers.

"I'm going down to the church, then out to the conservatory. Shall I come back here before I head home?" Abby asked.

"You don't need to do that. I'll help Candace and make a few calls, then I'll head back home. I'll be fine," Mary assured her sister.

"If you need help maneuvering through the snow, I'll be here," Candace said. "Before you go, Abby, take these with you." She wrapped a fistful of cut flowers in floral paper and tied it together. "Take these to the church. They'll be good for a couple of days, and maybe they'll cheer someone up."

"Thanks." Abby accepted the bouquet. She sniffed the flowers and smiled. "They've cheered me up already."

SEVERAL PEOPLE had congregated in the church meeting room. Janet hurried forward to take the flowers from Abby. She handled all the flower arranging for the church.

"Lovely," she said, sniffing the flowers and turning toward the kitchen. Abby followed her.

"Hear anything from the searchers?" Abby asked.

Janet took a vase out of a cupboard and carried it to the sink. "Nothing new. A group went out about seven this morning. Doug and Rev. Hale went with them, along with several men from town and all the sheriff's deputies. They're searching around Oyster Inlet today. How's Mary doing?"

"Fine. She brought me to town. I'm going out to the conservatory. Just thought I'd check here first. If there's anything I can do . . . if they need another searcher, I'm available."

"You can help me put together some lunches for the searchers. The Green Grocer donated a slab of ham."

"Put me to work," Abby said, washing her hands.

For a half hour, Abby and Janet sliced ham and made sandwiches. As Abby wrapped them, Janet got out a large container of cookies.

"Someone's been busy cooking," Abby said.

"With everyone stuck at home yesterday, a lot of people kept busy baking. Food donations have been pouring in from all directions," Janet said.

Abby left Janet to store the lunches and drove over to the school. When she honked her horn, Sandy and Bobby waved and started toward her.

Sandy opened the front passenger door. Her face was red. Her short hair was dark with moisture and plastered around her face. She puffed out clouds of frosty air with every rapid breath.

"I'm glad to see you. Mind if we come along with you now? I'm pooped."

"I'd love to have you come with me. Hop in," Abby said. She got out to open the trunk for Bobby's sled.

"That was super neat! I can't wait to come back with Dad tonight. You want to come sledding with us?" Bobby asked her.

"Thanks for the offer, but I think I'll pass this time." Bobby was always generous and didn't want anyone left out of anything. Abby enjoyed outdoor activities, and sledding sounded like fun, but she didn't want to break into their father-son time.

"Okay." He removed his hat and gloves and climbed into the backseat of her small car.

"I hope we won't be in your way," Sandy said as Abby turned left onto Primrose Lane.

"You won't. I'm happy to have the company. Bobby's my right-hand assistant, you know," she said. The young boy had proven to be a willing student and diligent worker over the months he'd been helping Abby at the conservatory after school.

"He loves helping you out there," Sandy said, turning to look over her shoulder at Bobby.

Abby looked at her young friend in the rearview mirror. His hair was sticking up in spikes and his face was flushed from the cold and exertion. His grin warmed her as if the sun had suddenly come out.

"I WAS AFRAID OF THIS," Abby said, shaking snow off one of the rhododendron bushes growing along the path around the conservatory grounds. "Frozen leaves. See how translucent they are," she said, showing Bobby and Sandy. "These plants are pretty hardy. They'll survive, but with the snow cover and ice, many of the birds can't reach their food sources. Then there's the problem of fresh water. Let's check out the stream, make sure it's not frozen over."

"I can break through the ice," Bobby said.

"That might help for a while, but this cold is supposed to last all week. The birds are hardy, though. They'll manage, but it wouldn't hurt to supply some fresh water for the wildlife. Let's go to the lookout platform."

They shook the snow off bushes as they went along, but their efforts made little effect on the habitat. Ice and snow completely covered the deadfall maple tree.

"Insects lay their eggs in the dead tree as it decomposes," Abby explained. "Birds feed on the eggs and larva. There are similar deadfalls in the forest all over the island. Right now, they're all covered with snow and ice. Ground birds won't be able to find food and many of the birds that make their homes in the treetops have come lower, seeking shelter out of the cold wind. They need food sources. In this cold and snow, the voles and slugs and small animals go to ground, looking for shelter. Raptors, like owls, hawks, falcons and eagles feed on them, so they're low on food sources."

"That's terrible. What can we do?" Sandy asked.

"Abby told me the birds are good at finding food," Bobby told his mother. "Can we put out some seed and suet around the island?" he asked, turning to Abby.

"It wouldn't hurt," she said, proud that her young protégé had listened and understood her lessons. Bobby would make a wonderful ornithologist or just about anything he set his mind to. "Most of the islanders have backyard bird feeders to attract birds. Birds will come to the easiest food source. My concern is that they supply healthy food for the particular bird types," Abby said.

They reached the observation platform, which was covered with a foot of snow. Climbing up on it, they looked out over the conservatory acreage. Snow blanketed everything. As the three stood silently looking and listening, the woods were eerily silent. Abby knew the birds huddled together on lower branches of trees and down in pine and fir trees, their feathers fluffed out for warmth. In the extreme cold, their systems slowed to conserve energy.

"Remember you showed me how to make birdseed and fruit decorations for the trees?" Bobby asked, looking up at her expectantly. "Maybe we could make some at school."

"That's a great idea," Sandy said, beaming at her son. "We have an assembly scheduled with a talk on early spring plants with a master gardener from San Juan Island on Wednesday. Maybe he could postpone his presentation. I could check and see. Could you come show us how to make feeders? I'll call and set it up, if you're willing."

"I promised the school I'd give a lesson and demonstration about the local birds to the students. Perhaps I could do it this week. At least we could make sure people put out the proper feed," Abby said.

They trudged back through the snow to the conservatory building. The collapsed flight cage came into view, reminding Abby of the narrow escape of the rough-legged hawk. She wondered if it had been back looking for food.

The food Abby had left for the hawk was gone. Whether her hawk had returned or some other raptor found it, at least it had provided a meal. Inside the conservatory's work building, they filled a large tub with warm water, hoping the warmth would keep it from freezing for some time, and carried it out near the end of the flight cage, next to the box she'd put out before. She put out a good chunk of raw hamburger that she'd had for the recovering hawk. If it wasn't strong enough to hunt, especially with the weather conditions, perhaps it would come back.

After they carried suet and birdseed out to the platform and placed some on downed logs along the way, they headed back to town.

As Abby took extra care on the snow-packed road, Bobby leaned forward from the backseat and touched Sandy's shoulder. "Hey, Mom, you can tell the principal that your class can do reports on making seed things for the birds, as an English project."

"Yes, they could," Sandy said, reaching over her shoulder to pat Bobby's hand.

"Following that reasoning, the science class could do a project to monitor the birds' feeding habits," Abby said. "I'd like a copy of that report. And social studies could study it as an environmental exercise. I don't know how a math class could use it."

"*Hmm.*" Bobby cocked his head. "Maybe they could make a formula to figure out how many seed things they can make. What do you call them anyway?"

"Feeders," Abby said. "And there are several different kinds we could make if I can get the supplies."

Bobby looked up at Abby. His earnest concern touched her heart. "The school's just gotta say yes," he said.

"I'll call the principal this afternoon and see if I can get permission," Sandy said. "At least my class can do it."

Abby smiled. She loved Bobby's tender heart. "I don't know how they could refuse you," she said. The birds would be fine, but she always welcomed a chance to make people aware of the island's wonderful bird population. This storm provided an excellent opportunity.

MARY WAS READY to go home when Abby, Sandy and Bobby returned to town. Abby wanted to visit Terza, so Sandy and Bobby decided to go home with Mary, and Abby left them at the flower shop.

Terza was sitting at the small table in the study, going through her leather-bound guest register when Abby arrived at the inn. Terza looked up and smiled when Abby entered the room.

"Any luck finding your anonymous correspondent?"

Terza shook her head. "Martin remembers all these people,

but he only eliminated a few. We don't know how long ago this person was here." She marked the page with a slip of paper and closed the register. "We missed you at breakfast this morning."

"And I missed Martin's delicious cooking and your wonderful hospitality, but I have to admit, it felt good to be home with Mary and sleep in my own bed. I enjoyed staying here, though. Your rooms are so luxurious, I felt very pampered."

"I'm glad. It's always good to be in our own home. I appreciate that you came to help us. Martin has stopped trying to change our luck. He said last night that he realizes how blessed we are. Now this new mystery has him perplexed, but at least it is a good puzzle. Another piece came in the mail today," she said.

"Really? That makes five? So you're only missing two pieces?"

"Yes, but then we have to figure out what the puzzle means. Martin says the pieces are old, but not valuable, so the puzzle itself will not bring us good fortune."

"Do you remember which room you found the lost piece in?" Abby asked.

"Yes. It was the white elephant room, where the Nivens stayed."

"Have you looked through their room to see if there are any more puzzle pieces?"

"Not yet."

"If you want, I'll help you look."

"I hate to take up more of your time," Terza said.

"Are you kidding? I'm curious to see what it all means. Sandy and Bobby went with Mary, and the roads are pretty well cleared, so I'm sure she'll get home fine."

Terza rose. "All right. We can go now." She put the guest

book on the registration table before they went upstairs. At the door to the rear bedroom, she fished a set of keys out of her pocket and opened the door.

This room was decorated with an elephant theme. The wallpaper was a soft green with a pattern of pagodas and graceful ladies with parasols. A white elephant formed the base of a table lamp and a beautiful bronze elephant on the dresser held a decorative clock with his trunk. It looked old. Several paintings depicted a story of a white elephant first with a farmer, then with the farmers' children, and then decked out in finery, carrying an emperor.

"I love the way you decorated the rooms. I've seen the goldfish and I was in the lovely pheasant room. What theme did you use in the other guest room?"

"It has pandas in a bamboo forest," Terza said. "We wanted to keep our Chinese traditions. We are fortunate the Victorian English and Americans like to decorate with Oriental style and art."

"You've created an atmosphere that's beautiful and restful and gracious," Abby said. "Has Mary seen your upstairs rooms?"

"Yes. When we first opened the inn, before her accident. We opened the house with a reception for the islanders. Mary gave us a beautiful bouquet with orchids and chrysanthemums and bird of paradise for the dining room."

"I'm glad. It would be difficult to bring her upstairs now."

Terza had cleaned the room. The bed was made and clean towels were folded neatly and stacked on the bathroom counter.

"I'll check the drawers," Abby said. She started with the antique tiger maple highboy, removing all the drawers. Each drawer had its own enclosed compartment. Bending down,

Abby peered in the top one. It was dark enough that she couldn't see clearly. Taking a tissue, she reached in and ran her hand around the inside. She came up with a single, white shirt button. Setting it on top of the dresser, she went to the next one. She found a little dust, but nothing more.

"You certainly keep things clean," Abby told Terza. "I wouldn't think to clean in here."

"I don't clean there after every guest, but I try to do a complete cleaning every couple of months."

"Do you take every piece of furniture apart when you do that?"

"Yes. That's how I found the ivory piece. It was down in the chair. It had fallen through to the bottom. I had to take out several tacks to get it out."

"So someone feeling around the cushion wouldn't have found it."

"Perhaps not. I think when I turned the chair on its side, it slid down where I could feel it."

"It won't hurt to double-check, but I doubt if we'll find anything in the chair," Abby said. She moved to the bedside table, which had two drawers. It matched the dresser and had the same type of drawer compartments. She found a scrap of paper with a list of island sites. "How long ago did you scour this room? Do you keep a schedule?"

"Yes. It was, let's see, I think early December, so it's due for another thorough cleaning next month. I do two rooms each month."

"So the time before would have been early October?"

"Yes."

"Then it's probable your anonymous guest stayed in this room between early October and early December."

Terza was feeling down in the chair cushions. She stopped, plunked down onto the chair and looked at Abby. "Yes. I never thought of that. Of course." She covered her mouth with both hands, but Abby could see her wide smile. "You're a genius," Terza said.

"Simple deduction, Mr. Watson," Abby quipped in a low voice. At Terza's confused look, she laughed. "Sherlock Holmes," she explained.

"Oh." Terza giggled. "You are better than Sherlock Holmes," she said.

"I wish," Abby said. "He always solved his mysteries."

"But that was make-believe," Terza said.

"True. Too bad all mysteries can't be solved so neatly, but we'll figure this out. After all, puzzles are made to be solved, right?"

"Right," Terza said, but she didn't look convinced.

CHAPTER ✿ THIRTEEN

As she started home for lunch, Abby saw Henry's sheriff's car and several of the searchers' cars parked in front of Little Flock, so she stopped. A group of tired, disheveled-looking people were seated at tables in the meeting room, eating a late lunch. Henry was deep in discussion with two men Abby didn't recognize. She didn't want to intrude, so she went into the kitchen, where Rev. Hale had his sleeves rolled up, cleaning up coffee supplies.

"Good afternoon," she said. "Looks like you got stuck with KP. Do you need some help?"

The pastor looked over his shoulder at her and smiled. "No thanks. I'm almost finished. How are you and Mary doing?"

"Fine. The roads are pretty well cleared, so Mary brought me into town to get my car."

"Good. We're still using the church as a meeting place and command post for the island. I think we've reached all the residents with food and prescriptions. Thankfully, no one was seriously injured during the storm."

"Have they found Dr. Clark?"

Rev. Hale shook his head. "Not yet. The search teams came in for lunch and to regroup. They sent up a helicopter to look for him this morning. It's like the man disappeared into thin air. Henry thinks he might be injured, where he can't walk out or call out for help. Henry's cautiously optimistic. He won't give up until he finds him."

"If he could get to it, I'd think he'd return to his rental car, unless it wouldn't start. I can't imagine he would have gotten lost walking back to town, even in a storm."

"A person can get disoriented in the white-out conditions we had. The whole situation's strange. No one knows for certain who the man is. I tried talking to the young man who came here looking for him. He won't open up. He must know something. I can't imagine what they're hiding, but it's not helping the searchers find him. We've had a prayer vigil going since he was discovered missing. The Lord knows where he is, and we're just trusting He'll lead us to him."

"That's the best help of all," Abby said. "You and Henry and the searchers are doing your part. I'm sure the Lord will answer our prayers."

"Yes. In His time." Rev. Hale dried his hands on a towel. "Would you like some lunch? We had ham sandwiches to send out to the searchers, then Martin brought over a big pan of turkey and rice. It's really good. He's been so concerned about Dr. Clark, he's been keeping the searchers fed."

"Thanks. I'll grab a plate and go talk to Henry."

When Abby went out into the meeting room, the searchers and deputies had gotten up from the table, leaving Henry alone to finish his lunch. She filled a plate with food and got a cup of coffee, then went over to his table.

"You look tired," she said as she sat down across from him.

As if reacting to her comment, he ran his hand through the white fringe of hair rimming his bald head. "I am, a bit. More frustrated than tired."

"Rev. Hale was just telling me Dr. Clark seems to have vanished from the face of the earth."

"If the man is anywhere on the island, we'd have found him by now. He can't have left, unless he had a boat hidden somewhere, but I can't believe that. Even a complete novice wouldn't have gone out in that storm."

"Did you find out anything from the car rental agency?"

"His driver's license lists an address in Springfield, Illinois. It's an old address. He gave the Chois a post office box address in Chicago. I tried getting information from Terry Jones." Henry shook his head. "He claims he's never met the man— that he conversed with Clark on the Internet. I have no reason to interrogate him. As far as I know, there's been no crime and no reason for suspicion other than their secretive behavior."

"They do seem to be taking privacy to extremes." Abby took a bite and thought for a moment as she chewed. "What about the cliff caves on the north side of the lighthouse?"

"We did a visual search from the air. He didn't fall over the edge or we'd have seen him. We checked the top of the cliffs. He would have needed ropes and equipment, and there's no sign of a recent descent. We haven't scaled the cliff. Too risky. The face is ice covered. Getting to the caves will be difficult without experienced cavers." Henry sighed wearily. "I'd hoped our crew could find him. I may need to call for help."

"Taking a wild guess here, he could be holed up inside a cave and can't get out, for the same reasons you can't get in," Abby speculated.

"That's a possibility. If he's a caver or a rock hound, I'm

hoping he packed supplies, at least to keep him warm and hydrated." Henry picked up his empty plate and stood. "I'd better get back at it. How's Mary?"

"Fine. She came into town this morning, but I think she headed home with Sandy and Bobby already."

Henry nodded. "Maybe I'll stop by and say hi before I head out. I hope we find our missing tourist long before Mary's winter festival. I heard the fire department's supposed to be cooking bratwurst. I wouldn't want to miss that."

THE MYSTERIOUS AURA surrounding J. D. Clark occupied Abby's thoughts as she got into her car. She had a hunch they would find him if they could discover his mission on the island. She put the car in gear to back out of her parking spot when her cell phone rang. Putting the car in park, she picked up the phone. The LCD display identified Sandy McDonald as the caller.

"Hi."

"Hey, I got permission," Sandy said.

It took Abby a moment to figure out what Sandy was talking about. Then she remembered. Bird feeders at the school. "Good. When?"

"Wednesday morning during first period, if that's good for you. About nine o'clock. As it turned out, our other speaker canceled because of the weather. Margaret was happy to have your program now and reschedule the master gardener."

Margaret Blackstock was the school secretary. She kept the kindergarten through high school running like a well-serviced engine. "I can do that," Abby said. "I'm on my way to the conservatory. I'll get what suet and birdseed we have." Abby began making a mental list of items she'd need.

"Let me pick up supplies for you. What do you need?"

"That would be a big help. The conservatory will cover it as part of our education program. Could you pick up several large jars of peanut butter, three large boxes of coarse cornmeal, two large bags of raisins and all the suet they have from the Green Grocer? We could make paper cup suet logs, if you want to buy paper cups, and I'll get a roll of rattan cord from Mary." It was important to have bird-friendly supplies that a bird could peck through in case it became entangled. Abby rattled off a few more items.

"Bobby and I will go shopping right now. Thanks, Abby. This means a lot to Bobby, and I know the students will love this."

After she hung up, Abby drove to the conservatory. She loaded a twenty-pound sack of wild birdseed, ten pounds of black sunflower seeds and several blocks of suet into the trunk of her car.

Abby went to her office and logged onto the Internet. She did a global search for the words *geology, fossils and Clark in Illinois*. She scrolled through dozens of Web site listings that included Lewis and Clark, Clark Street, Eliza Clark, and a deceased Joseph B. Clark. She was almost ready to give up when she found a link to a site that mentioned the name Clark in relation to an article on wooly mammoths.

Her attention caught, Abby sat straighter. Following that lead through several layers took her to an online journal by *RocksterMan*. In the archives, she found an interview with J. D. Clark, PhD.

Abby read the interview with interest. RocksterMan referred to a scientific paper on the effect of climate on the preservation of Pleistocene period fossils in the American Midwest. *This isn't your average blog,* Abby thought. She followed and occasionally posted on several blogs by birders and ornithologists. It was a good way to keep up on the birding community. RocksterMan obviously referred to geology, and not rock music. Clicking on the link to the article, Abby found J. D. Clark's byline. He was associated with the Illinois State Museum, which just happened to be located in Springfield, Illinois.

Excited, Abby found a phone number and called the museum. When a receptionist answered the phone, Abby identified herself as Dr. Abigail Stanton, Associate Curator of the Nature Museum at Sparrow Island and asked for Dr. J. D. Clark. She was crestfallen when the receptionist told her Dr. Clark was no longer associated with the museum, until the woman elaborated that Dr. Clark had taken a position at the University of Chicago. Unfortunately, she did not have information on how to reach him.

Back to the drawing board. Abby brought up the University of Chicago Web site. She went straight to the online catalog for the Department of Geophysical Sciences. Clark wasn't listed. Disappointed, she ran a search of the document for Clark. She found lots of references, but no J. D. Clark and no geologist. At the bottom of the catalog, she found a date. The catalog was a year old.

Abby placed a call to the university's geology department. She got an answering machine in the Dean's office. Frustrated, Abby left a message, giving her official name and title. "I'm trying to locate Dr. J. D. Clark," she said. "I believe he's associated with the university. Dr. Clark is here, on Sparrow Island,

and he's missing. We've had an unexpected snowstorm. He went out the day before and didn't return to his lodging. He's been missing now for two days. He could be injured. If we knew where to look, it would help. Could you find out his mission on the island and help us locate him?" Abby suspected the university wouldn't divulge information to her about the man's whereabouts. "If you can't give information to me, please call Sgt. Henry Cobb or the San Juan County Sheriff's Office. They can verify that Dr. Clark is missing." Abby left Henry's cell phone number and the telephone number for the sheriff's office.

Sighing, she hung up. At least she'd identified their missing man. There was a good chance that he was on some kind of a geological field study, although she still didn't know where to look.

Abby closed up her office and returned to town. She stopped at Holloway's Hardware to purchase livestock feed mixture for the school bird feeders. She was filling a sack with field corn kernels from a bin when she heard voices in the next aisle. She recognized Aaron Holloway's voice, but she didn't immediately recognize the other voice.

"I don't know where you'd find a GPS system around here. You probably have to take the ferry to San Juan Island or even the mainland," Aaron said.

"Don't have time. Maybe someone has one I could borrow," the voice said.

"Could you find what you need on a topographical map?" Aaron asked. "I have a U.S. Geological Survey map that might show what you're looking for."

"Won't work. It doesn't have the right kind of legend," the other voice said.

"You could look online. You can find anything on the Internet," Aaron said.

"Do you have a computer I could use?" the man asked. Abby identified the unknown voice. It was Terry Jones. She hadn't recognized him. His voice was normally a bit surly. Aaron was about Terry's age, and he had no reason to be on guard with the merchant who was being so helpful. But why would Terry want a GPS device, unless . . .

Abby hit her head with the heel of her hand. Of course. The notebook in Dr. Clark's room must have held GPS coordinates. Terry must have seen the notations when he barged into Clark's room.

Abby paid for her purchases and hurried to the Bird Nest.

When Abby entered the bed-and-breakfast, Terza and Martin came out of their rooms to greet her.

"Martin, could you let me in to Dr. Clark's room please? I think I figured out how to find him."

"Yes." Martin started up the stairs. "You are good at solving puzzles. I hope you're right," he said. "We've been praying for Dr. Clark." He shook his head. "He's been missing too long."

"I hope I'm right about this puzzle," Abby said as Martin unlocked the door to the guest room.

Abby hurried over to the bedside table. The notebook was gone. She turned to Martin.

"Did you see the notebook that was here? Did you or Terza move it?"

"We never move guests' belongings," Martin said.

"It was here when we looked with Mike." She hadn't pointed it out to the deputy or to Martin at the time. She thought the scribbles on it had no significance. Now she realized she'd been wrong.

She looked inside the drawer, then around the floor and under the bed. Martin looked in the dresser and checked the trash can. He turned to face her, forking his fingers through his hair.

"It's not here, Abby."

"No one has come in here since we searched the room?" she asked.

"No one that I know about. I have the only master key. The rest of the keys only work on one room and the front door in case we lock the door at night, although I don't lock the doors. No one on the island would break in."

"True. No one *from* the island, anyway," Abby added.

Martin's brows raised. "You think someone broke into this room?"

"I'm afraid so," she said. "Not from outside. I think Terry Jones got in and took the notebook."

"We must call Sergeant Cobb."

"I'll call him. I have other information for him. Thanks, Martin."

First, I'll talk to Terry Jones, she thought as she left the bed-and-breakfast and hurried back to the hardware store. At four o'clock, it was already getting dark. As she approached the door, Aaron came out carrying a heavy bag of feed. He said hi and kept going to the pickup truck with the Summit Stables logo on the door. Lindsay Buckminster said hi and followed behind him. Abby went inside and looked for Terry Jones. She didn't find him in the store.

"Hey, Abby, do you need something?" Aaron said, coming up behind her.

"I was looking for Terry Jones. I heard you talking to him a little while ago."

"He just left. He looked something up on my computer, then took off."

"He must have found what he needed then," Abby said. "You didn't happen to see in what direction he went?"

"No, but he bought nylon rope, a rock pick and a couple of carabiners. He's part of the search for that missing man, you know. I was out helping yesterday."

"I'm surprised they haven't found him yet. Thanks, Aaron." Abby went out to her car, then called Henry from inside, where she could talk without being overheard.

"Sergeant Cobb," he answered.

"Henry, I found out about Dr. Clark. He's on staff at the University of Chicago, probably in the geology department. I got an answering machine at the university, so I left a message and gave your number. I hope someone calls you soon."

"So your deduction about geology is right. I wonder if we missed him somehow."

"There's more. I saw a notebook with scribbling in his room. I didn't connect it to anything initially, but I think it might have been GPS coordinates."

"Can you get it? We can run the figures and see if we come up with a location. We're just wrapping things up for the day. It's too dark to keep searching, unless we can pinpoint his location tonight."

"I had Martin let me in his room. The notebook is gone. I think Terry Jones took it. He used Aaron's computer at the hardware store, then bought rope and climbing equipment. Find him and he might lead you to Dr. Clark."

Abby heard a long, weary sigh. "I hope he isn't foolish enough to go looking in the dark. We don't need two missing men. Good work, Abby. We'll be on the lookout for him."

Abby hung up, then bowed her head, right there in her car, and asked the Lord to guide the searchers to the missing man and to keep them safe.

Abby couldn't believe how quickly the day had disappeared. As she drove home with all the bird feeder supplies, she hoped Mary was in an understanding mood. Abby hated to smell up the kitchen, especially since it was too cold to open the windows, but she needed to melt down the big chunks of suet to prepare it for the feeders for the school program. Mary was always accommodating, but she hadn't brought such a large project home before. There were over two hundred children at the school, and they would all want to make a bird feeder. Mary's kitchen would be a disaster before she finished and cleaned it up.

CHAPTER ❧ FOURTEEN

ABBY AND MARY WERE IN the kitchen Tuesday morning, cleaning up after the suet rendering project when the phone rang. Abby wiped her hands and answered it.

"The last two pieces came this morning," Terza said, her accent so thick with excitement over the telephone, it took Abby a moment to understand her words.

"You found the rest of the puzzle?"

"Yes. In the mail. Two packages came at the same time— one had two pieces in it. Martin's trying to figure it out. Can you come see?"

"I wouldn't miss it for the world. We're just cleaning up here. See you soon."

"Was that Terza?" Mary asked after Abby hung up the phone.

"Yes. They received the rest of the puzzle pieces. Now they need to solve it."

"I'd like to see that. Maybe I'll come too."

"Let's take separate cars. Then I can go out to the museum for a while. With Hugo gone, I feel like I should check on things out there. I also told Wilma to take a few days off."

"Wilma agreed to take time off?" Mary asked, incredulously. Wilma loved her job and took her duties very seriously. She acted as receptionist, bookkeeper and general girl Friday at the museum, allowing Hugo and Abby time to work on their projects.

"I had to twist her arm," Abby said, "But I assured her the museum would be nearly deserted. She said she might spend some time at home making baskets. They sold out at Christmas. I told her we won't have any visitors in this weather."

"True. Neil said the only passengers on the ferry are locals. Maybe people will get out this weekend. I wouldn't mind having some tourists come to our snow festival, although it's planned for the islanders. Are you ready to go? I can't wait to see this puzzle solved. Let me get my jacket." Mary wheeled off to her room.

ABBY FOLLOWED MARY'S VAN into town and parked in front of the Bird Nest. Martin saw them coming and hurried out to make sure Mary could maneuver her way through the snow and up the sidewalk to the ramp Martin had added the previous year.

"I'm glad you came," he said. "Maybe four heads can figure out the puzzle. Terza and I are bumped."

"You mean stumped?" Abby asked.

"Yes. We can't figure it out. It could be anything."

"What do you mean?" Mary asked.

"Come. I'll show you." Martin led them into the study,

where Terza sat at the table, arranging and rearranging seven engraved ivory shapes.

"You see, the puzzle looks like a running man. If she changes it like this"—he moved the pieces around and made it look like a rabbit—"it makes a different form. There are at least two thousand forms. What form should we make?"

"Perhaps it is the puzzle itself that has meaning," Mary suggested.

"That's possible, however the puzzle pieces came with sayings." Martin picked up the cards. "The note with the sixth piece says 'Chance is always powerful; let your hook be always cast.' And the last note finishes the saying. 'In the pool where you least expect it, there will be a fish.'"

Abby repeated the two phrases. "Remember the Bible story where Jesus had the disciples cast out their nets, after they'd been fishing all day with no catch, then they caught so many, the nets were breaking? This saying reminds me of that. Who knows what the Lord is doing, but nothing is chance. They couldn't find any fish, then He blessed them, and they had so many they couldn't haul them in."

"With all respect, I don't think that's what the Chinese proverb refers to," Martin said.

"Maybe not, but it applies. We're supposed to help others, without thinking about what we'll get in return. You and Terza do that all the time. It sounds to me like this mysterious guest wants to return a blessing and lead you to some sort of treasure or reward."

"So they're supposed to go fishing?" Mary said.

"Not literally, but it certainly indicates there's more," Abby said. "Terza, did you narrow down the possible list of guests who could have sent this?"

"Yes, I did. Between October and early December, there were ten different guest bookings in that room. Only five of the bookings were Chinese. Martin's uncle's wife's sister's nephew and his wife were here. Then my cousin's husband's parents. A young couple stayed here on their honeymoon, then there was a man who came to Seattle on business and our friend Lin Wong suggested he stay here. The last guests were a young woman who is a student at the university and her grandmother. The grandmother spoke no English, so the young woman wanted to stay here, where the grandmother could speak to other Chinese."

"Which of them do you think would send the anonymous puzzle pieces?" Abby asked.

Martin took hold of the back of a chair and looked down, shaking his head. "Not a single one of them."

"LET'S EAT AT the Springhouse Café tonight," Mary said after they left the Bird Nest. "Maybe Henry can join us."

"All right. I'll meet you there at five." Abby watched her sister get into the van, then she drove out to the Nature Museum.

Wilma hadn't been there. Abby didn't expect her until Wednesday. She went around checking all the displays and thermostats. Everything was working. The inside temperature was an even sixty-five degrees, more than double the outside temperature. They usually kept the thermostat set higher, but Abby had decided to close the museum until life on the island got back to normal.

Abby tried calling the University of Chicago again, and spoke to an assistant who didn't know Dr. Clark. All the staff were either in classes or meetings, but she understood the urgency of finding the doctor and promised to pass on a message.

Frustrated, Abby turned to a stack of mail. There was nothing urgent, but she managed to compartmentalize her thoughts and handle most of the pending correspondence.

Getting outdoors always helped when she felt restless, so she bundled up and went outside. Taking a quick hike around the grounds, Abby listened for the sounds of the forest. A light breeze soughed through the evergreen branches, whistling and sighing softly. Abby pulled the turtleneck of her sweater up high against the chill and zipped her jacket. Her glasses fogged up. She wiped them off with her gloved hands.

As she walked, she observed the condition of the forest and the open areas. Most of the birds and small animals were bedded down or denned up together for warmth. Abby loved the winter woods, when the maples and alders stood proudly bare, their trunks and branches stripped to their bones, graceful and statuesque against the dark green pines and firs. In winter, the undergrowth died back, allowing passage through the dense forest. Now blanketed in snow, the forest looked like an enchanted playground for rabbits and deer and woodland creatures. Abby knew the beauty held danger and hardship for those same animals, but God had endowed his creation with remarkable tenacity, and most would adapt to the unusual weather and survive.

Somewhere in the woods a *chip-chip, chip-chip* sounded. Abby listened, straining to pinpoint the little winter wren's location. Abby called back with a small squeaking sound, hoping to attract the only other forest inhabitant she'd heard. The hardy little bird's chirping stopped for a few moments, then resumed again. Abby peered intently, but couldn't see the elusive, small brown bird, even against the stark white snow. Still, the sound of its *chip-chip* gave her the special joy she always felt when she heard a birdsong. The winter wren preferred insects and their eggs, but would settle for a bit of sustenance from birdseed. Abby brushed the snow off the top of a log and sprinkled some seed that she'd brought along. Perhaps her little friend would find it.

Farther along the path, Abby spotted some freshly chewed branches. The deer had been at work. She reached the observation platform and climbed up to look around. At first, she saw nothing moving. She took out her binoculars and looked slowly around. A movement caught her eye. She focused on the bare top of a tall, dead alder tree. Perched on a high branch, the large, bulky shape of her rough-legged hawk stared back at her. She knew he couldn't see her, although his eyesight was keen. He looked healthy. He turned his head to the side. Suddenly he rose up, spread his wings and dived, straight and sure and fast toward the forest floor. She tried to follow his flight, but lost him against the dense dark trees. She hoped he'd caught his prey.

Satisfied that all was as well as could be, she headed back to her car.

When she got to town, she had to park half a block past the Springhouse Café. Mary's van was already there.

It was a good thing Mary had arrived early. Several people were standing waiting for tables. In the gift shop people wandered around, looking while they waited. Abby greeted people as she made her way through to the table where Mary was already seated.

"Goodness. It looks like everyone had the same idea," she said as she sat across from Mary.

"Everyone had cabin fever after being cooped up for a couple of days. Henry just called. He said they found the missing man."

"Hallelujah! What a relief. Thank You, Lord," Abby said. "Where was he?"

"I don't know any details yet. He'll tell us when he gets here.

"Did you see all the new snowmen?" Mary asked.

"Yes. They sprouted up in a hurry."

"After school, a bunch of high school and junior high students swarmed all over town, offering to build snowmen for the businesses."

"I saw a group at the firehouse. They were having a great time. I'm sure the firemen will get a charge out of it. We're so fortunate to have such a great group of young people," Abby said. "I also saw our hawk. He looked to be in good shape."

"Good. I bet he's happy to be free," Mary said. She waved toward the door and smiled. "There's Henry now."

The sergeant made his way to their table and sat next to Abby, across from Mary. He had shaved and changed into casual clothes, but the long search had taken its toll. He had dark smudges beneath his eyes. He reached over and squeezed Mary's hand.

"Boy, you're a sight for sore eyes," he told her. "After all that white and hiking over hidden rocks and logs and slippery slopes, I could sit here and feast on your pretty face all night."

"Henry, you are a tease," she told him.

"Nope. I mean it." He turned to Abby. "I sure appreciate your help," he said.

"You're welcome. You look exhausted. How'd you end up finding him?"

Henry rubbed his hand across his mouth and down his neck. "I got a couple of hours of sleep at the station," he said. "A combination of things, all instigated by you, led us to Clark. Terry Jones did not return to the inn last night. I waited for him awhile, then took a couple of deputies and went back out looking for him. We didn't find him until this morning. He had coordinates, but no GPS, so he was going by what he found on the Internet. He got out in the snow at night and got confused. We found him cold and exhausted on the northside of Mount Ortiz. We got some coffee and a protein bar down him, then I mentioned possible charges for breaking and entering and stealing Dr. Clark's notebook. He opened up real fast." Henry shook his head. "Fortunately for him, he was very penitent. I was tempted to put him in jail for obstructing our search. He could be in a lot of trouble, but Dr. Clark declined to press charges. He wants to keep everything quiet."

"So what's he doing here?" Mary asked.

"He's here on behalf of the university, checking out a report of a significant fossil in a cavern on the island."

"Really? Wow. Did he find one?" Mary asked.

"Not just one. He found an entire graveyard of them. The coordinates on the notebook Jones produced led us right to a cave at the top of a hill northeast of the lighthouse. We had to dig through the snow and brush, but we found the entrance. I sent Artie Washburn down into the cave to investigate. He couldn't believe he'd never found that cave before. He said he's been caving around here for most of his life. He found Clark asleep. He'd run out of food, but he had water, a sleeping bag and a bunch of tools that he'd packed in case he decided to spend a few nights on site. He'd parked and walked in to the site, so no one would follow him. Said he started back to his car Saturday just after dark and realized he'd forgotten something, so he returned to the cave. Then he got busy and lost track of time. When he came out and saw it was snowing, he decided to wait it out in the cavern. He said it never occurred to him people would be worried. He's been happily digging while we've been searching."

Mary stared at Henry, appalled. "What a thoughtless man," she said. "You could have been injured out searching for him. You could have been out helping other people."

"Yes, but we couldn't take a chance. He did say his find would bring a lot of money to the island when he returns with a team to dig up the skeletons. He also asked that we keep this quiet. He doesn't want every rock hound and fossil collector in the world descending on this find. The land is privately owned and the owner has offered it for sale to the university, who sent Dr. Clark to authenticate the find and assess its value. He's very excited."

"I can understand that," Abby said.

"I hope they don't turn the island into a three-ring circus with their excavations," Mary said. "We don't want that kind of notoriety."

"Amen," Henry said. "We don't want the extra traffic and the liability of people crawling all over the cliffs looking for fossils either. Dr. Clark promised me that the university would keep the find quiet until after their excavations. They'll make the announcement from the university's museum when they're ready to unveil them."

"Well, at least that's one mystery solved successfully," Abby said. "What about Terry Jones?"

"He's a graduate student from North Dakota who caught wind of a possible discovery from an obscure comment on an Internet chat room. He came here to find Clark and get on his team. Since he helped find him, I believe Clark will be more open to his petition. Especially if it will help keep him quiet about the find."

The two men in question came in and sat a couple of tables away. They were deep in conversation and seemed to be getting along. Abby was glad neither was a criminal. She'd had her suspicions because of their secretive behavior. A lot of other people on the island had voiced similar suspicions. *Just proves, you can't judge people on outward appearance. Like the Scriptures say in Luke 6:37, "Do not judge, and you will not be judged."* She would try to remember that.

CHAPTER ❦ FIFTEEN

Nine o'clock Wednesday morning, Mary sat in her wheelchair at the end of a long table in the cafeteria of Green Harbor Public School. Finnegan lay next to her. The children kept looking at him, but they didn't try to pet him. Sandy had explained to the students that Finnegan was a service dog and he was on duty, which Mary appreciated.

"Be sure you don't leave loops that the birds could get caught in," Mary said, as she showed several students how to tie a string hanger on the large paper cups they would fill with the rendered suet, shortening, cornmeal, peanut butter, seed, corn, barley and fruit conglomeration they'd made in large mixing bowls from the cafeteria kitchen.

Abby showed the entire group a log feeder, made by hollowing out a fairly thick tree branch, drilling holes in the sides so the birds could get to the suet packed into the hollow center. She explained different kinds of feeders that the students could make at home with pinecones, milk cartons, liter pop bottles and small log sections. For their emergency purposes, however, they were making fake log feeders with large paper cups.

Abby went from table to table, showing each group how to cut the bottoms out of the cups, so the birds could feed from the tops or the bottoms, then pack the suet mixture into the cups. The mixture was crumbly, but packed together easily.

Mary's table completed their feeders in no time. Most of the children at her table were middle school age. With all of the students and the teachers participating, they would cover the island with bird feeders. Sandy had bought enough cups for each of the 278 students to make a feeder.

Mary watched a table of first graders across from them as the children painstakingly tied the string handles onto the cups and carefully filled their feeders. She had to smile at one little boy who had his tongue stuck out the side of his mouth as he concentrated on tying a knot.

Abby went around making sure each child completed a feeder to take home. The children responded to Abby's instructions enthusiastically and clamored for her attention. She was patient and worked easily with the students. Mary hadn't seen this side of her sister before. Although she was at ease with Bobby, Abby was accustomed to teaching serious university students. Mary admired Abby's flexibility and easy nature with the children. She tried to imagine Abby lecturing at a symposium of scientists. Mary shook her head. She couldn't picture her casual, easygoing sister in such a scholarly situation.

Near the end of the hour, the teachers had the students clean up and put the extra materials into boxes. As the students filed back to class, they carried their feeders to hang on a tree near their home. Mary smiled and waved at the younger children, who bore their creations so proudly. She understood their pride of accomplishment. Even the storm and the crisis for the wildlife came with unexpected blessings.

AFTER THE SCHOOL PROGRAM, Mary went to Island Blooms. She drove slowly around town, admiring the new artistic renditions of Frosty the Snowman. The businesses had very imaginative snow creations, while the houses on Harbor Seal Road and Kingfisher Avenue had more traditional snowmen. A snowman had appeared outside the Green Grocer wearing one of Archie Goodfellow's royal-green butcher aprons and a Green Grocer cap and pushing an old-fashioned dolly with a wooden vegetable crate on it. The snowman had the prerequisite carrot nose. Mary wondered what he'd used for the brown eyes and bright red smile. The crate was filled with round orange pumpkins with green stems. Archie currently used a newer, metal dolly, so Mary supposed this was one of the old pieces of equipment that Archie used to add ambiance to the store. He had old tins and glass milk bottles and other collectibles that were reminiscent of the past.

Al's Garage really made Mary chuckle. An old clunker car sat out front and a snowman was protruding out from under the car wearing a pair of greasy old boots.

Mary's cell phone rang. She waited until she got inside Island Blooms to call back. It was Patricia Hale.

"Hi Patricia, what's up?" Mary asked.

"I just saw your car go by," Patricia said. "Are you at Island Blooms? We need to have a meeting. Can we come over there?"

"Let me check." Mary covered the mouthpiece. "Candace, do you need my help for a while? The festival committee wants to come here for a meeting."

"No problem," Candace said. "It's been quiet so far, and we don't have any weddings or funerals or anything."

"All right." She uncovered the mouthpiece. "Candace doesn't need me, so you can come over any time. I'll make sure there's coffee."

"More winter festival planning?" Candace asked after Mary hung up.

"Yes. We only have three days. Have you thought of any way Island Blooms can be involved?" Mary asked.

"I have several craft ideas. In fact, I'm hoping you can help me with them, if you're not too busy with the committee. If you are, I can find another helper," Candace said.

"I don't have any committee duties that I know of. In fact, I thought I'd mind the store, where it's nice and warm."

"Well, first, I thought we could do the crafts in the park. We could do it from here, but it will be more fun out there, don't you think?" Candace asked.

"Definitely. You can set up a booth in the park. I just don't see how I can wheel this chair around in the snow. I need skis instead of wheels," Mary said, grinning. "Now that would be a sight, wouldn't it? All the children would want rides."

"We'll just have to work something out, but here's what I have."

Candace showed Mary three simple crafts for children to make flowers out of paper plates and colored construction paper. "I figure if we clear an area and put down a tarp, we can set a table on it, and it will be a good height for children to work. Plus I ordered little pots of primroses and grape hyacinths. That would give people a little start on spring for about fifty cents apiece."

"That's terrific! You're brilliant. I thank the Lord for you everyday, Candace. You're doing a wonderful job here."

Candace blushed. And again, Mary counted her blessings. Candace was high on the list. She'd stepped into the role of manager after Mary's accident, and Island Blooms was flourishing under her care.

"We're here," Janet called out in a loud, jovial voice. Finnegan sat up and pricked his ears up. He looked at Mary and gave a little *woof.*

"It's okay, boy. You're off duty," she said, scratching his ears.

Finnegan nuzzled her hand, then went over to a corner to lie down out of the way. He knew from experience that too many feet around Mary could be dangerous for him. His tail had been stepped on more than once.

"I'm so excited, I can hardly stand it," Janet said, pulling up a chair next to Mary at the worktable. She gave them all a smug grin.

Ida and Patricia took seats at the table.

"What?" Mary said, and Ida and Patricia echoed the query.

"I talked to Keith Gordon at the Dorset. He sent out a special e-mail invitation to the people on his preferred guest list. He's offering a weekend package for our winter carnival, and the Dorset is completely booked for the weekend."

Mary looked at Patricia, whose stunned expression matched her own dismay. "But Janet, we've planned a small festival for the islanders. We aren't prepared for an influx of tourists."

"Why not? Keith wouldn't put out such an invitation if he didn't think it would be a great event. He has a reputation to uphold, you know," Janet responded.

Ida put on a brave smile. "We'll just have to make sure he isn't disappointed."

"How will we do that?" Patricia asked.

"We'll put our heads together right now. That's how," Janet said.

Mary sighed. "Okay. What's done is done. Now we've got to produce. So let's go over our list. What have we got?"

Patricia opened her loose-leaf notebook and read off all the local businesses and craftsmen who had committed to participating. Mary was astonished at the community enthusiasm.

"What about food?" Ida asked. "I know the Springhouse is doing coffee and hot chocolate and the chef is planning to make funnel cakes. They're yummy!"

"Kari Dryson promised to make Kari's Creams for the occasion. They're always a popular treat," Patricia said.

"I'm not going to eat for the rest of the week, so I can have one of her cream puffs and a funnel cake," Ida said.

Mary laughed. "My mouth's watering, too, but you're slender enough to pull it off. I'll have to diet for the next month."

"Course, that's not counting the bratwurst and chicken sticks. Duncan Grady and Bob McGuire have teamed up. Duncan's providing his big barrel drum cooker for the occasion, and Bob said he'd provide some real hot sauce and a fire truck in case they have to put out a fire."

"Oh dear. I'd better keep James away from there," Patricia said, rolling her eyes. "He loves the hot sauce, but then he has terrible heartburn. He claims it's worth it, but when he suffers, I suffer with him."

"Maybe we can offer antacids. Too many funnel cakes will do that too," Janet said, grinning.

Patricia laughed. "Good idea." She took a sip of coffee and set down her cup.

"We need a name for our event," Ida said. "I've been calling it a winter carnival. You call it a winter festival, Mary. We need something catchy."

"Like what, Ida?" Janet asked.

"How about calling it a snow fest?" Patricia said.

"I like that. It sounds more, oh, I don't know, fun," Ida said.

"Sounds good to me," Mary said. Janet agreed.

"Good." Ida sat back with a smile and crossed her arms.

"What are we going to do about all the snowmen?" Patricia wanted to know.

"What do you mean?" Ida asked.

"You really started the snowball rolling, so to speak, with your snowman at the Springhouse Café, Ida. Everyone on the island seems to have a snow creation of some sort. We have all these gorgeous snow creatures, and no one to judge them. I mean, we talked about people competing, but we never actually announced a contest. We should judge them and give out certificates for the best ones."

"I agree," Mary said. "I love going around looking at all the snowmen."

"Trouble is, no one on the island could be impartial. We all have a stake in this. We need someone who doesn't live on Sparrow Island," Patricia said.

The ladies stared at each other with blank looks. After they eliminated everyone on the island, Janet suggested Mary and Abby to come up with judges from San Juan Island.

"I don't know about volunteering my sister," Mary said.

"You don't have to. I'll call her," Janet said. "We need at least three judges. And we need prizes and categories."

"Oh dear. This is getting complicated. I sure hope we have

enough time to get this together. Can we pray about it?" Mary asked.

"That's the best idea we've had yet," Patricia said.

WHEN ABBY ARRIVED at the museum after lunch, Wilma was hard at work. As she bent over her work, the overhead light shone on her long salt and pepper hair, pulled today into a neat bun on top of her head. She looked up from her desk and smiled when Abby entered the museum.

A CD of soft, harmonic music mixed with recorded bird-calls played over the loudspeaker, giving the museum the ambiance of a stroll through the winter woods.

"Good morning. Any calls or visitors?" Abby asked.

"Not a soul. It's so quiet, it's almost spooky," she said, laughing. "Were you expecting a call?"

"Not really. And certainly no visitors. It's still too cold for people to get out. There isn't much to do here, if you want to take the rest of the week off," Abby said.

"Thanks, but I have some bookkeeping to catch up on," Wilma said. She leaned back in her chair. "Besides, I needed to get out of the house. I made five baskets over the weekend and the past two days, so the snow was a blessing in that way, but I got my fill of twisting and pulling cedar bark, wild cherry bark and fibers. I used up most of my supplies. This summer, I'll have to gather more bear grass and nettle fibers, but at least I'm well stocked with baskets for the season.

"Good for you." Wilma made beautiful cedar bark Indian baskets in the tradition of her Native American ancestors. During tourist season, the baskets were in big demand at Bayside Souvenirs and at Island Blooms and festivals in the area. "I think I'll catch up on some documentation myself,"

Abby said. "I need to order supplies for the conservatory too. I used up all our supplies at the school this morning, teaching the students to make bird feeders."

"That sounds like fun. I made fresh coffee," Wilma said.

"Thanks. I could use a cup." Abby headed back to her office and Wilma returned to her work.

Abby adjusted her glasses and waited as her computer booted up. She opened a file on the rough-legged hawk they'd been nursing back to health. Bringing the file up to date, she recorded the storm, the collapse of the flight cage and the bird's escape. Then she recorded her sighting of the bird hunting and diving toward prey. She was satisfied that the bird's recovery had been complete.

Printing the report, she filed it in her file cabinet. That task completed, Abby allowed her thoughts to return to Martin and Terza's puzzle, which had been pressing on the back of her mind all afternoon.

Puzzles had solutions, and Abby couldn't leave a puzzle unsolved.

Martin said the tangram had thousands of possibilities, but their anonymous correspondent had one particular solution in mind. The proverbs had to point out the solution. What could they mean?

"Search and you will find it. What is unsought will go undetected." That could have meant the puzzle piece in the room.

"Chance is always powerful; let your hook always be cast. In the pool where you least expect it, there will be a fish." Could something be hidden in the fish room?

She loved the themes Terza and Martin had chosen for their rooms. They could have used flowers, but they'd chosen different animals instead. Birds, pandas, fish and elephants. All had significant meaning to the Chinese culture. By coincidence, she had stayed in the bird room, but not just any birds. The pheasant in the wallpaper was a very rare, endangered bird.

The pheasant, the goldfish, the panda and the elephant. Those meant something to Terza and Martin. What did they mean to their anonymous guest?

Abby had her hand on the phone to call Terza when it rang. "Sparrow Island Nature Museum. Abigail Stanton speaking."

"That was fast. You must have been sitting on the phone. This is Janet. We need your help," she said. "The committee met and, well, you've noticed all the snowmen around town. We need judges."

"Hold it. I can't be a judge. I have conflict of interest issues. Island Blooms has a lovely snow girl."

Janet laughed. "I know. I was just there. We don't want you to be a judge. We want you to get judges for us. We were thinking about your birding society friends from San Juan Island. I bet they owe you a few favors."

"I don't know, Janet. They've helped me with bird counts more than I've helped them. Besides, it's such short notice."

She might as well have addressed her objections to the moon. Janet didn't recognized the meaning of the word no. "All right. I'll see what I can do."

"Great. I knew we could count on you."

Janet could count on her dogged determination, is more the case, Abby thought. After they hung up, Abby dialed Terza. She would call her acquaintances at the San Juan Islands Birding Society later.

When Terza answered, she said, "This is Abby. I've got an idea about the puzzle. Would it be all right if I come by?"

"Oh yes! Please come."

"I'm just leaving work. Is it all right if Mary comes too?"

"Yes, yes. I'll put on a pot of tea."

Abby hung up and called Mary. Henry was there. They promised to meet her at the Bird Nest in fifteen minutes.

Abby went out front. "I'm taking off for the rest of the day," she told Wilma.

"Have a good evening."

Abby said good-bye and hurried out to her car. She couldn't wait to take another look at the tangram.

CHAPTER ❧ SIXTEEN

MARTIN, TERZA, MARY, Henry and Abby gathered around the Chois' dining room table, eager to solve the riddle of the tangram puzzle. Martin laid the seven pieces on the table, in no particular order.

"Those look old," Henry said. "Is the puzzle itself valuable? Could it be a gift from this anonymous benefactor?"

"I doubt it is valuable," Martin said. "I'm no expert in antiquities, but I've seen many puzzles just like this one. It may be a few generations old, but it is common. I had one like it as a boy that belonged to my father's father."

"What happened to yours, Martin? Do you still have it to compare the two?" Henry asked.

Abby hadn't asked Martin to compare puzzles. Leave it to Henry to go into investigative mode. He was good at ferreting out facts and putting them together. She'd thought of that when she asked to include him tonight. She knew he loved puzzles as much as she did.

"I no longer have mine," Martin said. "I gave it to a young boy years ago."

Martin didn't say, but Abby suspected he had given it away after their only child was killed in a tragic accident. Martin and Terza rarely talked about that time, and had, in fact, put it behind them, but Abby knew it had been a difficult time for them. Martin had no son to whom he could pass on a family inheritance.

"All right, it's time to solve this puzzle. According to the first card, this puzzle is meant to honor you. So I've been thinking about the proverbs on the cards. The first proverb had to do with finding the missing piece that was left here in the bedroom. 'Search and you will find it. What is unsought will go undetected.' I believe that meant the puzzle piece in the room. Because of your thorough cleaning habits, you happened to find it before the riddle came in the mail, or at least before you opened the mail. What did the next proverb say?"

"I have the cards here," Terza said, taking them out of her pocket. She opened the cards and set them on the table. Out loud, she read, "Chance is always powerful; let your hook always be cast. In the pool where you least expect it, there will be a fish."

"I think that's the clue. The fish," Abby said. "You found the lost piece in the elephant room. All your rooms have animal themes. Your anonymous guest must have learned that and tied the puzzle to your room themes."

"I thought of that, too, so I tried making a fish with the pieces," Martin said. "The problem is that I can make a lot of fish with the tans." He began arranging the tiles and formed a simple, rather bloated looking fish.

"What are you looking for?" Mary asked. "Is the fish supposed to lead you to something else?"

"It must. If the puzzle isn't the treasure, it must be a clue," Abby said. "Your guest went to a lot of trouble to send you this puzzle."

"Could it have a mathematical solution?" Henry asked.

"Yes. I'm afraid I'm not an expert in the mathematics of tangrams," Martin said. "If the solution is numerical, we may never solve it."

"Perhaps the fish refers to the room with the fish. Maybe something's hidden in that room," Abby said.

"But what? We have to know what we're looking for," Martin said. He rearranged the tans, coming up with a fancier fish. He flipped the various pieces back and forth, trying to find something that made sense.

"What about the Chinese characters on the pieces? Maybe the right configuration has a message," Mary suggested.

Martin and Terza studied the fish. "I don't see anything," Martin said. He began flipping pieces. "The message could be on the other side of the tans," he explained.

Again, he and Terza studied the fish. She shook her head. "It doesn't make any sense," she said. "It's no use. We're never going to figure this out."

"The possible combinations are infinite," Martin said. "Your idea is logical, Abby. If the puzzle leads to something hidden in the goldfish room, perhaps Terza will find it when she cleans again, after Dr. Clark leaves."

"Or you'll figure it out when you're an old man," Terza said. She gave her husband an affectionate smile. "Whatever it is, we don't need it. We've been blessed with a riddle to occupy our minds and good friends to help us with all our problems. Our prayers have been answered getting rid of the raccoons in the attic and find the missing guest."

"That's a passel of blessings all right," Henry said.

They heard the front door open, and the two inn guests came in. Seeing them, the guests walked over to the dining room.

"Good afternoon," Dr. Clark said. "We'll be leaving in the morning, but I want to apologize for all the concern I caused. It never occurred to me that anyone would be worried about me. I'm afraid I lost all track of time or weather." He shrugged his shoulders and looked embarrassed. "Sometimes I get so involved I forget to eat or sleep."

His apologetic smile reversed Abby's previous impression of the man as uncivil and self-absorbed. Knowing about his quest made her sympathetic to his cause. She became completely engaged when it came to her bird studies. "I've done the same thing," Abby said.

"You must be Dr. Stanton," he said to Abby. "Sergeant Cobb told me you were the one who deduced where to find me."

"I merely made an observation, Dr. Clark. We looked in your room to see if we could find a clue to your whereabouts," Abby said. "You could have been lying in a crevice or cave somewhere, injured. Your ivory sample gave me the clue, although I didn't realize it for a while."

"Yes. Please call me J.D. I'll be spending a great deal more time on the island this summer and I'd love to visit your museum and talk with you." He turned to Henry. "I'll see that a donation's made to your search and rescue organization. I'm afraid I put them to a lot of needless work."

Standing behind J.D., Terry refused to look at anyone, but stared at the floor until J.D. stepped aside and drew him forward. "I'm grateful to Terry too," he said. "I apologize for his somewhat unorthodox methods, Sergeant, but his intentions were honorable. He tried to rescue me and still protect my mission. I suppose you've all heard why I'm here?" he said.

"Apparently you've discovered some rare fossils," Abby said.

"Yes. Something I'm not anxious to reveal to the world just yet. I hope you understand." He gave each of them a studied, rather stern look.

"We all understand," Mary said. "Your find is remarkable. We don't want undue attention drawn to the island either."

"Thank you. I, in turn, will try to be unobtrusive when I return with a team." He looked at the fish configuration on the table. "Speaking of ivory," he said. "That looks old. Is it a family heirloom?"

"I believe it is several generations in age, but not of our families," Martin said. "We received it as a gift."

"May I see a piece?" J.D. asked.

Terry looked uncomfortable and tired. "I'm going to turn in," he said. "I'm sorry for my trouble," he told Henry.

"Don't make it a habit, son," Henry said in a low voice, for Terry's ears.

"Yes, sir." To J.D. he said, "I'll see you in the morning."

J.D. gave him a brief nod, but his attention was on the puzzle. Martin handed him a piece. He looked at it, turning it over and examining both sides. "Probably elephant ivory," he said. "I find all artifacts made of ivory or bone fascinating," he said. "The Chinese are among the most accomplished and artistic with ivory. I have a modest collection, myself. If I may be so bold, may I ask what you are trying to solve?"

"A riddle," Martin said. He didn't seem inclined to say more.

Abby considered the paleontologist. Solving ancient puzzles was his business, just as hers was discovering modern puzzles concerning birds and seeking future solutions. He might have some insights, and a new perspective often helped. Besides, she believed the final clue was in his room. They couldn't investigate without his permission. "Let your hook always be cast. In the pool where you least expect it, there will be a fish," Abby recited. "That's the proverb that came with the puzzle. It seems to indicate a clue's hidden in a fish."

"Or in a room. My room's filled with fish," he said.

"That's possible," Abby said, pleased that he took her bait. "I think the riddle's associated with the room themes," she said. "The pieces came in separate mailings, and one piece was found in the room with the elephant theme."

"Perhaps the reference to fishing is merely a message to keep seeking. Have you tried an elephant?" he asked, sitting down at the table, clearly intending to stay to help solve the puzzle.

Martin began rearranging pieces to form an elephant.

"Try moving the parallelogram there," Henry said, pointing to the pieces.

"Yes, I see it," Mary said, leaning forward to point, getting into the game. "Put one of the large triangles there."

With a bit more rearranging, a crude elephant took shape. Henry, Abby and J.D. went to stand behind Martin and Terza, looking over their shoulders.

"Does it say anything?" J.D. asked.

"Yes. Light . . . something about light," Martin said.

Terza flipped over a triangle. She hesitated a moment, then picked up another triangle the same size and switched them.

"That's not it," Martin said. He picked up the square and turned it a half turn, then replaced it. A satisfied smile settled on his face, easing his frown of concentration. "I don't know if this is the solution, but at least it finally makes sense."

"Well, what does it say?" J.D. asked impatiently, when Martin just looked at them with a grin.

Terza leaned over and stared at it. "Light is good from whatever lamp it shines," she said. She looked around the room, then up at Martin.

"We have lamps all over the inn," he said.

"What kind of clue will a lamp give us?" Terza asked.

All of the room's occupants stared at each other.

"Light gives illumination," Mary said.

"Light could refer to truth," Martin said.

"Your word is a lamp to my feet and a light for my path," Abby quoted. At J.D.'s blank look, she smiled. "That's from the Bible. Psalm 119, verse 105."

"I don't see how that has anything to do with the riddle," J.D. said.

"You're probably right. We need some kind of illumination to figure this out though," said Abby.

"Like the illumination of our flashlights to find the raccoons hiding in the attic," Terza said.

"I suggest looking in all the lamps and light fixtures for another clue," Henry said.

Abby was still thinking about the fish. "Cast your hook. There will be a fish," Abby repeated to herself. Then it hit her. It couldn't have been clearer if it had fallen on her head. "It *is* in your room, J.D. May we go look?"

"By all means. Let's see if you can solve this puzzle."

Abby and Henry looked at Mary.

"Go on. I'll wait here. Just come tell me what you discover," she said, waving them away. At Terza and Martin's hesitation, she shooed them away too. With J.D. leading the way to his room, they all trooped up the stairs. He unlocked the door and went inside, letting them all follow.

His pack sat on the floor at the end of the bed. His clothes were heaped in the corner. Ignoring the signs of his return, Abby turned toward the dresser.

"The cast bronze fish sconces," she said, pointing to the small antique metal globes with cutouts forming fish shapes on either side of the dresser mirror. "Are those lamps?"

"Oh!" Terza covered her mouth with her hands as she stared at the lamps, wide-eyed. "Yes. I never thought of those. I dust them, but I never take them down. We don't use them as lamps. Too old," she said. "I would be afraid of fire."

"Your guest must have figured that out. Henry, you're tall enough. Can you reach inside them?" Abby asked.

"Certainly." He stepped forward and reached up. He lifted the oil lamp off the wall and handed it to Martin. It had a lid. Martin lifted the lid and peered inside.

His face fell. "There's nothing there but the oil receptacle," he said, looking at Terza.

Abby caught the wave of disappointment that crossed Terza's face before she schooled her features.

"Wait. There's another one," Abby said. "Henry, would you please lift down the other lamp?"

Henry took down the second lamp and handed it to Martin. Holding the small globe, he looked at Terza, whose eyes shone with anticipation. She nodded encouragement.

Martin took the lid off the lamp. His eyes grew wide. He reached in with his fingertips and pulled out an ornate key.

"But, that's the key to my father's mother's trunk," Terza said. "How did it get in the lamp?"

"Someone put it there on purpose," Abby said. "Someone who sent you puzzle pieces with proverbs for clues. If that person had the key, then whoever it was had access to the trunk."

"Martin, can we look in the trunk?" Terza asked. "If you bring it to the dining room, Mary can see us open it."

"Are you sure you don't want to open the trunk in private?" Abby asked. "It might be something personal."

"No," Martin said. "I don't believe anyone would go to so much trouble to hide something to harm us. You helped us solve the riddle. Now come share our discovery. I will bring the trunk to the dining room, as Terza requested."

Martin went back to the attic stairway while Terza hurried the rest of them back downstairs to the dining room. In the time it took Martin to get the trunk, Terza flitted like a nervous butterfly, clearing the table of the puzzle and getting everyone seated. Abby hoped Martin would hurry, before Terza wrung her hands into knots.

CHAPTER ❦ SEVENTEEN

I T SEEMED A LONG TIME, but it was actually only a few moments later when Martin came into the dining room, carrying the small, ornately carved trunk. Terza wiped off the bottom of it, before Martin set it on the table.

Martin rubbed his hands together. He looked at Terza. "Ready?"

She nodded solemnly and handed him the key, which she'd been holding.

Martin inserted the key into the antique lock. When he turned it, the lock sprung open. He lifted the lid slowly, as if something might jump out at them. When nothing happened, he opened it all the way and looked in.

"Papers," he said. He reached in and took out a modern manila envelope.

"We didn't put that there. What's in it?" Terza asked, rubbing her hands together. "Hurry, Martin. Open it."

His hands shook slightly as he opened the flap of the envelope and pulled out a sheaf of papers. He set the bundle on the table and picked up the handwritten note on top. It was penned in the same careful handwriting as the anonymous cards. Martin stared at it for a moment.

"Please, Martin, read it out loud," Terza said.

Martin took a deep breath.

Honorable Mr. Choi and Madame Choi. I am glad I found you, and now you have found this. I wanted to give it to you in person, but I was concerned that you would refuse my humble gift. I am a very wealthy man today, but once I was a child with no family and no future. Your generosity gave me the chance to receive an education. Your kindness taught me humility. Your letters to an orphan boy gave me value. I want to give all that back to you. I have no parents, no elders to honor and support except you. Please accept this token of my esteem. It is signed, Tan Jinghuan.

"Tan Jinghuan?" Terza repeated. "Martin! That is the child from the Christian orphanage."

"You're right. And the tangram must be the puzzle I sent to him as a gift. I remember, because I wanted him to have something of his own. The orphanage gave him his last name. Tan Jinghuan is equivalent of John Doe in English," Martin explained. "I thought the tangram would give him something of substance to give honor to his name."

"It sounds as if you were right," Henry said.

Martin handed the letter to Terza, and picked up an official looking document. "This says we own two thousand shares of

Global Data Technologies, Incorporated. I don't know what this company is, but that's a lot of stock. We can't accept such a valuable gift." Martin set the stock certificate on the table.

Terza picked up a handmade booklet, like a child's school report. "He kept a school notebook. It starts a long time ago."

Terza silently read the first page. It had crayon drawings of animals and a rough building and yard with stick figures playing catch with a bright yellow ball. Tears formed in her eyes and ran down her cheeks. Abby knew Terza hated to show emotion in public, so the letter must have been very distressing. She wanted to soothe her friend. She wanted to spare Terza and Martin the humiliation of expressing their deep emotions. Obviously, this gift touched them deeply.

Dr. Clark stepped away, then turned and went quietly up the stairs. Mary backed her wheelchair away from the table. Henry nodded to her and started to turn away.

"Wait, please," Terza said. "Let us explain."

"You don't have to," Abby said. "This is something private. We should leave you alone now. If you wish, you can tell us some other time or you don't have to tell us at all."

"We want to tell you. This is a moment of great joy," Martin said. "This boy, we adopted many years ago through an international children's organization. We sent a small amount of money every month, and the organization provided a place to live and education for the boy. We sent gifts once in a while. Nothing of any value. They didn't want one child to have more than the others. When he turned twelve, I sent him my tangram that my father gave to me and his father gave to him. We had no child to pass it on to. Terza agreed with me that we should give it to this boy, who had no parents."

Martin took Terza's hand and gave it a brief squeeze. She

looked up at him with a tremulous smile. "Now we have the puzzle back, but I wish he had kept it. I'm glad our little gift made him happy," she said, through shining eyes.

Martin scanned through the notebook that had a handmade cover. On the last page, a faded photograph of the boy in a white shirt and black pants, wearing a graduation cap, was glued to the page. He looked at it and passed it back to Terza. "He was smiling at the camera. He looks strong and healthy."

"We have a copy of that picture." Terza got up and went into their private rooms. She came back out a moment later with a carved cedar box.

The box held a thick stack of photographs and reports from the orphanage that included handwritten thank you notes from the child in a handwriting that advanced from juvenile and unformed to precise. "This is what they sent us over the years. Here is the last picture of him when he graduated, before he left the orphanage." She held the picture up. It was identical to the picture in the envelope. "They told us he would become an apprentice to learn a trade. Then the correspondence stopped."

"What a blessing to know you affected that child's life in such a profound way," Mary said.

Terza stared at the picture. "He was here, in our home," she said. "I didn't recognize him, and he didn't tell us who he was." She blinked and looked down at her lap where she was wringing her hands together. Abby knew what it cost her to hold in the turmoil of emotions roiling through her. She suspected Martin was dealing with the same emotions.

"Do you remember him now? You must have spoken with him," Mary said.

Terza pressed her fingers against her temples for a moment.

"He had to be the businessman who came because of our friend, Lin Wong's recommendation," she said. "But he gave his name as John Wong. I thought that was a funny coincidence, but I didn't ask. I didn't want to embarrass him. I remember he was very pleasant and polite."

"He gave us a false name so we wouldn't recognize him." Martin frowned, staring out the window, as if considering this new information. "I do remember him. He was astute." Martin sat tall, his head high as if he were pleased by his guest's acumen. "He played a game of chess with me and he won."

"Martin's very good at chess," Terza said.

"Why do you suppose he put the stocks in the trunk? Did you show him the attic?" Abby asked, still trying to put all the puzzle pieces together. It seemed somehow unfinished to her. Terza's forehead wrinkled, then her eyes opened wide. "Martin, you showed him the trunk. Remember?"

"You're right. I'd forgotten." He shook his head. "All these clues and puzzles make my head turn."

Abby smiled. She thought he meant it made his head spin. She didn't correct him.

"I served tea after the chess game," Terza said. "He complimented us on our Chinese decorating. He knew all about Chinese antiques and which ones fit the Victorian period of the house."

"Yes, I remember. He admired the detail and artistry in the carved wood and inlays. He said the antiques are important reminders of our heritage. He asked if our pieces were family heirlooms."

"Martin told him about several pieces that came from our ancestors. I mentioned my trunk. One of my ancestors carved the design, so it is unusual. Martin brought it down from the attic to show him." Terza's eyes glistened with moisture. "I never imagined he was our orphan. He has no family."

"He has us," Martin said. "We would have welcomed him."

"You did welcome and honor him, as you do all your guests, Martin." Henry said.

"Yes, but we would have given him greater honor," Martin said.

"Perhaps he will come back someday," Abby said. "He did realize your family's important to you. That's why he chose the trunk to hide his gift. He knew you'd discover it sooner or later, even if you didn't solve the puzzle."

"Yes, that must be it." Terza turned away and Abby saw her wipe her eyes before she turned back to face them. "I would have given the trunk to him," she said.

"I'm glad he came," Martin said. "It is good to have a grateful spirit, but the gift is too grand. We will send back the stocks."

"No, Martin. We cannot turn down his gift. He accepted our gifts. I don't want his stocks either, but we must allow him to do this. It is for his honor." She sighed. "It's not fair. I want to see him."

"Yes. I would trade all of this for a chance to meet him and have him in our home again," Martin agreed.

"Did he leave an address?" Abby asked.

"I will look." Terza got up and brought the guest register to the table. She turned back through the pages to late October. "Here it is. The address is California," she said. She read off an address in San Francisco.

"That is the address on the stock certificate," Martin said. "That proves he is the man, but it doesn't tell us how to find him. I'll write a letter to him at the address, but I'm afraid he won't get it. I don't know whether to address it to John Wong or Tan Jinghuan."

"Can you contact your friend, Lin Wong, and see if he knows? Could they be related?" Abby asked.

"I don't think so. The boy had no known relatives." Martin said. "I'll do that first thing tomorrow."

"Good. That's a start. Now we'd better leave. It's getting late." Abby stood. "Thank you for sharing that with us. We'll pray for you to find your adopted young man."

"I won't sleep tonight. I'll be praying for our . . . our orphan."

"No," Martin said. "He is our son. I will tell him that in a letter and pray he gets it."

THURSDAY MORNING, Abby sat at her desk, tapping her pen against her chin, wondering what she should do. She'd prayed for guidance during her morning devotions, but so far, she hadn't received an answer.

She knew what she wanted to do, but she had no reassurance that God had given her that desire. Abby knew herself well. If there was a problem, she felt compelled to solve it, whether God had that in mind or not. She'd learned from a few times when she had pushed ahead on her own that her way wasn't always best.

She tried to be patient. A packet had arrived at the museum with details of a proposed new conservation program. Abby read through the thick document, but she had a hard time concentrating.

Part of her job entailed grant writing for funding to keep

the museum and conservatory operating. This program looked promising. She opened a file on her computer and began listing the items she'd need to research for the grant. The cooperative effort included measures to preserve certain wetlands for a variety of invertebrates as well as birds and mammals. The conservatory grounds covered a boggy area that fit the criteria. She worked for a while, getting the grant file organized. She had several weeks, so it wasn't urgent.

She saved the file, then got up and paced, trying to listen for God's still, small voice, to figure out what to do. Finally, she decided to take a walk to see how the birds were faring in the cold. Sometimes she listened best when the whir of machines and artificial light didn't distract her.

Shutting down her computer, she let Wilma know where she was going. At the back door, she glanced at the indoor-outdoor thermometer. The numbers made her shiver. Twenty-seven degrees. Usually in the winter, her windbreaker over a sweatshirt was sufficient, but today she put on her winter coat, hat and gloves and went out.

A few minutes later, as she trudged up the icy path she and Bobby and Sandy had packed down with their boots, she was glad she'd dressed for the outdoors. The weatherman had misread the storm, so the blizzard took them by surprise, but he'd been right about the sustained arctic cold front. It looked as if the cold would keep the snow around at least through the weekend and Mary's Snow Fest.

Unlike earlier in the week, today the birds were chattering up a storm. A convention of chickadees and nuthatches congregated on the maple log, busily feeding where she had spread suet and seeds. The sight and sound of the birds cheered her. Although she loved watching wild birds at Mary's backyard feeder, as a scientist, she subscribed to the belief that the birds could fend for themselves naturally, and the strongest and healthiest would survive, which was best for the whole species in the long run. The unusual cold would not last more than a few days—a week at the most—and the snow would melt away, uncovering the birds' food sources. So what had the extra provisions accomplished? she wondered. When was it appropriate to interfere and when should she keep her nose out of situations? She wasn't thinking about the bird feeders that the students had made. As long as the feed they used was appropriate and uncontaminated, the birds would be fine and enjoy the students' kindness. She was thinking of a more personal situation. Helping the Chois get rid of raccoons in the attic was beneficial to their welfare and their business. Helping them solve the tangram puzzle was harmless and fun and led them to discover a treasure meant for them. Should she interfere more by helping them find their anonymous benefactor? That bordered on personal interference. *Father, show me what to do*, she prayed silently.

She went on to the observation platform, where she surveyed the scene with binoculars. Off to the north, a shrill *kyak-kyak-kyak* caught her attention. Swinging around to look, she focused in on a movement against the skyline and her breath caught in her throat. Just above the trees, she spotted a gyrfalcon, distinctive by the yellow V on its underside formed by its legs and feet in flight. For a moment she stared in awe, taking in the beautiful sight. She hadn't seen that particular bird before and the sighting was uncommon, as the gyrfalcon rarely migrated so far south. Looking to see what caused its distress, she saw her rough-legged hawk flapping its wings menacingly from its perch atop a bare, lightning-scarred treetop, warning the gyr away from its territory. The gyr generally hunted from the ground, which may have been why she hadn't seen it before. Spellbound, she watched until the gyr flew off toward Paradise Cove and the hawk settled on its perch.

She hoped the gyr would stick around for a while so she could find and observe it again. She couldn't wait to tell Hugo about the sighting. For a few moments, she forgot the problem that had absorbed her thoughts late into the previous night and all morning.

Abby completed the path around the conservatory grounds and returned to the museum near lunchtime. Suddenly hungry, she decided to drive over to the farm and check on her parents. She chuckled as she thought of her mother, who wouldn't be a bit fooled by her timely appearance. Her mother loved to interfere in her life by making sure her daughter took time for lunch. Though she had to admit the Stantons were careful not to coddle or get overly involved with their daughters' lives, she loved being pampered on occasion by Ellen Stanton— especially when the soup pot was on. And today certainly would be that kind of day.

CHAPTER ❧ EIGHTEEN

"Umm, let me guess," Abby said, sniffing as she removed her coat at her parents' kitchen door. "I smell vinegar and onions, beef, beets and rye bread. Am I right? You made borscht and fresh Swedish limpa bread, didn't you?"

"I did. I had a premonition you might stop by. Come in and get warm. It's freezing out there," Ellen said, motioning for her daughter to come in by the stove.

"Colder than freezing," Abby said. She removed her gloves and stuffed them in her coat pocket. "Dad shouldn't be out working in this weather." He and Sam had been working on a piece of equipment when she arrived.

"I'll call them in for lunch, soon as I set the table."

"Here. Let me do that," Abby said. She gave her mother a hug, then went to the sink and washed her hands.

She was carrying a stack of soup bowls to the table when her father came in.

"Smells good in here," George said. He removed his coat and boots.

"Where's Sam?" Ellen asked. "Isn't he joining us for lunch?"

"He had an errand to run in town. Said he'd grab something at home."

Abby helped her mother serve the food while her father washed up. When they were all seated at the table, George gave thanks for their blessings.

"To what do we owe the honor of your company?" he asked when he finished praying.

"I was out walking the trail at the conservatory and it's cold out there," Abby said. "I knew Mom would have the soup pot going."

"Just when does our daughter need a reason to come see us?" Ellen said. "I'm glad you decided to stop by. We don't see you often enough."

George gave Abby a wink. "Thought you might be checking up on us old folks. Making sure we're all right. 'Course, we're better off than most. Especially with Sam here."

"I know. You've managed fine, even with all this white stuff all over everything," Abby said.

"So tell us about your adventures this week. I hear you got rid of the critters at the Bird Nest. I'm sure Terza and Martin are relieved," Ellen said. "What about their other puzzle?"

"We solved that." Abby told them about the gift their mysterious guest had left for them, and their tie to the orphaned boy who grew up to become successful.

"How gratifying," Ellen said. "We don't usually get to see how our actions affect others. So they did get to meet him when he stayed at the inn. Do they know which guest he was?"

"They're pretty certain who he was, and they have sketchy

memories of him. They're both wishing they could get to know him instead of receiving a gift that means little to them."

"You going to help them find him?" George asked.

"I don't know," Abby said. She suddenly realized that this question was the reason she'd come to her parents' home for lunch—not the soup and bread, which was delicious, but the insight they were so blessed with. "Solving a puzzle is one thing. Interfering in a relationship is another. I don't know what to do," she said, looking to her parents for guidance.

"*Hmm.*" George rubbed his chin. The stubble on his face showed he hadn't shaved for several days. *The sudden storm gave people a feeling that they were on a time-out from normal life, suspended in the surreal world of white and cold. Me included,* Abby thought.

"Seems to me there's a history but no personal relationship, and that's the problem. You can't interfere in something that doesn't exist," George said.

"Terza and Martin have such kind hearts, I can see how this would distress them," Ellen said. "Terza's experience of losing a child gives her special empathy for people who are hurting. She and Martin take the call to hospitality in the Bible to special lengths with their guests, giving some of them help and comfort beyond a room and a great breakfast."

"That's true. I saw that staying there. When they discovered the hidden gift from their benefactor, they were more interested in the pictures and his notes and all the things he'd done in his life than the stocks. Terza was in tears."

"Oh dear. Terza never cries," Ellen said.

"I know. There was a scrapbook of the boy's childhood at the orphanage," Abby said. "In it were pictures of him and the school and some of the letters they'd sent to him. That's the gift they cherish more than the stocks, which are probably valuable. They described the years of supporting this orphan boy, that the amount was small, but they were able to watch him grow and learn. When he graduated from the orphanage school, they lost all contact with him. They never knew what happened to him after that."

"So the puzzle gave them answers to old questions about this boy who disappeared from their lives. I can see how the gift's a mixed blessing. How wonderful for them to know they helped the child, and yet meeting him would be better than getting a reward for their help."

"Exactly. They didn't do it to get a reward. They did it to give the boy a chance. They gave to him out of the kindness of their hearts," Abby said.

"So what does the kindness of your heart tell you to do?" Ellen asked.

"I want to find him for them."

"And then what?" George asked. "What if he doesn't want to meet them?"

"I thought of that. That would be worse for them. But I think he does want to meet them. Otherwise, he wouldn't have come to the island and stayed at the Bird Nest. He could have just mailed the stocks to them. Right?"

"I think you just resolved your own doubts," George said. "The puzzle opened the mystery, but it isn't solved yet."

"Exactly. Martin and Terza welcomed him as a guest, but they didn't know who he was. If they had, they might not have accepted his gift," Abby said. "In fact, Martin wanted to return the stocks, but Terza said that would hurt his honor. They would never do that."

"If you can find him, at least you could tell him how much

he means to them," Ellen said. "It'll be up to him whether to come meet them or not."

"Martin wants to return the tangram puzzle. He gave it to the boy as a gift. Now the man gave it back, but Martin doesn't want it. He wants him to keep it," Abby said.

"You may not be able to find this man," George said.

"I certainly won't find him if I don't try." Abby finished her soup and put down her spoon and napkin. "Hope you don't mind if I eat and run. The soup was delicious, Mom. Thanks. For the food and your advice." She rose and carried her empty dishes to the sink.

"I don't recall we gave you any advice," George said.

"Oh, you did." Abby gave each of her parents a hug. "You listened and asked questions and steered me to the answers. Now I need to get back to my office and do some surfing."

"Surfing? Not in this weather," Ellen said, wide-eyed.

Abby laughed. I love the outdoors, but I don't go ocean surfing even in good weather, Mom, so don't worry. I mean searching on the Internet. It's amazing the things—or people —you can find there."

BACK AT HER DESK, staring at her computer screen, Abby found a few references when she typed Tan Jinghuan into her search engine, using the last name first as was customary, but nothing seemed to fit. She typed in the name John Tan. Hundreds of pages of references appeared on her screen. She scrolled down through several of them, clicking on links. A surgeon, an engineer, a professor, an author, an innkeeper . . . that gave her a moment's pause. Wouldn't it be interesting if he'd gone into the same profession as the Chois? She followed that lead for as far as possible and concluded it was not the right John Tan.

Tapping her fingers against the computer mouse, Abby considered her search. This was not the best way to narrow a search. She changed tactics and typed Global Data Technologies, Incorporated, into her Internet search engine. The company came up on her screen right away. The stock symbol GBDTI took her to a stock quote that stunned her. She double-checked to make sure she had the right stock. As of that moment, the stock was down three cents to $258.53. Down? A quick calculation made the Chois' stock worth just over half a million dollars.

Abby let out a whoosh of breath and sat back. She'd been thinking the stock might be penny stock or worth a couple of dollars a share. She doubted Martin and Terza had any idea that their gift was so valuable.

Would that make a difference? Should she tell them? Abby decided that was not her place. They could look up the stock on their own. Abby guessed that they might not do anything with the stock. If they knew it was valuable, they might want to donate to some charities. But revealing the value wasn't her goal. She wanted to find their donor.

A link from the site gave her the company profile. She clicked on it.

The company name came up. It was located in Los Altos Hills, California. The stock had listed San Francisco. Doing a map search, Abby found what looked like a small town south of San Francisco. If the company owned the location, the property alone would be worth many mega-millions.

The profile gave a phone number and business summary. The company provided Internet advertising and sales venues, but specialized in data storage systems for large entities.

Key executives. Now she was getting somewhere. To have

that kind of stock, the Chois' young man must have a high position in the company. She looked through the executive list for Tan Jinghuan or Jinghuan Tan or John Tan or John Wong or John Doe or John anybody. Nothing.

Below the Key Executives was a hot link to "View Insiders." Abby clicked on the link and a page came up with a list of major holders. Seven individuals, all either officers or directors of the corporation, were listed. She clicked on each name. From the information given, she was certain none of them were John Tan.

A list of top institutional holders followed. Most were fortune five hundred companies or mutual fund and management groups. She supposed it was possible the donor could be an individual or an employee of the company who bought the stock, but it seemed unlikely. The man was giving away half a million dollars to strangers, even though they had given to him when he needed help. She was getting frustrated.

Out of curiosity, Abby looked up several long-standing charitable organizations that helped children. One Christian organization pictured mission projects all over the world. India. Africa. Latin America. The Middle East. Europe. The testimonials and pictures of the children touched Abby's heart. She gave to her church and to missions and many worthwhile programs, but this affected an individual child's life. She'd seen firsthand the impact Martin and Terza had had on one young boy. She wanted to have that kind of impact on a child.

Abby couldn't believe how little a sponsorship cost. For the price of dinner at a nice restaurant once a month—not an expensive one—a child could receive an education and some essential help. There were other projects, like providing clean water, farming aid and health aid.

With no children of her own, and sharing costs with Mary, she could afford the little bit extra, over and above what she already gave, to support a child. The thought gurgled up inside of her, giving her a feeling of anticipation. She'd seen the collection of pictures Terza had saved of Jinghuan Tan. She could see pictures of a child and watch that child grow and know she was helping.

Abby decided right then that she would support a child. She remembered her mother once calling that "giggle giving," when the Lord touched your heart for a special purpose, and you gave, out of spontaneous joy, just because the opportunity was there. It might not have been so easy for Martin and Terza, however. They came to the United States from Hong Kong years ago. Abby didn't know much about that time in her friends' lives, but she suspected supporting the boy had been a sacrifice. Knowing them, they'd given freely and wholeheartedly. They were generous people.

She printed out the information so she could check more thoroughly. She wanted to make sure she gave to a group that handled the finances wisely and spent most of it on the children. She wanted a Christian group that would give the child hope, as well as food and education. This didn't help her find the Chois' donor, but it made her realize how easily she could help. And it gave her a real insight into their feelings for this person who had risen above poverty and become a success.

What kind of a man was Tan Jinghuan? she wondered. Had he learned the values of giving and helping others? It would seem so. Did he learn about God? Did he find faith, so he had the strength of the Lord to help him in his life? Martin and Terza must be thinking of all these questions and many more. How she would love to bring them the answers.

She wondered if he lived in China or the United States. If he'd come to the states, or become westernized in his dealings, he might have changed the way he presented his name. Martin and Terza used their given names first and their surname last. That would make the man Jinghuan Tan or John Tan.

He'd said he'd become wealthy. She wondered how wealthy he'd become to give away such an expensive gift. Abby refused to consider that she might fail in this effort, but she had to acknowledge that he might be hard to find.

CHAPTER ❦ NINETEEN

ABBY DEBATED WHETHER to call Terza to inquire further about their benefactor. She had no idea how the couple was responding to their discovery or if they would be offended by her questions. Still, they had been willing to share the discovery and the story with Mary, Henry and her.

Discouraged that her Internet surfing had produced no discernable leads, Abby shut down her computer and went out to the conservatory lab. She put on gloves before she took a plastic bag with a small nest down from a shelf that held several abandoned nests she'd gathered early in the winter. Few species reused their nests. They were easy to spot in the woods after the deciduous trees and bushes had lost their foliage.

Abby collected and cataloged feathers. In a successful nest, where a brood had hatched, she'd find feathers from the nestlings. Some nests contained feathers used in the nest construction.

The bag identified the nest as collected from a western red-cedar tree. She removed the nest, placing it on her work surface. Carefully deconstructing the nest, Abby identified it as a cedar waxwing nest. She could tell the bird species by the location, materials and construction of the nest. It was a fairly common, cup-shaped nest made of twigs and grasses, moss and bark. Often nests contained hair, leaves, thread or yarn or any material available. Robins and swallows used mud as mortar to hold the nest together. Some species used spider silk or insect egg cocoons to knit their nests together.

Using tweezers, she removed feathers and bits of shell, checking to make sure the inner lining was intact. DNA could be extracted from the nest's contents and cataloged, although she would not do that now. She sealed the samples in plastic bags, labeled and dated them.

Setting them aside, Abby studied the details of the nest. Although she couldn't be certain without observing the nest-making, the cedar waxwings were one of only a few species that would take materials from abandoned nests. She suspected some of the materials were recycled, which saved the birds a great deal of time and energy, a trait she admired.

Considering the aspects of conserving time and energy, she had been wasting hers trying to find an individual with a common name on the Internet. She was not employing her resources or deductive reasoning. She completed her observations and list of materials, cataloging them and storing them in separate plastic bags. She put the project components and findings in her filing system, stripped off the gloves and tossed them in the trash, then locked up the lab building and returned to her office. It was only four o'clock. She still had time to call Terza before their mealtime.

When Terza answered, Abby said, "This is Abby. Hope I'm not interrupting your dinner."

"No. Martin went to the mainland for supplies. He isn't back yet."

"I promised Janet I'd ask if he'd make apricot tarts for the Snow Fest."

"He already decided to make some extras, so the ingredients are on his shopping list."

"Great. How are you doing? Did you have a chance to ask your friend about Tan Jinghuan or John Wong or whoever he is?"

"Martin was going to see his friend today and ask. I'm not sure I want to know. I go back and forth. We lost him once, a long time ago. Now we almost found him, and again we've lost him. You know? I keep thinking about him. It hurts my heart."

"I'm so sorry." Abby wasn't sure what to say. Martin and Terza were grieving for a child they lost all over again—this time, an adopted child whom they'd never met. She softened her voice. "Terza, do you want to find him?"

"I think yes. But then I think, what if he doesn't want to meet us? What if his gift is to him like paying a debt?" As she spoke, Terza's accent grew more pronounced. Abby heard a little catch in her voice.

"If that were so, he wouldn't have left the pictures and his journal pages," Abby said.

"That maybe is true," Terza replied. "Yes. I want to meet him. Martin, I'm not so sure, but he is asking his friend about this man, so I think yes."

"You and Martin are always generous to everyone. I'm asking God to be generous to you and to help you find this man. Will you let me know what you learn from your friend?"

"Yes. I'll call you. Then we will know better how to pray. Thank you, Abby. I'm asking the Lord that we can meet our Jinghuan too."

That cemented Abby's resolve. She would do her best to locate this man. With the Lord's help, if He was willing, the Chois would find this son of their hearts.

Abby looked up the phone number of Leanne Van Hoesin, president of the San Juan Islands Birding Society. Dialing the number, she sat back. Leanne loved to discuss birds. With the storm, she would have plenty to say before Abby could make her request.

WHEN ABBY GOT HOME, Mary was in the kitchen, preparing dinner.

"Give me a minute to change, and I'll come help you," Abby called out before she bounded up the stairs. She'd taken a quick walk out to the observation platform at the conservatory and gotten her pant legs wet. Though mostly dry, it made the denim stiff and cold.

Abby dropped her clothes in the laundry room, then washed her hands at the kitchen sink.

"Looks like you have dinner almost ready," she said. Water was boiling in a large pot on the stove and marinara sauce was warming in another pan. Mary was sitting at the table, slathering garlic butter on French bread.

"I had time," Mary said.

"I got your judges for the snowman contest. Three of the San Juan Islands Birding Society board members are going to do it. I had to promise a special program for them in April, but Leanne Van Hoesin, Wulf Walkenhorst and Maureen O'Leary all graciously agreed to help us out."

"I'm sorry. I should have told Janet to call someone else."

Abby laughed. "As if Janet would have changed her mind. It's fine. I love an opportunity to talk about birds."

"Well, I could have tried," Mary said, a twinkle in her eyes. "I talked to Judge—or I should say Daniel—Swink and he promised to come." She grinned. "He's a character. I bribed him with Mom's lemon pie. I'll have to tell her. He wants to eat it with Mom and Dad."

"That'll be interesting," Abby said. "But he won't be an easy judge."

"That's all right. I wouldn't want to have to pick. We have some terrific snow creatures. I'll have to call William and have him take pictures for *The Birdcall.*" Mary gave her a pleading look that said "don't shoot me."

"By the way, I sort of volunteered you to drive the judges around."

"Me? Judge Swink wouldn't fit in my car, let alone the other judges."

"You can drive Mom's Lincoln. She won't mind, and it's the closest thing to a celebrity car that we have around here."

"I suppose." Abby took lettuce and radishes out of the refrigerator and picked a tomato from a bowl on the counter. Setting a cutting board on the table, she sat across from Mary. "This Snow Fest is turning into quite an event."

"I'll say. I'm amazed, myself. Everyone in town wants to take part in it."

"That's one of the things I love about living in such a small community. Everyone wants to help, and no one wants to be left out," Abby said. "Can your committee handle everything?"

"I'm sure they can." Mary set aside the butter and knife

she'd been using. Abby noticed a slight frown on her sister's forehead.

"They? I realize you can't move tables and do the physical setup. You are planning to attend, aren't you?"

"I'd like to." Mary looked up Abby. "Have you noticed all the snow out there?"

"There's a lot. That's why we're having a Snow Fest, is it not? It'll be cold, but we'll all bundle up." Although Mary wasn't big on outdoor activities, Abby couldn't imagine she wouldn't want to participate in the event she'd helped plan.

"It's not the cold. I have that wonderful down lap blanket I can wrap up in. It's the snow. I can't roll through it. I know Henry and Neil and James would clear the park for me if I asked, but they've got their hands full with all the problems related to the snow." Mary made a dismissive gesture with her hand and managed a smile. "It's okay. I can mind the shop while Candace runs a booth in the park. We're expecting an influx of tourists to the island for the day, so I'm sure I'll see plenty of people."

"Of course. I suppose all the stores will be busy." Abby hadn't considered her sister's logistics plight. It was like Mary to play down her own needs so she wouldn't inconvenience others. "I wouldn't be a bit surprised if Janet and Patricia have already thought of that and made some kind of arrangements." And if they hadn't, Abby intended to put a bug in their ear, although she wouldn't let Mary know her plans.

Mary gave Abby a cheerful smile. "I think I'll start baking tonight after dinner. I promised I'd make brownies and cookies."

"I'll help you," Abby said, just as the phone rang. "I'll get it," she said, jumping up. She answered on the third ring. "Hello. This is Abby."

"Hello. It's Terza. Oh dear, are you eating dinner now. I didn't look at the time."

"Not yet. Did Martin get home?"

"Yes. He's making dinner now. You asked me to call and tell you what our friend said." Terza didn't sound excited. Her voice sounded flat, disappointed.

"Yes. What happened? What did he learn?" Abby prompted. She heard a sigh on the other end of the phone.

"He didn't learn anything," Terza said. "At least nothing that will help us find Jinghuan, only that it was him. He met Jinghuan at a business conference. When they talked, he told Jinghuan that he lived in Seattle. Jinghuan told him he wanted to visit the San Juan Islands, and Lin told him about our bed-and-breakfast. Lin was pleased that Jinghuan came here."

"But Terza, that's wonderful! Now you know for certain which guest he was," Abby said. "Did he say what kind of business conference?"

"No. Martin didn't ask him any more questions, but Lin Wong works with computers. He makes programs, I think. Very important businessman. He has rich clients. Maybe . . . no, he didn't say Jinghuan was a client. So maybe Jinghuan does the same kind of work."

"Perhaps. Has Lin heard from Jinghuan since then?"

"No. And he doesn't know how to contact him." Terza sounded disheartened.

"If Martin talks to his friend again, have him ask where the conference was and when. Don't give up, Terza. The Bible says in Proverbs 13:12 'Hope deferred makes the heart sick.' I can hear that sickness in your voice. But then it goes on to say, 'but a longing fulfilled is a tree of life.' Whenever things seem hopeless, I remember that. The Lord has opened the doors of this blessing. He hasn't closed it yet."

"That is just how I feel, Abby. My heart feels sick. I should be so happy that we heard from him. Why can't I be satisfied with this unexpected gift?"

"Because you adopted this child in your hearts. Keep telling yourself that you reached out to this lonely boy, and he felt loved so much that he searched for you and tried to return your love. Maybe he doesn't know how. Maybe he's afraid that you have forgotten him."

"Never!" Terza said.

"I know that. Now we have to make him know it. Keep praying for God to bring him back to you."

"I will. We will. Martin and I pray this every morning and every night, and my heart prays for him all the time in between."

"Good. The prayer of a righteous man—or woman—is powerful and effective. The Bible says that in James 5:16. Mary, my mother and I are praying too."

"Oh, Abby, God just has to hear all those prayers."

"He does, Terza. You can count on it."

CHAPTER ❦ TWENTY

AFTER THE DISHES WERE cleaned up, and Abby started the dishwasher, she wiped her hands and turned to Mary. "I'm going to do a little work on the Internet tonight. I'm trying to find John Tan. Terza said he's somehow associated with the computer technology industry and the stock he gave them is from a successful technology company."

"Good. If anyone *can* find him, you will. I feel so bad for them, getting so close to knowing their adopted son, then realizing he slipped right through their grasp. Unbelievable." She shook her head. "I'm going to read for a while, but first I'll sit here and pray that the Lord leads you right to him," Mary said.

Abby leaned over and gave Mary a kiss on the cheek. "Thanks, sis. That's all the help I need."

Abby booted up her computer at her desk in the upstairs study. The room had an upholstered chair, where she sometimes read her trade journals and scientific periodicals, oak bookshelves and a matching lateral file cabinet that held her copious personal papers and photographs of her field trips and sightings over the years.

She wasn't sure where to start, but Martin had been able to confirm Tan Jinghuan's connection to the computer technology world, and Terza thought it had more to do with software or the Internet than computer equipment. Their friend had met Jinghuan at a conference, so she ran a search for computer technology conferences. Hundreds of possibilities came up. Since the company specialized in data storage, she tried narrowing the field by adding that to her search. Another level of conference listings came up with as many possibilities as before. She picked one, and it led to another list of upcoming trade shows. Since she needed a conference that had already taken place, the lists weren't much help.

Abby returned to the financial listing for Global Data Technologies. Because of the stock, it was the only common thread she had.

She skipped past the areas she'd already searched and clicked on company events, hoping for something linking Jinghuan to the corporation. She found references to SEC filings, financial reports, changes of officers and directors and the annual report. She clicked on the links that seemed to have the most potential. An hour later, Abby removed her glasses and rubbed her eyes. Every listing she'd chosen had led to a dead end.

Abby put her glasses back on and glanced at the time. Almost nine o'clock. She would work another half hour. Going back to the main page, she tried headlines. There had to be something there.

The corporation seemed to be all over the news. Words like

gains and *strategies* and *record earnings* sprinkled the headline links. She followed a few stories, which all gave glowing reports of the company's future. That was good for Martin and Terza. Their stock was poised to go up.

Abby was getting nowhere. All she'd done was eliminate a few more places to look. Where was her logic? She couldn't seem to form a hypothesis or a plan. An hour and a half had passed as she'd lost herself in following Internet rabbit trails. Discouraged, she logged off the Internet and shut down her computer. Perhaps a good night's sleep would clear her thoughts and give her a fresh approach.

Although the hour was late, Abby felt the need to end her day in Scripture, to help regain her perspective. She sat in her favorite reading chair and picked up her Bible, which was on the table beside it. Opening to a reference from her morning devotions, she turned to the book of Habakkuk. In chapter one the prophet seemed to be arguing with the Lord, then the Lord would answer his complaint. The exchange began in chapter one. It began, "How long, O Lord, must I call for help, but you do not listen?"

All right, she thought. *I haven't been searching for Jinghuan for very long, but I've prayed and asked for Your help, and Terza and Martin are praying. Will You answer our prayers?*

She believed God answered all prayers, but she knew the answer wasn't always what she wanted. *Lord, please give me a word to let me know I'm doing the right thing to keep looking for this man*, she prayed. She continued reading.

"Then the Lord replied: 'Write down the revelation and make it plain on tablets so that a herald may run with it. For the revelation awaits an appointed time; it speaks of the end and will not prove false. Though it linger, wait for it; it will certainly come and will not delay'" (Habakkuk 2:2–3).

Abby set her Bible down in her lap and stared across the room, seeing nothing but the words written on her mind.

Wow, Lord, I know this is not talking about finding a long lost orphan, but are You speaking to me? she prayed. The verses told her to write down the revelation—what she knew—and make it plain, so she could see what was in front of her, then look and wait for the Lord's revelation. *It will certainly come. . . .*

"Thank You, Lord," she prayed out loud. "I wasn't expecting such a fast answer, but I shouldn't be surprised. You are always faithful."

She opened a new page in the notebook she kept for Bible notes, and began jotting down everything she knew about Jinghuan Tan and all the avenues she'd already explored. Tomorrow she would begin again, and look to see what the Lord would reveal.

FRIDAY MORNING, Mary wheeled around the end of the cereal aisle at the Green Grocer, looking for the chocolate and peanut butter oatmeal bars that made a great quick lunch. Scanning along the shelves, she wondered why store managers felt the need to play musical chairs with their merchandise. Just when she knew where to find something, they moved it. She finally spotted it, on the upper shelf. Using her easy reach metal gripper, she grabbed the box of protein bars to pull it down.

"I'd be happy to help you with that," a gruff male voice said behind her. He didn't sound happy at all.

Mary recognized Archie Goodfellow's voice. She swiveled around to face him and smiled. "No need, but thanks." She held up her shopping tool. "As long as it's not too heavy, I'm fine."

"Glad to hear it," he said. He planted his massive hands on his hips and looked at her. Finnegan stiffened next to her, alert for her command. She reached out to put her hand on his head, letting him know she was fine. The last thing she needed was for her faithful service dog to go after her grocer.

Archie glanced at Finnegan and stepped back a few inches, appearing less threatening, but he wasn't deterred. "I got word that your committee's putting on a winter carnival and a snowman competition. It's not a bad idea. The city council discussed it last night and we decided to support your event in the park, but you should have consulted us first. You're using town property, you know."

"Yes, but it is public property," Mary said. "No one else has asked to use it, have they?"

"No, but that's not the point. You all elected a council to approve things like this."

"Oh dear. I'm sorry, Archie. This all happened so fast, I'm afraid we didn't think about that. I'm so glad you voted to support the Snow Fest. It's not a true carnival, you know. There won't be any rides that require permits, or anything like that. We'd like to use the electric hookups at the park to keep coffee and cocoa hot—that sort of thing. Is that all right?"

"There is a use fee, you know. It's twenty dollars. You'll have to pay that."

"Of course. We'll be glad to." Mary fished in the side pocket for her purse. "I can pay you right now," she said.

"No. You have to pay the County Public Works Department. They handle the park maintenance."

"I'll take care of it this afternoon."

"Good. Next time, you need to bring your proposal before the council a month in advance and get the proper authorization," he said. He turned to leave, then turned back.

"Anything I can do for you?" he asked.

"No thank you," she said, giving Archie a sweet smile. "Finnegan and I will be fine."

"Well, then, I'll let you get back to your shopping."

Mary let out a sigh of relief as she watched Archie walk away. As soon as he went through the swinging door to the back of the store, she let out a little chuckle. "A month's notice, he says, Finnegan. As if we knew a month ago that this blizzard was coming."

Finnegan stared at her with his intelligent, brown eyes, as if he knew exactly what she was saying and agreed with her.

"We'd better get moving. I need to take the groceries home, then run out to Public Works to pay this fee. We sure don't want the county after us for a violation. What was it Clare Boothe Luce said? 'No good deed goes unpunished'?"

Wondering what other obstacles they'd be facing, Mary wheeled down the aisle toward the milk section, Finnegan right by her side. She hoped there weren't other problems they hadn't considered. After all, they just wanted to put a positive spin on their most unusual circumstances.

AFTER STAYING UP LATE, Abby overslept. She hurried through her morning routine. When she got to her office, before she even booted up her computer, she called Terza. "I wondered if you'd discovered anything more about your anonymous guest," she asked.

"Not very much," Terza answered. "After we talked, I told Martin your questions. He called his friend Lin Wong after dinner and asked for the date and place where he met Jinghuan and if he knew who Jinghuan worked for. He said they met at a conference in September in Sunnyvale, California, where all the computer companies are located. Jinghuan didn't tell him who he worked for. Lin said he was asking about Seattle and places to live, so Martin thinks he might be moving here. Martin wants to go look for him."

"Seattle's a big place. If he's there, he could have moved to any of the surrounding cities," Abby said.

"That's what I told Martin. He could spend the rest of his life looking for Jinghuan. That's not good. I told him we must keep praying that he will come back here."

"That's the best advice you could give him," Abby said. She thought about sharing the verses she'd read last night, but the Scripture said the revelation awaits an appointed time, and Abby had no idea when that time would be. Tomorrow or ten years. "I'm praying for that too," Abby said.

"Thank you, Abby. You're a good friend."

After Terza hung up, Abby grabbed her coat and gloves and went outside. True to the forecast, the temperature had not topped freezing, although this Friday morning it hovered at thirty one point eight. If the sun broke through the thick, high cloud cover, the snow would begin to melt. For Mary and the sake of the Snow Fest, Abby hoped the cold would last through Saturday. One more day, then it could warm up.

Abby walked out to the observation deck, looking for signs of birds and other woodland creatures along the way. Most of the snow had fallen off the larger bushes and the trees, and bits of leaves and shreds of bark littered the snow where birds had gleaned berries off the bushes. Freshly cut and shredded stems proved the deer and rabbits were out scavenging. Looking out over the grounds from the deck, Abby breathed deeply and inhaled the crisp air. There in the center of nature, she felt the presence of God, and she raised her face to the sky. "Dear Father, You are a kind, loving Father, and we know You long for all Your children to come to You. You adopted us when we were lost. You understand the longing in Martin and Terza's hearts to know this orphan child who has become a man. Right now he's lost to them. Please, Lord, bring him back here. Bring them together to have the joy of caring for each other now. Amen."

Talking to God in the solitude of His creation always filled Abby with deep peace. She felt that now as she walked back to the museum. The crisp air, the sharp scent of pine and fir, the symphony of nature filled her with God's presence in His universe. She felt renewed and optimistic, anticipating what the Lord would do next.

Back in the office, Abby returned to her Internet search for Jinghuan Tan. She logged onto the financial pages of Global Data Technologies, Inc. With a time frame of September, she went to historical prices, to see any dramatic changes, but the growth had been even and constant. Headlines were current. She couldn't find a history there. She tried Profile, Key Statistics, Industry Center, Blogs and Competitors. All listed current statistics, events and companies. Company Events had historical reports and reports of SEC filings. She'd looked there before, but now scanned backwards to September.

Dates and SEC filings were listed, but this section gave a description of the type of reports. She scrolled through the items going backwards from October to September. Quarterly Report. Change in Directors. Financial Reports. Entry into a Material Definitive Agreement. She clicked on that last one.

It was dated September 15th. Abby scanned the contents.

. . . Global Data Technologies, Inc. (the Company),
entered into a letter agreement (the Letter Agreement)
with Tan ProTechT Resources Ltd. (Tan ProTechT
Resources) related to the purchase of . . .

Abby perked up. The Tan had to stand for Jinghuan Tan.
This had to be it. Global Data Tech bought Jinghuan Tan's
company. She read further.

The Letter Agreement sets forth the general terms upon
which the Company would, in exchange for $15 million
in cash and shares, acquire 100% equity interest in Tan
ProTechT Resources. The parties have substantially
completed negotiations . . .

Excited, Abby ran a search for TAN ProTechT. Pages of
links came up. Here it was. News of the sale. It listed J. P. Tan,
principle owner. No wonder she couldn't find Jinghuan. He
went by initials. This had to be him. Jinghuan P. Tan. The
words of Habakkuk came back to her. *For the revelation awaits
an appointed time.* The time had come!

"Thank You, Lord," she said out loud. "Now please help me
find him."

It seemed the man was some kind of genius according to
the news reports about his development of data storage and
security for huge organizations and corporations.

Following link after link, Abby pieced together a picture of
J. P. Tan's adult life, from a biography of his stellar college
career to his rise in the telecommunication industry. There
were articles about him, but no current interviews or pictures.
She could write to his company, but it might not reach him.

Unfortunately, there was no information to help Abby contact the illusive man.

Abby printed out several articles for Martin and Terza. She'd gone through a number of pages in the search results, and the trail began to repeat. She was about to log off when a word caught her eye.

One link that listed Tan had the word *Foundation.* Clicking on it opened a Web site for The Rebecca Tan International Children's Refuge Foundation.

Was it a coincidence? Did Jinghuan Tan have a wife or daughter? She looked through the Web site pages. The foundation's mission was to find shelter and education for homeless children all over the world. Abby saw pictures of children in Asia and Africa and South America and even the United States. The method of support was similar to what Martin and Terza had done for Jinghuan. She clicked on a page for fundraisers. A lovely dark haired woman was speaking at a podium to an auditorium filled with people. In the background, a young Chinese man in a suit and tie stood watching her.

Jinghuan. Abby was certain it was he. It had to be.

There was an 800 number to call. Abby picked up the phone and dialed. A woman answered the phone.

"Children's Refuge Foundation," she said. "Would you like to make a donation or support a child monthly? We accept checks or credit cards."

"I might, but that isn't the purpose of my call today," Abby said. "I'm Dr. Abigail Stanton of the Sparrow Island Nature Conservancy, and I'd like to speak—"

"I'm sorry, but this foundation doesn't make donations to other foundations. All of our funds go to help the children," she said, interrupting Abby.

"Yes, I understand. I'm not looking for a donation. I have some information about Rebecca and Jinghuan Tan's family. If I could speak with one of them?"

"That won't be possible. I must take another call now."

"Wait. Please take my name and phone—"

Click. The woman had hung up the telephone.

Well, what did you expect, Dr. Stanton? Abby asked herself. The woman probably thought she was looking for a handout. No doubt Jinghuan received lots of calls looking for money. Abby shook her head. Now what?

There had to be a contact name or an address to send donations. She scrolled through several Web pages until she found an e-mail link.

Now, how to attract the right attention to her message? How did he address the letters to Martin and Terza? She'd written it down somewhere in her notebook. Abby got her purse and took out the small spiral notepad that she carried.

He'd addressed the letters to Choi Ching-kuo and Choi Furen. Applying that to their last name, she wrote:

To Tan Ching-kuo and Tan Furen. She hoped that wasn't incorrect and didn't insult them. If J.P. was, indeed, Jinghuan, he would know this was regarding the Chois.

Choi Ching-kuo and Choi Furen solved the tangram elephant and found the key to unlock your gift. They are honored by your gift, but grieved that they have lost you again. The greatest honor you could give would be yourself. Please come to meet them. They are praying for this blessing. I am praying too. Yours most sincerely, Abigail Stanton, a friend.

Abby left her e-mail address, her telephone number and the name and phone number of the museum.

Please, Lord, let this message reach Jinghuan, she prayed.

She found an address and jotted a note with the same message, and addressed the envelope to the Tans, in care of the foundation. As she kept scrolling through the Web site's pages, she found a phone number for people wanting to sponsor a fundraiser. Why not? Martin and Terza would surely like to help with this, and so would Mary and maybe Hugo. She called the number. A message machine came on.

"This is Abigail Stanton, of Sparrow Island, Washington," she said. "I am interested in putting on a fundraiser to support your foundation. Please call me at the Sparrow Island Nature Museum." She left her phone number.

She kept looking for any other contact information. There was none.

"All right, Lord, You led me to this. Please let this work. Please let the Tans find my messages and soften their hearts to come meet Martin and Terza. Amen," she prayed.

Abby put on her jacket, grabbed her purse and went out front, where Wilma was hard at work.

"I have a letter to mail before the last pickup. Do you have anything to mail? I'll run it into town."

"Yes. I have a stack of donation acknowledgements. Thanks." She handed the stack of neatly typed envelopes to Abby.

"I'll see you later." Abby said good-bye and hurried out to her car.

CHAPTER ❦ TWENTY-ONE

GOOD NEWS FOR THE coastal region," the weather girl announced on the early edition of the Friday evening news. She pointed to the weather map with swirling clouds and arrows. "The cold is finally leaving our region, heading east into Idaho and Montana tomorrow. Lows tonight will only get down to freezing, then expect a warming trend, with highs tomorrow reaching thirty-eight in the afternoon. As the low pressure system moves east, it will bring moisture to our area. There's a sixty percent chance of rain or snow showers tomorrow, tapering off in the evening. The temperatures will increase into the forties Sunday and Monday with clearing skies. The extended forecast calls for . . ."

"Oh dear," Mary said, sitting in the living room, watching the news with Abby. "That's not good news for us. I hope it doesn't warm up too soon. Snow showers would be fine, but not rain."

Abby sat on the couch holding a decorative pillow against her chest. "Maybe it will miss us," she said, always optimistic.

"Ida, Janet and Patricia have worked so hard to put this festival together, it'll be a shame if it rains," Mary said.

"And you. You've put hours and hours into this event. Besides, we'll never eat all those cookies and brownies you made."

"We could always take them to church for coffee hour," Mary said. "Everyone on the island is excited about tomorrow though. Too bad we couldn't hold it earlier in the week, when it was still so cold."

"You've done a terrific job in five days. I don't see how you could have held it any sooner," Abby said. "We'll just have to pray that it works out. I'd hate to see Bobby disappointed. He's so excited about the sled races. He told me his dad rounded up a bunch of plastic disks for sledding. Bobby asked me to be in the races. I told him I couldn't until after lunch, since you roped me into playing chauffeur to the snowman competition judges."

"I'm sorry. I didn't think about you competing in the sledding," Mary said. She realized she should have asked her sister before volunteering her. She hadn't thought about Abby having other plans.

Abby chuckled. "Don't be sorry. You gave me a good excuse. Besides, I think Bobby was being polite, asking me to race. I don't have the energy to compete against those kids."

"Don't sell yourself short," Mary said. "I appreciate your help. Now if the cold will just hold out for another day."

"As long as it doesn't start raining, we should be all right," Abby speculated.

"How's your search for Martin and Terza's benefactor coming?"

"I hate to be too hopeful—I don't want to jinx it—but I think I found him."

Mary tsk-tsked and shook her head at Abby. "Now you sound like Martin. You prayed about this. If God answered your prayer, it's a sure thing."

"*If* being the operative word." Abby told her about the foundation named after Rebecca Tan. "I sent messages every way I could. Now I'm praying at least one of the messages will get through and he'll decide to contact them."

"Wow. Wouldn't that be something? They could gain an adopted son and daughter-in-law too." Mary's children meant the world to her, and she'd seen Terza's tenderness for children. After being childless for so many years, Terza would be over the moon with joy. "Oh Lord, please let this work out," Mary said out loud.

"Amen." Abby added. "That's what I'm praying. They might not even be around to get my messages, but I mailed a letter to them at the foundation. They should get it eventually."

"Are you going to tell Martin and Terza?"

"I don't know. Not yet. I don't want to get their hopes up. But I printed out information about Jinghuan and his wife. I'll give that to them." Abby stared at the fire crackling in the fireplace for a moment. Then she took a deep breath, as if changing gears. "Now how about you? Are you ready for tomorrow? Is there anything I can do to help tonight?" Abby asked.

Mary knew Abby had taken the Chois' puzzle and discovery to heart. She added a little prayer that Abby's efforts would be rewarded with success, for her joy, as well as for their friends.

"I promised to make a large pan of lasagna for lunch at the

church for the judges," Mary said. "You're invited too. Patricia's taking care of the Caesar salad and garlic bread. Janet's making a dessert and Mom's bringing in a lemon pie for Judge Swink."

"I'll help you cook. Let's make a little extra, so we can put some in the freezer for next week."

"Sure. It's just as easy to make a lot as a little." She didn't need help with the cooking. She'd become very adept at working from her wheelchair in her remodeled kitchen, but she welcomed her sister's help. They could get it done a lot faster and have the time together.

"How about setting up tomorrow morning? Who's doing that?"

"Ida, Janet and Patricia are in charge of the park setup. They told me not to worry about a thing. Just to show up tomorrow morning at nine with lots of warm layers. I'm to take the lasagna to the church, then go to the park. I have no idea what they've arranged. Have they talked to you?"

Abby shrugged. "Not to me. I have no idea. Sounds like you'll be spending the day outdoors though. I sure hope it doesn't rain."

"Me too."

TO SAVE MARY A TRIP, Abby dropped off the lasagna at 8:30 Saturday morning on her way to pick up her mother's Lincoln. As she drove past Holloway's Hardware, she saw the bustle of activity at the park, half a block back off of Shoreline Drive. She spotted Sam's and Rick's pickup trucks parked at the west end of the park near the picnic tables and the small pavilion area. Pastor James and Doug Heinz were also there, unloading folding tables from the back of Rick's truck. Janet was standing near the pavilion, bundled up with a bright red stocking hat, a matching knit scarf around her neck and a clipboard in her red gloved hand. She was pointing to a spot as Rick carried a table in the direction she pointed.

Abby slowed to take in the sights of downtown Green Harbor. The streetlamps were still on, and someone had draped garlands of greens and red ribbon on the lampposts, giving the town a winter holiday air.

Considering the island's limited resources, Abby was amazed at how well the streets and sidewalks were cleared of snow. It had been piled between the sidewalks and curbs, making white berms next to all the snowmen and streetlamps. Green Harbor looked lovely and clean. The snow gave it a special charm. For a moment, the sight gave Abby a pang of longing for the white winters of upstate New York, even though she loved Sparrow Island. She especially loved being with her family. She sped up, her parents' farm her destination. Her mother's kitchen would be warm and welcoming and there'd be fresh coffee and rolls, still warm from breakfast.

MARY COULDN'T BELIEVE her eyes when she pulled into the handicapped parking at the park. A wooden ramp led from the parking area to the pavilion. Henry was already there and must have been watching for her, as he immediately came over to her car. He picked up a piece of plywood and set it in place for her wheelchair to roll onto from her lift. She rolled down her window.

"Good morning," she said. "This is amazing."

"It is, isn't it? Bobby McDonald has been here all morning making sure the men laid this out correctly," Henry said.

"Bless his heart. Here. You can take my extra blanket and my umbrella, in case it rains." She handed them to him, before she activated the lift to get out of the van. Finnegan jumped down beside her, ready to help.

Henry walked in the snow beside the ramp as Mary wheeled down to the concrete pavilion. Cedar poles and beams created an open enclosure over the pavilion. Ida stood beside a table that faced the bronze pole clock in the middle of the park.

"Hey Mary, this spot's for you," she called out, smiling like she'd just won a grand prize as Mary approached the enclosure. "You're in charge of the Little Flock table."

She waited until Mary wheeled up to the table. "What do you think?" she said proudly.

Mary looked around with wonder. A large banner was strung across the front of the pavilion. Reading it from the back side, Mary made out First Ever Sparrow Island Snow Fest.

To her left, close enough to pivot her wheelchair, a table was set up for Island Blooms flower art. At their end of the park, spots had been cleared and tables set up beneath brightly colored canopies and tented stands. She saw Wilma Washburn setting out her beautiful baskets. At the far end of the park, across the expanse of pure white snow, Lindsay Buckminster was hitching her horses to her hay wagon.

Mary took a deep breath. The air chilled her nostrils and filled her lungs with sharp, zesty air, invigorating her senses. She smelled charcoal and looked over to see a large black barrel barbecue with the rounded lid raised and smoke billowing from the pit. Soon the cooking bratwurst sausages would entice everyone from miles around with their tantalizing smell.

"Unbelievable! This is everything I imagined and more," she said. "You and Janet and Patricia have done a fabulous job! I hope someone's taking pictures."

Ida laughed. "Patricia has her digital camera. She's been shooting pictures of the setup. William's over there." She pointed toward the fountain with the sculpted metal dolphins. Their newspaper editor was bundled in a full-length coat, with a long wool scarf around his neck and a hat on his head. "He's recording the entire event. He said he's going to publish a special edition dedicated to the snow and the Snow Fest."

"You'd better wrap up, before you get cold," Henry said, unfolding her down lap blanket and reaching over her shoulder to lay it over her legs. She looked up into his eyes and smiled.

"Thank you," she mouthed. He smiled back, his eyes twinkling. Then she saw the blue tarp. Someone had covered the open beams of the pavilion roof with a large blue plastic tarp. "I guess I won't need my umbrella."

"Henry's idea," Ida said. "He and Rick got up on ladders and put that up."

Mary heard a familiar honk and looked over. Abby had pulled up in their mother's big Lincoln. She waved, turned around and drove off. Mary glanced at her watch. The ferry would arrive in a few minutes, bringing the snowman judges and possibly a boatload of visitors. Come what may, the festivities were about to begin.

ABBY SPENT TWO HOURS driving the judges around the island, viewing every snow creature. Leanne and Maureen had discussed the attributes of each snowman, pointing out to the men the merits or weaknesses of each creation. Wulf and Daniel had nodded, mumbled noncommittal sounds and marked their papers. Abby was certain the four judges would not reach a consensus on any of the snow creations.

She was glad the island was small and the roads few by the time she dropped them off at Little Flock, where they would eat lunch and compile their scores. Declining to join them, she left her mother's Lincoln parked in front of the church and hiked over to the park.

She found Mary surrounded by a group of tourists who were sipping hot spiced cider and nibbling on funnel cakes. Next to her, Candace was bent over, helping three children make paper plate and construction paper flowers. Her long, strawberry-blonde hair hung down around her shoulders, adding a layer of warmth. She was chatting with the children, seemingly oblivious to the cold.

"Those look good," Abby said, eyeing the funnel cakes. "Want one?"

"I sure would," Mary said. "I've been watching people eat them all day."

"Have you been sitting here all morning?"

"No. I took a break and went to the store to warm up a bit."

"Good. I'll be back in a few minutes."

On the way to get the cakes, the smell of roasting bratwurst drew Abby to the pit cooker. She bought two bratwurst rolls, then went to the Springhouse Café booth, where Ida was deep frying the doughy funnel cakes in an electric fryer. The smell of sweet frying dough reminded Abby of going to the county fair every year with her parents.

"Cinnamon sugar or powdered sugar?" Ida asked.

"Powdered sugar," Abby said. "That's the only way."

"Oh no. It's much better with cinnamon sugar," Ida declared.

"So how's business?" Abby asked. The park was filled with people tromping around in the snow.

"Unbelievable. I never expected this many people to turn out."

"You can take credit for the success. And your snowman competition is wonderful. I can't believe all the beautiful creations all over the island."

Ida blushed. "Thanks," she said. She lifted the golden brown cakes out of the fryer and placed them on a paper plate covered with waxed paper.

Abby paid her and headed back to Mary. She pulled up a chair and sat next to her sister, handing her the sandwich and cake.

"Yum. Thanks. I'm starving."

"Where's Henry? Why didn't he feed you?"

Mary grinned and pointed to the far end of the park, where Henry and his deputy, Mike Bennett, were playing the part of draft horses, pulling children on inner tubes.

"Aha. Looks like they got roped into helping."

Mary laughed. "Literally."

Mary's cheeks were rosy red and her eyes sparkled.

"Are you cold?" Abby asked.

"Not bad."

"This turned out to be quite a shindig," Abby said.

"A total success, I'd say."

"You'd be right." She looked around at all the activity. Martin and Terza were helping Ana Dominguez show a group of children how to snow paint on mounds of snow. They were spraying colored liquid on the snow. *Only one thing would make it better*, Abby thought. But that wouldn't happen until later, if at all, although she prayed it would happen soon.

Abby finished her funnel cake and licked her fingers. "I need to work this off now. I'd better get over to the sled races before I have to go pick up the judges. Who's announcing the winners?"

"We're having Judge Swink do it. Janet and Ida spread the word for people to gather here at one thirty for the awards."

Abby glanced at her watch. "I need to get going, then." She wiped her hands on a towelette and put on her gloves.

CHAPTER ✿ TWENTY-TWO

Heading out across the park, Abby came upon Janet and Doug Heinz standing beside a portable fire pit, a cheery blaze sending waves of warm air and tiny sparks dancing toward the sky. They were surrounded by children and their parents, with stretched-out coat hangers extended over the fire to roast marshmallows. Janet helped a child put his gooey marshmallow between graham crackers and chocolate squares. She handed the finished s'more to the child, who stuffed it into his mouth.

Janet looked up and waved at Abby.

"Cushy job you've got," Abby shouted.

Janet grinned. "You bet. Gooey too."

Abby laughed. The funnel cake was sticky enough for her.

The Green Harbor PTA had a booth selling meat pasties and curly fries. Sandy was working the booth with another teacher and a parent. The fries smelled so good, Abby wished she wasn't full. She passed the St. Christopher's Church ladies with all kinds of knit mittens, hats and scarves. It looked like they were doing a good business.

She stopped for a moment to admire the mounds of painted snow artwork under Ana and Terza's instruction. Martin and Ana were each standing behind a child, who had a squirt bottle aimed at a snow mound. Martin's child was painting stripes.

Terza had just finished with a child, who was proudly posed next to her snow flower painting so her mother could take her picture.

"What's in those bottles?" Abby asked Terza.

"Kool-Aid," she said. "We tried diluted gelatin, thinking it would set up better, but it kept jelling and clogging the sprayers.

"Well, it looks like you're having as much fun as the children."

"Oh, we are!" Terza's smile and soft brown eyes had regained the serenity that Abby loved and admired so much.

"You seem more relaxed today," Abby observed. "I'm glad."

"Martin and I were given a great gift, and instead of being grateful, we wanted more. We are so thankful for a peek at Jinghuan's life, that he found success and a place for himself in this life. Now we pray that he has the peace we have in knowing the Lord. That is our prayer."

Terza's simple prayer brought a lump to Abby's throat and squeezed at her heart. For a brief time, Martin might have lapsed into the traditions and superstitions deeply ingrained in his childhood, but his faith had risen to overcome the old ways. The Chois' humility and faith shone above their desire.

Abby had some news to share with them, but had decided she would tell them later what she'd discovered about Jinghuan and his wife Rebecca.

"I will pray for Jinghuan's peace too," she assured Terza.

A child came up to do a snow painting. "I'll see you later," Abby said. "I promised Bobby I'd go see his sled races."

Terza gave her an astonished look. "Are you going sledding?"

Abby laughed. "Not today. No time. If the snow hangs around, I might go sledding with Bobby later."

As Abby neared Green Harbor Public School, where the sled races were being held, the big wooden Summit Stables hay wagon and horses went by, filled with red-cheeked, smiling revelers wrapped up like presents in fleecy blankets. Lindsay waved at Abby as they passed.

"Abby!" Bobby yelled as she came around the school toward the hill in back. "Come on! Hurry!"

At least a dozen kids and parents stood around, waiting a turn on the sleds. Four competitors were hiking up the hill, pulling or carrying a variety of sleds.

Although Abby got a lot of outdoor exercise hiking around the island for her bird studies, she felt a bit out of breath by the time she reached Bobby and Neil. It must have been the bratwurst and funnel cake, she reasoned.

"Whew. Looks like you've got a great turnout," she told her young friend.

"Yeah! Isn't this neat?" Bobby was so ruddy-faced his freckles blended together. His ears were red where they peeked out from under his stocking hat.

Abby watched as the racers jumped onto their sleds and careened down the hill. On the sidelines, people yelled encouragement, egging them on.

At the finish line, the winner jumped off his sled and raised his gloved fist in the air, shouting his triumph. His face was as red as his knit hat. The others were just as red.

"Want to race, Abby?" Bobby asked. "I'll let you cut in front."

"Thanks, Bobby, but I've got to pick up the snowman judges and take them to the park. They're announcing the winners at one thirty."

"Oh yeah? I hope José wins. He and his dad worked hard on theirs. Did you see it?"

"Yes. It's one of the best, in my opinion." Abby squeezed his shoulder. Leave it to Bobby to want his friend to win. He'd worked hard on his own snowman and helped with several others around town.

"Keep up the good work. I'll see you later." Abby shared a smile with Neil, who was busy getting the next group ready. Then she headed off toward the pavilion. At least it was all downhill this time.

A CROWD HAD GATHERED around the pavilion, waiting to hear the results of the snowman contest. Mary thought it was interesting that the snow sculptures around the island showed the various personalities of their creators. Some were simple snowmen, borne of the joy of playing in the unexpected white gift. Some were works of art, revealing their maker's creativity and imagination. Many of the creators seemed determined to outdo each other, even without a formal contest. That seemed especially true of the businesses in town, which was natural, she supposed. Running a business required a bit of competitive spirit, as well as a desire to serve, in order to succeed.

A cheer went up when the judges arrived in Ellen's old Lincoln. The panel looked solemn, befitting their serious deliberations as they walked up to the pavilion. Mary wheeled to the sidelines, so she could hear them announce their decisions. She looked around. They hadn't designated anyone to introduce the judges. She caught Abby's eye and gave her a nod toward the microphone. Abby raised her eyebrows. Mary nodded.

Abby gave her a little frown, but dutifully stepped forward.

"By default, it looks like I have the privilege of introducing our esteemed judges," she announced, which earned a chuckle from the audience.

"Keep it short," a man in the back said in a voice just loud enough to carry. Everyone laughed.

"All right. We are fortunate to have such a prestigious group of judges." Abby introduced them all. The audience applauded, and a few people whistled their appreciation. "Now Judge Daniel Swink, from the San Juan County Courthouse, will announce the winners."

"Thank you, Abby," the judge said as he took the microphone. "Let's get right to it. We had two divisions. Commercial and residential," he said. "We'll start with the residential. Let me tell you, this wasn't easy. You all did a fine job with your snow creations." He turned to Leanne, who handed him a clipboard.

A whale pod snow sculpture won for being The Most Beautiful.

The crowd applauded and whistled as Joanne Flemming made her way forward.

"Congratulations," Leanne said, handing her a light blue certificate with a silver border and snowflakes. The judges had signed it with silver ink.

"Thank you," Joanne said, smiling.

Mary could see the sparkle in her eyes as she turned to the audience and held up her certificate. *A simple piece of paper and a little recognition. We couldn't have had a better prize if we'd awarded money*, Mary thought.

"Next, for the most creative, we have José Bondevik with the fishermen and their catch of the day."

A screech went up from the audience.

"We won, we won, Dad!" José screamed. Mary looked out and saw Bobby jumping up and down beside José, practically beating him on the back. Bobby had left the sledding to be with his friend. José grabbed his father's hand and dragged him toward the pavilion.

"That's a very fine snow sculpture, young man," Judge Swink said. "I assume that was supposed to be you and your father?" he asked, reaching out to shake José's hand.

"Yeah. Dad helped me make it."

"Good job," Wulf said, also shaking José's hand.

José proudly carried his certificate back to the audience where Bobby and Neil waited.

The judge announced the list of winners one by one, to great audience cheers and applause. He finally came to the last commercial award.

"The most creative goes to Archie Goodfellow from The Green Grocer, for the grocery man snowman," he said.

"Hey Archie, you gonna sell that handcart to me now?" a deep voice shouted.

"Yeah," Archie shouted back as he went up to the pavilion. "The price just went up. After all, it's valuable now."

The crowd roared as Archie raised his fist in the air. Mary had to laugh. Abby was chuckling too. Archie looked over at them and winked, which made them laugh even harder.

"Now there's a man whose bark is definitely worse than his bite," Abby said, leaning down to Mary. Mary nodded.

Gradually the crowd dispersed, wandering off to the booths

with funnel cakes, brownies, s'mores, pies, coffee and hot chocolate.

"What a day," Judge Swink said to Mary and Abby. "Thanks for inviting me. I haven't had this much fun in ages."

"Are you ready to head back to the ferry?" Abby asked the judges. "It leaves in ten minutes."

"I'm going to visit with your folks this afternoon," Judge Swink said. "Your father promised to take me to the ferry after dinner. I can't pass that up."

"Leanne, are you all ready to go?"

"If you don't mind, Abby, we'd like to stay awhile and see all your booths." Lowering her voice, so only Abby and Mary could hear, she said, "I haven't had a s'more in years."

"You go on and don't worry about us," Wulf said. "The ferry's only a few blocks from here. We'll get there on our own. Personally, I'm wanting a brat with onions and hot mustard. The lunch was great, but it just whetted my appetite," he said. He was a big man, and Mary had no doubt he could down a bratwurst sandwich and a brownie too.

"Thanks so much for helping us out," Mary said.

"We enjoyed it," Leanne said. "Besides, Abby promised us a program this spring."

"Just let me know when," Abby said.

As they wandered away, going off in different directions, Mary sighed. "I think we're done, except for winding down and cleanup. Thank goodness the committee found volunteers for that. I'm finished. How about you?"

Abby grinned. "If you say I'm done, then that's it. After all, you're the one who volunteered me for this job."

"I did, didn't I? Well, I'm not sorry. You did a great job. Was it difficult?"

"Interesting is more the word. They had a discussion at every snowman. Which category did it fit in, and the merits, the probable amount of time it took to make it, the tools used, on and on. You'd have thought they were all scientists."

"Then I guess you fit right in."

"I kept my mouth shut and just watched. Perhaps I'll do a paper on my observations. The cognitive powers of the San Juan Islands Judicators."

"You wouldn't."

Abby raised her eyebrows. "Oh? Wouldn't I?"

CHAPTER ❧ TWENTY-THREE

As Abby looked out at the activity in the park, tiny snowflakes floated about in the air like little white gnats in a soft breeze. She looked up at the sky. Overcast, but not threatening. The air felt slightly warmer. This snow she could handle. It wouldn't last long.

What a week. Strange noises, intruding raccoons, a missing guest, a world-class paleontological find, a freak blizzard, and a winter Snow Fest on Sparrow Island . . . When she listed the events of the past week, she suddenly felt tired. She chuckled. Mary was gathering her things. She looked up and gave Abby a questioning look.

Abby shook her head. "Nothing," she said. "I was just thinking what a full week we've had."

"Amazing, isn't it? I'm looking forward to an early night. I didn't sleep very well last night. I kept thinking of today and all the things that needed to happen. So here we are, and it's over. I wasted several perfectly good hours of sleep for no reason."

"Isn't that the way it usually goes? Why is that? I know you weren't anxious. You're not a worrier."

"No, it's more excitement and anticipation."

"Yes, that's it. Well, I'm not anticipating anything except getting back to work and cataloging my feathers and nests. That will keep me busy for a month."

"Don't forget, you have a program to present to the Birding Society."

"I'll talk about my feathers and nests."

"Nice and neat, huh? I know you'll spend hours preparing your program."

"Yes, but not tonight or tomorrow." Abby glanced out and saw Martin and Terza helping Ana clean up the snow painting booth. Although it was only two o'clock, the activities were winding down. The committee had planned on four hours, figuring that was about as long as people could stand the cold. A special family film was being shown at the school auditorium tonight, and the Community Center was hosting a potluck bingo night. The Springhouse Café had a dinner special and so did Winifred's, the fanciest restaurant on the island.

Out of her peripheral vision, Abby caught sight of a man, dressed in a formal wool greatcoat, walking across the park. He looked out of place. She glanced over and gasped.

"What?" Mary asked.

"Look," she said in a low voice, pointing toward the man. "I can't believe it. I think . . . that's Jinghuan. Oh." Abby clamped her lips together and sent a quick, silent prayer skyward. The man looked straight ahead, his steps purposeful. He looked so handsome. Just like the man behind Rebecca in the picture of the fundraiser on the foundation Web site.

"Are you sure?"

"Yes. I think so." Abby looked over to the edge of the park. Standing still, watching the man, was a dark haired woman in a long blue wool coat. *Rebecca.*

"I'm positive."

"Praise the Lord," Mary said, wonder in her voice.

"Amen." Abby stared, watching. She felt like an intruder on this very private moment, and yet they were in the middle of the public park. Besides, she couldn't have pulled her eyes away for anything.

Martin was bent down, putting things in a box. Something made him look up. He straightened up and froze. Terza looked at Martin, then turned to see what he was staring at. She grabbed Martin's arm, as if to catch her balance.

The man stopped a few feet in front of them and bowed. Martin bowed back, very formally. There was no doubt this was a momentous occasion. They talked for a moment. Martin reached out to the younger man, and they shook hands briefly. Then Jinghuan turned sideways and stretched his arm toward Rebecca. He beckoned to her and she walked toward them.

Abby watched Terza. She could almost feel her friend straining toward this adopted son and now adopted daughter-in-law, but she remained still. Terza waited for them to approach together. This young man, raised in China, was treating his elders with every outward sign of respect and honor. Abby imagined Terza drawing strength and peace from deep inside, restraining herself. Abby admired that in her friend.

Outwardly, from a distance, Jinghuan seemed calm and controlled. Was he nervous about this meeting? Did he wonder how he and his wife would be received?

"Abby, look at the wife," Mary whispered, as if they could be heard.

Abby looked. The woman walked carefully, almost leaning backwards. *Is something wrong with her?* Abby wondered.

"She's pregnant," Mary said, as if to answer Abby's thoughts. "Pretty far along, I'd guess."

"Oh. Oh my."

"Yeah."

Rebecca stopped beside Jinghuan and gave Martin and Terza a little curtsy. Then she looked down respectfully. Jinghuan took her hand and held it. Rebecca reached out with her other hand toward Terza. Terza responded, reaching out and taking Rebecca's hand. Even from across the park, Abby could see her friend's smile. Finally, Jinghuan picked up the box Martin had been packing and the four began walking away from the snow painting booth. They were some thirty feet away as they passed in front of the pavilion, headed toward the Bird Nest. Terza glanced over at Abby and Mary.

She gave only the slightest nod of her head, but Abby got the message and felt completely and totally thanked for her small part in bringing Jinghuan home to them.

SUNDAY MORNING Abby was seated between her mother and Henry on the last pew in church. The pew was shortened to accommodate a wheelchair at the end, where Mary sat with Finnegan curled up at her feet. Although it was still early, the church had a good crowd for such a cold, overcast day.

"I hear we're in for a thaw this week," Ellen said. "I'm glad. The snow's lovely, but I'm ready for it to go away."

"Me too," Abby said. "It stayed cold long enough for the

Snow Fest. Now it can melt away. I'm ready for daffodils and jonquils."

Ellen leaned forward to speak across Abby to Henry. "You're coming to dinner aren't you?"

"Wouldn't miss it," he said.

"Good." She glanced up. "Is that Martin and Terza's adopted son?" she whispered to Abby.

Abby looked up. Martin and Terza were walking up the aisle toward the front. Jinghuan and Rebecca followed behind them. They all slid into a pew about halfway to the front.

"My, he's handsome," Ellen whispered. "Beautiful wife too."

Abby nodded, her eyes on the foursome. How wonderful that they stayed and came to church with the Chois. Abby had no idea if Jinghuan was a Christian, but he had been raised in a Christian mission school.

The choir filed in and the organist began playing. Abby almost chuckled at their first song. "Whiter than snow, yes, whiter than snow . . . ," she sang with the chorus. She loved the old hymn, and it sure fit their week.

"What a week we've had," Rev. Hale said, following the first hymn. "The storm this week gave us a perfect object lesson about what we look like after the Lord covers us with His purity and we are washed clean. Fortunately, the Lord's white-as-snow covering is warm and loving, not cold and harsh, as some of us experienced. Especially those out looking for the man who was missing in the snow. Jesus gathers us into His fold and adopts us to be His own children."

Abby wondered if James knew Martin and Terza's adopted son had come home to them, but she didn't think so. Besides, he would never single anyone out as an object of a sermon.

That meant the Lord had a hand in this coincidence. She watched to see if the Chois or the Tans reacted to the sermon.

Martin and Terza glanced at each other, exchanging little more than a nod, but Abby knew that brief look spoke volumes. Beside them, Jinghuan glanced over at his wife. He pressed his shoulder against hers, and she pressed back, barely perceptible, but Abby was used to reading small signs. She sighed. *Thank You, Lord*, she silently prayed, rejoicing in His blessing.

The service ended with the congregation singing "Blessed Be the Tie That Binds," as a benediction. Abby couldn't believe how everything in the service celebrated the Chois' and Tans' reunion. Although they had never met in person, the relationship went back many years. Now they could explore and enjoy it to the fullest.

After the closing prayer, the congregation began filing out of the church. Abby stood with her parents, waiting to the last to leave, greeting friends and listening to everyone congratulate Mary for the great festival. Mary kept insisting she'd done very little. Abby knew better, but that was Mary, giving others the credit for everything.

Abby noticed Martin and Terza hanging back, waiting patiently. She wanted to hurry everyone up and push them along, so they could greet the Chois and meet their guests. She watched Terza's quiet peace and tried to emulate it, but gave up. She would never have that stillness.

Finally, the church emptied. Only the Stantons, Mary, Henry, the Chois and the Tans remained. Unsure quite what to do, they waited for Martin and Terza to approach them.

"Our dear friends," Martin said with a hint of a bow, "I am

honored to introduce our very special guests, our dear son and daughter, Wo qin ai de er zi, Jinghuan, he nu er, Rebecca." He introduced each of them, beginning with George and Ellen, the elders, to give them proper respect, then Sergeant Cobb, Mary and Abby.

"We are delighted to meet you," Abby said, making a little bow, not sure what to do, exactly.

Jinghuan bowed to them. "We are the honored ones," he said. "Most honorable Mr. and Mrs. Stanton, you have raised fine daughters," he said. Then he turned to Mary and Abby. "Madame Mary. Madame Abigail. We want to express our gratitude to you." He reached into his suit coat pocket and took out a folded piece of paper.

"This is why we came. You had to look very hard to find us." He unfolded the paper. Abby knew what it was.

"I'm so glad it reached you. I didn't know if it would, but I prayed you would see it."

"Your e-mail note let us know you were serious. When you said Choi Ching-kuo and Choi Furen were grieving because of my miserable self, I had to do something right away. I couldn't believe I could bless them, as you suggested, but Rebecca convinced me that we had to come find out." He gave his wife a smile and squeezed her hand. "We cannot stay today, but we will return. We have just moved to the Seattle area. When we come next time, would you honor us with letting us take you to dinner?"

"We would love to," Abby said, looking down at Mary, who nodded.

"We will have Choi Ching-kuo let you know when we can come." Jinghuan bowed.

As they began to step away, Rebecca reached over and gave

Abby a hug. "Thank you," she whispered. "Now our baby will have grandparents."

Abby hugged her back. "You bring that baby over to Sparrow Island often. We'll be happy to provide lots of aunties too."

Rebecca smiled. "We will."

Terza reached over and grabbed Abby's hand, giving it a squeeze. Abby saw the joy shining in her eyes. That was all the thanks she needed.

After they left, Ellen turned to Abby. "Well, daughter, it seems you've been busy."

"My mother taught me to do what I can to help others. I was just following her teaching," Abby said.

"You learned well," George said. "I'm proud of you both. Now, can we go home? I happen to know there's a lemon meringue pie waiting, not to mention pot roast with gravy and potatoes."

"Now you're talking," Henry said. "We'll be right behind you."

As they exited the church, the sun was attempting to break through the clouds. The snow had deflated several inches and the sidewalk was wet.

"It feels like spring out here," Abby said.

"It must be all of forty degrees."

"Exactly." Abby headed for her car, a spring to her step. Yes indeed, the storm was past, the puzzles solved. Poor Hugo missed it all. By the time he arrived home, the snow would be gone and he'd never believe all that had happened.

A NOTE FROM THE EDITORS

THIS ORIGINAL BOOK WAS created by the Books and Inspirational Media Division of Guideposts, the world's leading inspirational publisher. Founded in 1945 by Dr. Norman Vincent Peale and his wife Ruth Stafford Peale, Guideposts helps people from all walks of life achieve their maximum personal and spiritual potential. Guideposts is committed to communicating positive, faith-filled principles for people everywhere to use in successful daily living.

Our publications include award-winning magazines like *Guideposts*, *Angels on Earth* and *Positive Thinking*, best-selling books, and outreach services that demonstrate what can happen when faith and positive thinking are applied in day-to-day life.

For more information, visit us online at www.guideposts.org, call (800) 431-2344 or write Guideposts, 39 Seminary Hill Road, Carmel, New York 10512.